THIS EARL IS ON FIRE

By Vivienne Lorret

THIS EARL IS ON FIRE

The Season's Original Series

VIVIENNE LORRET

AVON IMPULSE

An Imprint of HarperCollinsPublishers

Excerpt from *The Virgin and the Viscount* copyright © 2016 by Charis Michaels.
Excerpt from *Love On My Mind* copyright © 2016 by Tracey Livesay.
Excerpt from *Here and Now* copyright © 2016 by Cheryl Etchison Smith.

EPub Edition AUGUST 2016 ISBN: 9780062446336

Print Edition ISBN: 9780062446343

Avon, Avon Impulse, and the Avon Impulse logo are trademarks of HarperCollins Publishers.

AM 10 9 8 7 6 5 4 3

To Marshall Brown,
for placing the broken pieces of a dream into my hands
and never doubting that I would find a way to fix them

The night before…

Liam Cavanaugh grinned at the corrugated lines marking his cousin's lifted brows. It wasn't often that Northcliff Bromley, the Duke of Vale and renowned genius, showed astonishment.

Bending his dark head, Vale peered closer at the marble heads within the crates. "Remarkable. Even seeing them side by side, I hardly notice a difference. The *fellows* will be fascinated when you present this to the Royal Society at month's end."

"It was pure luck that I had the original as well." Liam shrugged as if he'd merely stumbled upon the differences between a genuine article and an imposter.

Vale turned, and his obsidian eyes sharpened on Liam. "No need to play the simpleton with me. You forget that I know your secret."

Liam cast a hasty glance around the sconce-lit, cluttered ballroom of Wolford House, ensuring they were alone.

Fortunately, the vast space was empty aside from the two of them and a dozen or more large crates filled with artifacts. "By definition, a secret is that of which we do not speak. So lower your voice, if you please."

No one needed to know that he actually studied each piece of his collection in detail—enough that he'd learned how to spot a forgery in an instant.

"Afraid the servants will tell the *ton* your collection isn't merely a frivolous venture? Or that your housekeeper's complaints of dusty urns and statues crowding each room would suddenly fall silent?" Vale flashed a smile that bracketed his mouth with deep creases.

Liam pretended to consider his answer, pursing his lips. "It would be cruel of me to render Mrs. Brasher mute when she finds such enjoyment in haranguing me."

"She may have a point," Vale said, skirting in between two crates when a wayward nail snagged his coat, issuing a sharp *rip* of rending fabric. He stopped to examine the hole and shook his head. "Your collection has grown by leaps and bounds in the past few months. So much so that you were forced to purchase another property to house it all."

"The curse of immense wealth and boredom, I'm afraid."

His cousin's quick glower revealed that he was not amused by Liam's insouciant guise. Then, as if to punish him for it, he issued the foulest epithet known to man. "You should marry."

Not wanting to reveal the discomfort slowly clawing up his spine, Liam chuckled. "As a cure for boredom?"

Vale said nothing. He merely crossed his arms over his chest and waited.

It was a standoff now. They were nearly equal in regard to observation skills, but apparently Vale thought he had the upper hand.

Liam knew differently. He crossed his arms as well and smirked.

If anyone were to peer into the room at this moment, they might wonder if they were staring at matching wax figures. The two of them looked enough alike in build and coloring to be brothers, but with subtle differences. Vale's features were blunter, while Liam's were angular. And Vale's dark eyes were full of intellect, while Liam's green eyes tended to reveal the streak of mischief within.

"Marriage would do you good," Vale said.

Liam disagreed. "You're starting to sound like Thayne, always hinting of ways to improve my social standing."

The Marquess of Thayne was determined to reform Liam into the *ton*'s favorite pet—the Season's *Original*. In fact, Thayne had been so confident in success that he'd wagered on the outcome. *What a fool.*

"I never hint," Vale said.

Liam offered his cousin a nod. "True. You are a forthright, scientific gentleman, and I appreciate that about you. Therefore, I will give you the courtesy of answering in kind: No. I should *not* marry. I like my life just as it is." He lifted his hands in a gesture to encompass his collection within this room. "Besides, I could never respect a woman who would have me."

Vale scoffed. "Respect?"

"Very well. I could never *trust* a woman who desired to marry me. Not with my reputation. Such a woman would either be mad or conniving, and I want neither for a wife."

He'd nearly succumbed once, falling for the worst of all deceptions. After that narrow escape, he'd vowed never to be tricked again.

"Come now. There are many who care nothing for your reputation."

That statement only served to cement his belief. If his despoiled reputation were the only thing keeping him far afield of the *ton*'s conniving matchmakers, then he would make the most of it. And the perfect place to add the crème de la crème to his list of scandalous exploits would be at Lady Forester's masquerade tonight.

After all, he had a carefully crafted reputation of unrepentant debauchery to uphold.

Liam squared his shoulders and walked with his cousin to the door. "If the Fates have it in mind to see me married before I turn sixty, then they will have to knock me over the head and drag me to the altar."

CHAPTER ONE

The moment Adeline Pimm saw the body slumped against the doorway, she knew that London was a city full of adventure. Oh…and, of course, danger.

A series of indrawn breaths followed.

Father's gasp was more of a wordless exclamation as the man beneath the narrow portico of their rented townhouse tipped over the threshold and crumbled into his arms. Mother's accompanied a jolt of her limbs, an ever-preparedness to manage any given situation. While Adeline's stalled in her throat. Tiny grains of gooseflesh rose on her arms. Her skin tingled. And some strange force clutched her heart.

Her own response made little sense to her. After having been shielded from…well…*everything* for her entire life, a more understandable reaction might have been to faint, perhaps. Yet instead, she felt compelled to rush across the foyer to offer aid.

Her body answered this urge. Automatically she took a step forward. Unfortunately, so did her mother, effectively blocking her path.

Hildebrand Pimm—*Bunny* to all those who knew her—clapped a hand over her daughter's eyes. "Adeline, hasten to your room. This sight is too troubling for *your* eyes."

Not just any young woman's eyes, Adeline noted, but hers and hers alone.

She knew her parents loved her. They wanted to protect her. They wanted what—they believed—was best for her. And for the majority of the past twenty-two years, Adeline had rarely put up a fuss. Usually, she followed her mother's instruction without question. There had never been an ounce of discord between them, and even less rebellion from Adeline. However, since the last year or two, easy acceptance of the way her life always had been and always would be—so it seemed—had become unsatisfactory.

She wanted to take risks. She wanted adventure. Instead, she was cosseted and safeguarded from morning till night. Yet, as she had explained to them not long ago, if she was old enough for the marriage mart, then it was past time for her to stand on her own two feet. Or rather, in her case, stand firmly on one foot, while the other balanced on tiptoe.

Gently, Adeline lowered her mother's hand. "You promised not to coddle me any longer, remember?"

Beneath a frilled cap and a mass of light brown hair, much like her own, Mother's indigo gaze darted down to the tip of Adeline's shoe—the one with the extra inches of cork added to correct her limp, caused by an accident at birth. "Dearest, now is not the time to assert your independence. There is a man at our door, and we do not even know if he is alive."

"Aye. He's alive enough for now," Serge Pimm said, supporting the stranger's head against his barrel chest, his arms curled beneath the stranger's as he pulled him into the foyer. "Bunny, could you see to the door? And Adeline—"

"I am a grown woman, Father," she interjected before he could order her to her room as well. "I can help. And since the servants are not here, you need me."

After leaving their quiet country village, the family had arrived last night, a full day earlier than expected. Their coachman, Gladwin, had made a point of setting out before a storm had swept through Boswickshire. Unfortunately, the carriage filled with a half dozen of their servants had been delayed because of it. Not only that but, at first light, Mother had sent Gladwin and their tiger, Sean, to market with a list.

Normally, the absence of servants wouldn't have caused issue. Her parents, the Baron and Baroness Boswick, made a point of being models of self-sufficiency, unlike other aristocrats. In this particular moment, however, there was an unconscious man on the foyer floor.

Father glanced at her, a hank of thick salt-and-pepper hair falling over his forehead. His burly brows furrowed, and the spray of lines beside his brown eyes drew tight. "There's blood. A good deal of it."

In that instant, she realized he was not ordering her to leave. He was not shielding her as he'd always done. Instead, he was offering her a choice.

Without hesitation, she took a step forward. "I'm certain the blood won't bother me." After all, young women were no strangers to it.

Mother saw to the door and scurried over to the sideboard for a lamp. She had an uncanny ability to anticipate a need before it became apparent. Adeline wished she'd thought of it, because at first, all she could see was the top of the stranger's dark head, the sleeves of his blue coat, two long, immobile legs in speckled gray trousers, and a pair of muddied boots.

Yet as soon as Mother lowered the lamp to the floor, Adeline realized it wasn't mud on his boots. It was blood. *A good deal of it.* The speckles on his trousers were not mud either. Nor were the puddle-shaped stains on his waistcoat. And his face...

Adeline felt herself sway, the room spinning beneath her feet. She sank to her knees beside him. Crimson smudges covered his flesh, matting in the black slashes of his brows. All that she could see of his eyes were two swollen folds of flesh. Bloated and raw, the left side of his face looked as if it took the worst of the beating.

Her stomach roiled, though not in sickness. In anger. A surge of it gripped her lungs, turning each breath so hot that it scorched her throat. She glared at the gash splitting his bottom lip near the corner and yanked a lace handkerchief from her sleeve. "Who would do this to him?"

Father shrugged off his coat and tucked it beneath the man's head. "By the cut of his clothes, he appears to be a gentleman. Perhaps he was set upon by ruffians or thieves. Though with his gold watch chain in plain sight, I doubt it was the latter. Whatever the reason, they meant to be thorough."

She gently dabbed at the stranger's face, but the blood was sticky, like red quince jelly, and the handkerchief too dry for her ministrations to be effective. Thankfully, Mother brought a white glazed pitcher into view and handed it to Father.

"Thank you, Bunny. And see if there's a bottle of spirits in the—"

But Mother already had a bottle of honey-colored liquor in her other hand. Then, setting it down on the floor, she hastened up the stairs, likely preparing for the next unforeseen necessity.

Father poured a few drops of water onto Adeline's handkerchief before withdrawing his own. "Be gentle, child. We don't know how broken he is yet. When Gladwin returns, I'll send a missive to my Uncle Peirce and see if he is in town. When I was a lad, he was the best *leech* in three counties."

Father also had a knack for healing. Adeline had always wondered if she possessed that trait as well. Yet each time she'd attempted to assist a maid or footman who might have a cut finger or twisted ankle, they'd ended up trying to take care of her instead. As if her limp made her an invalid.

But she wasn't. She just needed a chance to prove it.

Beside her, the stranger's chest rose and fell in hitched, shallow breaths as if each one pained him. She settled her hand over his heart. Hard, labored beats met her palm.

Peculiarly, she already felt an inexplicable fondness for this stranger. As she tenderly cleansed his face, she felt somehow tethered to him. She didn't know where the abrupt, fledgling feeling came from. All she knew was that he needed help.

Right now, in this moment, he needed *her*.

"It will all be better soon," she promised on a whisper, a sense of certainty washing through her. "You were meant to find our door."

Since they'd arrived at such a late hour, they hadn't had an opportunity to see the façade of their temporary lodgings. With the first rays of dawn coming through the transom windows, they were just going outside when they'd found him instead.

"I've no doubt he was." Father carefully sifted through the blood and matted hair as he continued his examination. "Not many would have discovered him on their doorsteps for hours yet to come. Divine providence deals a fine hand when we least expect it, and likely when we need it most."

As Adeline nodded in agreement, an odd sensation occurred beneath her breast. Her heart wavered out of rhythm. It sped up for a moment, pounding hard and heavy, then slowed, but not to its original tempo. Instead, it matched beat for beat with the organ beneath her fingertips.

She lifted her hand and stared down at it as if it were a foreign limb. Then, like one pole of a magnet being drawn to another, she settled it over the man's bloodstained waistcoat once more.

"What is it?" Father asked, placing his own hand beside hers. "Is his heart fading?"

She swallowed. "I don't know how to explain it, but just now I thought I...Well, my own heart did the strangest thing."

Her gaze darted to her father and saw that his was equally startled. Then a knowing smile, of sorts, lined his countenance, appearing more worried and wistful than glad. "Then we will do all that is in our power to heal him."

She was close enough to her parents that she understood this expression. She knew their story. Knew a similar malady had struck her father when he first laid eyes on her mother.

This was why they'd been so understanding when Adeline had refused Mr. Wittingham's proposal. They knew she hadn't been thunderstruck by anyone yet. They even feared that, because of her deformity, she never would be, and that was the main reason they had agreed to let her come to the *treacherous city* of London in the first place.

"No." She shook her head, answering Father's unspoken assumption. She had no plans to fall in love and refused to resign herself to a life of more coddling. Which was precisely what any marriage would do. Her reaction was the result of eating her breakfast porridge too quickly. That was all.

But wouldn't it be just her luck if the only trait she'd inherited from her parents was a tendency toward overblown romantic notions?

A sense of panic flooded her. All Adeline had wanted was an adventure—to experience London as if she were just any other debutante, not a pitiable, feeble creature. Now, this strange feeling put that in jeopardy. She felt cornered, almost as if this man were threatening to take it all away from her.

Wanting distance, she scrambled to her feet. When her corrective shoe caught the hem of her morning dress, she stumbled back.

Righting herself, she reached out a shaky hand and waved it in his direction. "Perhaps we should send him away instead. H-he isn't well. And, well,"—she swallowed—"he should be at home. His home. Wherever…that…may…be."

"Oh dear, I feared this would happen," Mother said, rushing down the stairs to her side and placing a hand against her forehead. "This is too much of a shock."

A shock, indeed. And an unwelcome one at that. Though she wasn't entirely sure if her mother was referring to the man's injuries or to the fact that Adeline was experiencing the most peculiar sensation of…of…

Indigestion. That was all this was. Adeline couldn't acknowledge that it might be anything else, even if only to herself. Once was enough. And she would never admit that she *had* felt anything for the man lying supine on the foyer floor—not aloud, at any rate.

She would much rather pretend that the past five minutes had never occurred.

Yes. That thought calmed her.

Adeline slowly exhaled, forcing herself to relax. After all, once the stranger recuperated, then she need never see him again. Gradually, her breath came easier. Yet that uncomfortable pinching around her heart remained.

She shook her head, gently dislodging her mother's hand. "I am perfectly well. The stranger is our main concern. I should fetch more cloths…" Her excuse stalled the moment she saw the neat pile of fresh cloths her mother had brought. "Or perhaps a basin"—but there was one on the floor next to Father now too.

During her smallish bout of hysteria, Father had cleaned the blood from the stranger's head and face. Then he'd shifted, hovering over the body with his back to Adeline and Mother.

"His fingers are distended," Father said, proceeding with his examination, his movements concealed from their vantage point. "He gave back as much as he got, I imagine. There are no visible signs of broken bones. His arms appear sturdy. His ribs, however…A wealth of bruises tells me that he took quite a few blows to the left side, and"—Father hissed—"at least one in the shape of a man's boot."

The stranger issued a low moan. Heedless of the fear that caught her off guard minutes ago, Adeline rushed forward.

Again, she sank to her knees beside him. When she took his hand in hers, a warm, comforting feeling washed over her, as if this gesture were a habit of many years instead of a first touch.

She chose to ignore the sensation. "What can I do, Father?"

"Even if we knew where he lived, we could not send him away in his condition," he said, gazing at her with a measure of caution and worry.

She could see the struggle within him—the desire to protect her, competing with the desire to honor his promise of not coddling her. As always, she was grateful for his well-meant affection. However, she had a choice to make. Did she want to remain the cosseted, helpless girl that her parents saw? Or was she ready to prove herself capable of facing any circumstance?

It didn't take long to come to a decision. Adeline squeezed the stranger's hand. "Then we shall see to his care. *All* of us."

Liam Cavanaugh's cranial bones seemed to shift and throb like rock over magma. The flesh surrounding his skull and the pulpy gray matter beneath pulsed in a constant hellish fire of searing, unending pain.

What had happened to him?

He tried to remember, but consciousness was limited and somewhat hazy.

When he concentrated, all he saw were blurry fists plunging through shadows, white light flashing behind his eyes, and a gritty voice growling in warning, *"If you let her go, we could end this. Your choice, guvna."*

The effort caused agony to pummel him anew. He felt himself slipping away, falling into—what he hoped was—slumber. Though right this instant, death would not be unwelcome.

He didn't know how long he drifted—a moment, an hour, an age—until he came to a semblance of awareness. A memory greeted him in this next place.

"Liam, come here. Take your father's hand."

In this vision, he saw a frail old man lying against a brace of pillows in a massive bed of thick corner posts and dark, carved wood. His face was ashen, his eyes dimmed from the luminous green of a forest glade to the pale, cloudy hue of peridot stones.

"My bright boy, do not be afraid," he said, his voice nothing more than a rasp. *"When I am gone, you will not be alone. Mr. Ipley and the others will remain until you reach your majority. I have seen to it."*

The vision turned watery just before a small voice answered, *"But I don't care if the servants stay, Father. I don't want you to go."*

"Your mother is waiting for me. I can hear her call my name as if from the next room." Father closed his eyes, his mouth faintly curling into a smile. *"Come and give a kiss, son. Very soon, you will be the eighth Earl of Wolford. Be strong and promise you will remember all I have taught you."*

"I promise," the small voice said against a vellum cheek that was cold beneath his lips. And before Liam could back away, he heard one last breath. A raw, endless death rattle.

And the pain returned.

With a shock of clarity, Liam realized the moan was coming from his own throat. No wonder—it felt like his lungs were filled with shards of glass. Every breath was torture. He tried to move, but his limbs felt trapped, heavy. He tried to open his eyes, but darkness met him at every attempt.

"Shh…" a woman said as a cool, soft hand curled around his. "Do not be afraid. You are not alone."

This voice was unfamiliar. One of his servants? Not one that he could place.

Her tone was brushed velvet, soft, low, and lush, and more like a lover than a chambermaid. Somehow, hearing her made the next breath come easier. Yet to make sure that this sensation was not part of his dream, he squeezed the fingers in his grasp.

"Again," he said, wanting to hear that voice. His own was gravelly and coarse against his throat, scraping its way out.

A gasp answered him. The hand he held gripped his. "You are awake at last! I cannot tell you how worried I was… Well, we were *all* worried about you."

The *we* in her declaration bothered him. Since he did not recognize her voice, he didn't know the *we* of whom she was speaking. The simple answer was likely his servants. But which servants and in which one of his houses? And how had he come to be here, wherever he was?

There were too many questions and too much relentless pain to fight through in order to ask for the answers.

"More," he commanded, believing that the more she said, the more would be revealed. Besides, her voice seemed to offer a temporary respite from agony.

" 'More' of what? No, do not tell me. The answer should be simple," she said, apparently mulling it over while oblivion threatened him. "*More*. Oh yes, of course! I suppose you mean more water. Thus far, I've only managed to dampen your mouth with a cloth every quarter hour. We didn't want you to choke or cough, you see. Father says your ribs are damaged. Though I imagine you're quite thirsty now."

Father? Then she must be a servant's daughter. He wondered which one of his footmen was old enough to have a child who sounded both green and sultry at once. Though given that criteria, she could be anywhere between the ages of fifteen and five and twenty. The last time Liam had asked, Mr. Ipley had no children. As for Mr.—

Suddenly, her hand slipped out of his grasp. For reasons unbeknownst to him, his body jerked, attempting to follow her. A dire mistake. Instantly, the razor points in his lungs intensified. A tortured groan ripped from his chest.

"Lie still. Try not to move," she said, coming back to his side. A slight weight settled beside him. That was when he realized he was in a bed. Which bed or where, he did not know yet. Against her orders, however, he did move, enough to take an accounting of all of his limbs.

His hands and arms were stiff, sore, but nothing too terrible. His toes wiggled and his ankles rotated without any effort. A good sign. When he lifted one leg—albeit marginally—a sharp pain radiated upward and into his torso. He hastily abandoned the effort. For now. Yet he did lift a hand to his face, wondering why the room was so dark.

"Oh, please stop. You are injured, and I couldn't bear it if something else happened to you before you are well enough to leave."

Leave? What an odd thing for a servant to say. Why would he leave his own house?

When her hand grasped his arm, he forgot the question. The refreshing coolness of it penetrated a layer of linen that was likely his shirtsleeves. Though without being able to open his eyes, he couldn't be sure.

"We applied a salve to reduce the swelling and then bandages to aid in your healing," she said. Then tentatively, she directed his hand to his face and settled it against his forehead.

Coarse fabric met his fingertips—layer upon layer of an open weave that reminded him of cheesecloth. It covered most of his head, both of his eyes, and nearly one side of his face, including an ear.

An ear too? His pulse spiked with a heavy dose of worry. He could feel the throb of it behind his eyes.

Even though his limbs were intact, that said nothing about the rest of him. What lay beneath these bandages?

While he never wanted for feminine attention or admiration, he'd never considered himself a narcissist either. Only dandies primped or fussed in the mirror. The style and fit of Liam's clothes was the duty of his tailor and valet. Both a physician and a notable sportsman earned salaries to keep him in remarkable health. Yet when faced with the possibility of a deformity, he discovered a trembling, vain figure huddled in the corner of his mind, begging for a mirror.

What precisely had happened to him? The images of shadowed faces and fists that came to him were fleeting and exhausting. *"If you let her go, we could end this…"*

Her. Had this all happened over a woman? *Damn.* If he managed to survive, then he would have to live with Thayne's taunts for years to come. His friend was forever trying to make Liam more palatable to society and to abandon his more salacious activities.

If only he could remember his most recent assignation. Perhaps then he could pinpoint which woman had caused the upheaval and keep his distance in the future. But the effort caused an excruciating headache to pound beneath his temples.

Giving up, he lowered his arm.

"On the bright side, there is nothing broken—not even your nose—which Father said was quite a feat, considering how many blows you suffered," she continued, her voice a soothing balm, quieting his fears. Then something firm, cool, and smooth pressed against his lower lip. "Do you think you can manage a sip or two?"

Realizing it was the rim of a glass, he parted his lips in response. Straight away, blessed water quenched his mouth, slipping down his ragged throat. It was divine. Silken on his tongue and palate. Cold and wet at the corners of his mouth where it dribbled down his chin, saturating the linen at the base of his neck. He didn't care. He could gorge himself on it.

Had the finest wine or whiskey ever tasted so good? Smelled so clean and pure? He wasn't certain, but he doubted it.

Then too soon, she withdrew the glass.

"Oh, drat," she said on a huff and began pressing a cloth to his chin and throat. "I had hoped to be a better nursemaid. Who knew there was a certain talent required for assisting in the simple task of drinking?"

Even though her mopping was a little more vigorous than was comfortable in his current state, he found her self-reprimand somewhat amusing. While she batted away at the base of his neck, he chased the lingering droplets on his lip with his tongue, content for the moment.

Then her weight shifted as if she were prepared to leave him. He couldn't allow that, not when she was his only link to relief from pain and to the sighted world.

"Stay," he said. For good measure, he draped an arm across her legs, anchoring her to his side.

She stiffened, the slender muscles of her thighs contracting in a quick vibration, almost like a shiver. It didn't take her sudden indrawn breath to tell him that his action was improper. Sultry voice or not, she was a servant's daughter. And he never dallied with those paid to be of service...unless pleasure was their profession.

Not believing that was the case in this instance, he knew he should remove his arm. Instead, he splayed his hand against the whisper-soft fabric of her dress, finding comfort in her nearness. And finding the outer curve of her hip as well. Not only that, but he realized she was not wearing a dress after all. It was a night rail.

In his life, he'd had ample experience with women's various states of dress or undress. Though his preference was, most assuredly, of the latter.

As for the fabric beneath his fingertips, the soft, delicate weave was not the practical homespun he might have expected from one whose father worked in service but something more decadent.

A nervous laugh escaped her as she adjusted his hand more appropriately into her own but remained beside him. "Your glass is empty. Should you like more water—if you are willing to risk my clumsy efforts, that is—then I must cross the room to where the pitcher waits."

"Later."

"Hmm... That makes four words now." She shifted, her movements accompanied by the *clap* of a glass on a nearby wooden table.

He wondered if it was the mahogany Chippendale console at Wolford House in St. James or the walnut Hepplewhite commode in his rooms on Brook Street in Mayfair. The bedside tables he'd shipped to his new property, Sudgrave Terrace in Knightsbridge, were either marble-topped or bronze and would have made more of a *clack* instead...

His thoughts trailed off, surprising him. It was almost as if he could see by sound alone. Of course, he would much prefer having these bandages removed and his vision restored.

When she settled back, her fingers flitted over the top of his hand as if absently, touching each of his knuckles. "All day long and into the night, I'd wondered about the sound of your voice—wondered if I would ever hear it—and now my only reward is one command after another."

She didn't speak to him as a servant would, which added to his curiosity. And if it weren't for the low, teasing tone, Liam might have issued an apology for his rudeness. At the moment, however, all he wanted to do was listen to her and feel the jagged edges inside him go blissfully numb.

"How many words"—he dragged in a breath—"do you require of me?"

"I certainly have earned your *entire* lexicon, poor nursemaid or not. However, I will take only as many as you would give."

He felt a grin tug at his lips but also a cut that puckered his flesh at the corner. Halting before he ripped open the obvious wound, he merely answered her quip with one of his own. "Shall I begin...alphabetically?"

This time her laugh was not of the nervous variety but unreserved and inviting. "I would settle for your name."

Though somewhat puzzled, he grinned despite the twinge of pain it caused. "Do you not know it already?"

"Father said that if you knew your name, then we would not have to worry about"—she hesitated—"an injury we couldn't see. A more severe injury."

Alarm returned to him, undoing all the ease she'd provided. "What do you mean, exactly?"

So many bandages, even over his eyes. Could he have been blinded by whatever violence brought him here? Damn, he wished he could remember who did this to him.

She gripped his hand tighter, comforting and terrifying him with one small gesture. "Have you ever heard of amnesia?"

Other than the recent past, he recalled every single year of his life. And if that was her primary concern, then perhaps he could rest easier.

"Amnesia, you say? I'm not...certain I...remember what that is," he teased.

"It's a terrible disorder afflicting men who smirk at the women who sit at their bedsides. I believe it's caused by suffocation from a bed pillow," she answered directly, patting his hand.

Her quick parry drew a surprised laugh from him, which was shortly followed by a hoarse grunt of pain. He clutched his side. His lungs seized, tightening and burning. "*Rotter.* You should warn…a man…when you…intend to be…clever."

Her hands grasped his shoulders, urging him to lie back. "For all you know of me, I could be a wit, and every word I speak should first come with a caveat. Now be still. Try to breathe."

Impossible. He shook his head. "I can only breathe…when you're talking to me."

Apparently, agony was something of a truth serum. He might have felt embarrassed if it weren't for the spasms wracking him as he fought to sift air into his lungs. If he were amongst acquaintances, they would have mocked him ceaselessly, and he would have made a jest in return. He was forever playing the part of a gentleman with a head stuffed with bank notes and a tongue coated with quips and barbs.

He spent copious amounts of money on houses and various acquisitions. He supped on the finest cuisine. Indulged in lavish, hedonistic entertainments. He had everything a man could desire and was usually charming enough that people did not despise him for it. But right now, he felt…vulnerable. All he truly wanted was to hear the sound of this woman's voice.

"I'm certain you'll be able to breathe easier by the time you're well enough to leave," she crooned softly, but there was an edge of determination in her tone. This was the second time she'd mentioned his departure.

Her hands fussed over the bedclothes, tucking them tightly over his chest. A little too tightly for comfort. Then she began kneading his pillows. Again and again. They'd been perfectly fluffed before, but now they were lumpy and forced his chin to his chest.

On the other hand, it wasn't *all* bad. Each time she pushed and molded the feathers, her sweet breath rushed against his lips. The supple, unhindered weight of her bosom pressed against his chest in a combination that was half pleasure, half pain. And as she leaned over him, her hair fell across his face, enveloping him in a curtain of heavy silk and the hint of a perfume he did not recognize.

He focused on the scent, drawing it in bit by bit. It was pure and clean, reminding him of the white blossoms of a pear tree, the first of spring. It was light, almost as if a drop of dew had traversed the petals moments before it touched her skin.

A sudden hunger quickened low in his gut, surprising him. He was used to women and their rosewater, their cloying lily and lilac, and even lavender. Those perfumes were always applied liberally. Pungency concealed all manner of sins, or so some thought. But this fragrance—this unobtrusive essence—stirred him as well as calmed him. An odd combination that left him in need of more.

Despite his nursemaid's better efforts to the contrary, his body relaxed. Not only that, but her ministrations were invaluable at proving that his limbs weren't the only parts of him in working order. The quickening of his gut shifted southward.

"There now. That's better," she said as if with triumph. "I believe I've been successful in anticipating your need for a plumper pillow. Would you agree?"

He would not. His neck was already starting to cramp. His headache was returning. And if anticipating his *need* had been her aim, then her efforts would have been more valued a degree or two lower. *If she weren't a servant's daughter*, he reminded himself.

Thayne the Reformer would have been proud that Liam had bothered to do so.

"Your question," he began, drawing in another fragrant breath, "leads me to imagine that you are new to service…or that this is your first position as nursemaid."

"Truly? You believe that I am qualified to be in service?" She lifted away but settled beside him with a small but perceptible bounce. Her enthusiasm was evident.

Confused and a bit terrified, Liam asked, "You are…old enough to be in service, aren't you?"

She laughed, and he did his best to ignore the throaty, unreserved sound. "At two and twenty, I imagine I'm far too old to begin, but your words offer a most welcome compliment nonetheless."

A measure of relief filled him. "Then it is only your father in service."

Better and better.

"My father? Why ever would you imagine"—she went still, her breath suspended for a moment, until—"*Oh*. I realize the misunderstanding now. After all, we haven't made our introductions, have we? I'm Adeline Pimm. My parents are Serge and Hildebrand Pimm, the Baron and Baroness—"

"A gentleman's daughter?" he interrupted, shock and incredulity biting through him, making him wince.

"I am."

While her admission answered many questions, it also incited his anger. "Is this some sort of entrapment scheme? Spending time alone…in the bedchamber…with me, pressing your body against mine..." He was panting now. Seething. "Were you hoping that your parents would find us...in a compromising position that would force...our marriage?"

A similar circumstance had happened in his youth—a falsely innocent invitation that had turned into an ambush by the girl's parents. If not for Mr. Ipley's timely intervention, Liam would have been forced to marry when he was but a lad of seventeen. The young woman had been six years his senior and staring at a life of spinsterhood. Her only goal had been to become a countess. She'd cared nothing for him. And Liam, young, besotted fool that he once had been, had learned his lesson.

Now, more than ten years later, he was still wary of debutantes. They were a cunning lot.

"Compromising position?" Miss Pimm's voice rose as her weight left the bed. "I was fluffing your pillow!"

He scoffed. "You were doing far more than that...and you bloody well know it. No society woman of two and twenty is *that* naive."

Proof of that was in the way he still could feel the tantalizing press of her breasts, taste her breath against his lips and—*damn it all*—breathe in her scent! That was the work of a practiced beguiler, not an innocent. Which was why he preferred the company of expert courtesans and audacious widows, ones whose aim was pleasure without deception.

"For a man who doesn't even remember his own name, you seem to think you know quite a bit about me. You do not know the first thing," she hissed. "I would never marry you, regardless of the situation, compromising or not."

"Even to become a countess? I find that hard to believe." He felt his lip curl into a sneer that cracked open his cut. "I am Liam Cavanaugh, eighth Earl of Wolford."

By reputation alone, no respectable debutante dared to venture too close for fear of being tainted by association. And that was exactly the way he liked it.

"Well then, *Liam Cavanaugh, eighth Earl of Wolford*, I pity you. Not only because you are obviously an arse of the first order, but because you no longer have a nursemaid. Enjoy the rest of your night. I hope you do not become *too* thirsty." Then she closed the door with a succinct *click*.

Liam relished the sudden quiet. Hell, he even welcomed the pain. All the better to be rid of that exhausting bit of baggage!

But damn it all, he could really use another drink.

CHAPTER TWO

As was their habit in the country, the Pimms awoke at dawn. Or at least, Adeline believed the murky gray light beyond the windowpane was the rising sun. She had no view of it, however. All that greeted her was thick fog and an expanse of rooftops and dark windows. And when she opened the sash for an invigorating breath of morning air, all that greeted her was a fetid odor. Not even the stables at home or Mr. Doyle's pigs from down the lane smelled as ripe.

Adeline summarily closed the window.

Mother stepped into the chamber at the same moment and wrinkled her nose. "It will take some time for us to acclimate ourselves to the London air, I imagine. Your father warned me of it years ago, which was one of the reasons I was content to stay in Boswickshire after we married. Otherwise, I would have spent all my days preparing sachets, cloved orange pomanders, and flower vases for every room."

Mother had been content to remain her entire life in their hamlet. She'd been born on a nearby farm, where generations of her family had lived. In fact, her grandmother had once been a cook for Father's great-grandfather. Then one fateful day, shortly after Father inherited the barony, and while visiting his tenants, he met Mother and instantly fell in love. Or so the story goes. Mother's common birth had never mattered to him. Pimms always married for love.

Yet, in Adeline's opinion, their history was all too unvaried. For her life, she wanted things to change, starting with the fact that she would not marry.

"I hope you were able to sleep," her mother continued, crossing the room to the wardrobe while Adeline moved to the washstand. "With your window overlooking the street, I'd worried most of the night."

In the framed oval mirror, she caught her mother's troubled glance before turning back to her task. Adeline knew this trip was going to be hard on her mother. She'd spent the past two decades doing her best to shield Adeline from any sort of unpleasantness. In London there would be no way to do that, not even from a poor night's sleep.

"I slept fine, Mother," she said, pouring water into the basin. The truth, however, was that the clamor of horse hooves on cobblestone and the jangle of carriages had been constant until a mere hour or two ago. It hadn't helped her sleep. Not that she could have anyway. She'd been too busy fuming over the things their odious guest had said to her.

She glared in the mirror, the blue ring around her brown eyes turning darker from frustration. Liam Cavanaugh, eighth Earl of Wolford, had already made his mind up about her and her family. And his opinion of them was not favorable in the least. It was a first for Adeline—to be judged so harshly after a good deed.

Dipping her hands into the icy water helped to cool her head. Just as long as she didn't think about his insulting accusation.

"We will have to acclimate ourselves to a new schedule while we are here, as well," Mother said, lifting out a pale blue day dress and giving it a shake. "Like our neighbors, you'll be attending parties until the wee hours of the morning."

At last, a cheerful thought! A thrill shot through Adeline as she cast aside her irritation for more pleasant prospects. She couldn't wait to experience her first London party. Then of course, there were the shops, museums, the opera, drives through the park and even...*Rotten Row.*

A shiver stole over her as she lifted the facecloth away from her nape. Her bright eyes gleamed in the mirror. She'd read accountings of horse races there, and she truly wanted to see one. Not only that, but try it herself—her own hands gripping the reins, the horses under her command, the wind against her face—not forever tucked away inside a carriage. "Do you think we could ride through Hyde Park today?"

"Not today," Mother said. "A messenger arrived a short while ago with news that the servants will be delayed, possibly even until tomorrow. So we have a few errands to attend to."

Genuine concern turned Adeline's thoughts away from her own wishes for adventure. "What happened?"

"Nothing too serious. The storm lasted longer than expected, leaving the roads in poor condition. A carriage wheel broke in Banbury," Mother said, appearing distracted by the task of finding a pair of stockings from the tidy pile of underclothes that Adeline had unpacked. "The inns are full, but thankfully, they are able to stay with Mrs. Harvey's son until the repairs can be made. Though I can only imagine how Mr. Finmore must be grumbling now, checking the pocket watch your father gave him every quarter hour and imagining we are falling apart without him."

Their butler had been none too happy about Gladwin's impatience to set off for London before the storm, and more so, before the servants. He abhorred a change in schedule. "Then their delay will likely be a blessing for Mr. Finmore. He would have hated to know that we had an unexpected guest."

"You speak as if you expect the stranger gone soon."

Adeline didn't like the sound of that. "Of course. He cannot remain here. And…he isn't entirely a stranger any longer." At the reminder, she saw the reflection of her cheeks turn from a healthy pink glow to a feverish rose.

He'd touched her last night. It all started with his arm draped across her legs.

The gesture was understandable, she assured herself. Given his condition, he likely didn't want to be left alone. But then his hand traversed to her hip, causing all sorts of tingles to *traverse* her body. Wondrous, exhilarating tingles that felt like the first step of a new adventure.

She knew in an instant that it was dangerous to be near him. Yet she hadn't been able to leave his side. Hadn't been able to stop touching him in one way or another. It was as if every inch of her flesh craved his nearness. Even now, she wasn't entirely sure if fluffing his pillow had been for him or…for *her.*

Another rush of heat flooded her cheeks. Hastily, she picked up the drying cloth and buried her face, not wanting her mother to see.

"He awoke?" Mother asked and received a nod from behind the flannel.

Then Adeline busied herself with dressing, slipping into a chemise trimmed in pink ribbon, followed by her short stays, fashioned to fasten in the front.

From early on, she preferred clothing that didn't require assistance. By request, most of her day dresses were bib-fronted as well. It did not escape her notice, however, that Mother had chosen the only one with buttons along the back.

"That is good news," Mother said, finding the stocking's mate before walking toward Adeline. "Your father and I checked on him a short while ago and found him sleeping. Your father lingered behind to sit with him while I slipped down to the kitchen to make a pot of porridge and put the kettle on the fire." Gathering up the hem of the dress, she lifted it to Adeline's head.

Adeline looked pointedly at her mother. "I am able to dress myself. I have been for quite some time."

"I'm not trying to diminish your ability, dear. Merely enjoying the fact that I have you all to myself. At least for now."

Adeline wondered if her mother *had* noticed her reaction to Liam yesterday morning. The undesired potency of it still remained, lingering beneath her skin the way a too-hot bath left her warm long after slipping from the water. Which only served to remind her that the sooner they were rid of the earl, the better. She was about to say as much, but before she could, Mother slipped the dress over her head and spun her around.

"Did our guest manage to speak? Do you know his name?" Mother asked as Adeline pushed her arms through the short puffed sleeves.

When Mother began fastening the buttons down the back, Adeline's hair got in the way. It was a common enough occurrence that she lifted the heavy mass without thinking and tied it into a knot. But it slipped free, uncoiling like a fat rope. "We exchanged a few words, yes. He is the *Earl of Wolford*."

"Hmm… The last I knew of my daughter, she was not one to harbor prejudice over those who were born into the peerage, or even those out of it, for that matter. So I am left to assume it is not the title that bothers you but the man himself."

Adeline thought she managed to withhold mockery from her tone. Apparently not. Thinking back to last night, her irritation returned. "Once we made our introductions, he accused me of having ulterior motives for tending to him."

"I can see why you would take offense," Mother said, plaiting Adeline's hair. "In our village, no one has ever questioned our generosity. But perhaps our guest has not been quite so fortunate with his own acquaintances."

Adeline was unmoved. "Even after all I had done—remaining beside him day and night—his first inclination was to mistrust me."

With the braid finished, Mother placed a hand over the curve of Adeline's shoulder. "That tells us a great deal, does it not? A man who cannot trust the kindness of a stranger must have learned not to do at some time in his life."

Adeline grumbled, nursing her own wounded ego. Reluctantly, a fresh spark of concern kindled for that horrible man. "I suppose."

"There is another matter to consider as well. He is a man who awoke in a strange place, injured and unable to see. Perhaps *fear* could explain what resulted in a tense exchange?"

Bother. Mother was right. Adeline should have come to the same conclusion. After all, who wouldn't be frightened under such a circumstance? Now she felt as if she should have been more understanding instead of quick to temper. "Likely, he has hordes of people who are worried about him and will see to his care."

"I'm afraid to tell you that a missive arrived from Uncle Peirce earlier as well," Mother continued, returning to the wardrobe. "He recommended that we not allow the stranger to move or even to remove his bandages for another day, at least. He states that the blows to his head could lead to a sensitivity to light and sound that could be quite harmful. Perhaps even cause permanent injury. It seems as if he will be remaining with us for a short while longer."

Remain here *and* without the servants to tend him? No. That would not do. Adeline would be forced to see him again. The very notion caused wayward tingles to whisper over her skin. Her body, it seemed, was still ignorant of her decision to ignore her response to him. And blind to the threat he posed—

Adeline came to a halt on her way to the vanity for hairpins. Just now, she'd witnessed her doddering gait in the mirror and winced. Strange, but at times she forgot about her leg.

All at once, she realized that she had no cause to worry. After all, even if she did feel drawn to him, likely he would not want the attentions of a lame young woman. From previous experience, she knew there were only two ways that men reacted to her—pity or revulsion.

Of course, everyone in the village already knew about her limb. Liam Cavanaugh, eighth Earl of Wolford did not. Nor did anyone in London. If it were up to her, she would keep it that way.

Which meant that she would continue with her tasks as if she were like any other young woman—strong, capable, and completely unaffected by the memory of his touch.

Liam did not know what to think about Lord Boswick. By all accounts, he was just as informal as his daughter, immediately asking Liam to abandon all the *Lord Boswick* nonsense.

"You may address me as Boswick, Pimm, or even Serge if it suits you," he said a few moments ago, during his examination. And when Liam asked if he was a physician, he went into a lengthy explanation of an Uncle Peirce, listing all of *his* accomplishments.

Liam still didn't know if Boswick knew what he was doing. Or if he was a well-enunciating lunatic. Members of Liam's coterie did not poke and prod each other in order to heal a wound. They *hired* physicians for that sort of thing. *Nor*, Liam thought, embarrassed, *did they tend to a guest's chamber pot.* Not even his own valet would have done so. Then again, Neville was rather squeamish.

And while none of his acquaintances had daughters of two and twenty, he was certain they would never allow their offspring to play nursemaid.

"Have you no servants, Boswick?" he asked when his host returned to the room, clipped, heavy footfalls announcing his approach.

The baron stopped beside the bed and audibly slid the pot underneath—likely so that Liam would not have to hunt around in the dark for it.

"I do," Boswick said. "Unfortunately, the servants were first delayed by a storm and now—for I received word just this morning—due to a broken strut on the carriage."

Which meant they would both be forced to endure this intimacy a short while longer. Though Liam had to wonder if it disturbed Boswick at all. He certainly never let on that he was inconvenienced in any way. That notwithstanding, most members of the *ton* knew how to feign sincerity. They could smile behind their fans just as easily as plunging a dagger into your back without even a twitch in their countenance.

Yet with Boswick, there was no underlying tone of falsity or derision. In fact, he made Liam feel almost...welcome. What an odd fellow.

"And to answer the next obvious question," Boswick continued, "yes. I realize my practices and even my mannerisms are rather unconventional by society's standards. After all, I spent the first years of my life with nannies and tutors, like any young man who expected to inherit a barony. I saw my parents once a week for the required recitation of my studies, as is commonplace. At ten, I went off to school and returned home only for holiday. I barely knew my parents before they died. And in the years that followed, I discovered that the person who'd made the biggest impact on my life had not been my father but my—"

"Uncle Peirce," Liam interjected, coming to something of an understanding of his host. In fact, Liam's father had shared similar stories of his own upbringing. Perhaps that had been the reason his father had taken on the role of Liam's tutor himself. Liam had not known until he'd gone to Eton how unconventional *that* had been.

"Why, yes. An astute observation. My uncle's less formal demeanor left its mark upon me, I'm afraid," Boswick said from across the room. By the sound of it, he was pouring liquid into a glass. "I hope you forgive me if I made you uncomfortable. I'm not one to stand upon ceremony, but I will respect your wishes if you'd rather have your own physician. However, I do recommend that you remain here for another day, at least. Your injuries are severe enough that any strenuous activity might worsen your condition."

The news sent a fresh spear of alarm through Liam. And even more disturbingly, his first impulse was to wish for the sound of Adeline's voice—*correction*—Miss Pimm's voice. He would do well to remember that she was a marriage-minded debutante. Weren't they all?

Which posed a conundrum: how could he avoid her if he remained here?

It wasn't as if he was frightened of Miss Pimm and her wiles. Since the age of eighteen, he'd worked hard at becoming unpalatable to respectable families. What he had not managed to accomplish on his own, the scandal sheets assisted with the rest. Of course, there were always those who were more eager to forgive his venial sins in favor of his title and wealth. As of yet, he did not know if Boswick was one of those.

The uncertainty of it left him with the sense of being a trapped animal and at their mercy.

"Water?" Boswick asked, nudging Liam's hand with a glass. "Or would you prefer something to ease the pain?"

"I'd rather remain clear-headed, but thank you." Liam took the glass and lifted it—not without effort—to his parched mouth. When Miss Pimm had issued her final taunt earlier to hope that he wouldn't get too thirsty, a desire for water had all but consumed him before he'd faded into fitful exhaustion. Now, each sip felt like vindication. In fact, he would enjoy draining this cup in her presence, ending with a satisfied *ah*.

Unfortunately, lifting his arm high enough to drain it proved too painful. So he swallowed his last mouthful with a wince instead.

"Shall I send a missive to your physician?" Boswick asked as he took back the glass.

"No. That won't be necessary," Liam answered, surprising himself. The truth of it was, he rather preferred Boswick's straightforward methods over his own physician, Fortier's, tendency to fuss.

"Then one to your family. Surely, they must be concerned by now."

Liam shook his head, suppressing a wry grin. "My family and close acquaintances are accustomed to my frequent absences. Sending word would only cause undue alarm to my Aunt Edith. I would, however, appreciate if you'd send word to my steward, Mr. Rendell."

"Rendell?"

Curious about the surprise in Boswick's voice, Liam asked, "Do you know of him?"

"Yes. In fact, we rented this house through Rendell. He was courteous and—out of respect—never once passed along the owner's name. Now, I can only presume this is your property." Then Boswick recited the address in Knightsbridge.

Liam nodded as certain aspects of how he came to be here fell into place. "Then that explains the reason I ended up on your doorstep instead of my own. Sudgrave Terrace is my property—though my living quarters will be in the middle bay—for when I am in this part of town."

"This part of town? How many houses do you own?" asked a familiar velvet voice from the doorway. Or at least, where he imagined the doorway stood. Liam wondered how long she'd been listening and if her curiosity about his estate was something he should be warned against.

"Adeline, you have better manners than that," Boswick said in an undertone of reproof.

"Perhaps, but I wish that I'd lingered in the hall a moment longer, and then I would have heard you ask him, Father." Her tinge of playfulness returned on a laugh. It had gone absent during the moments before they'd parted hours ago. Then she'd left Liam, irritated, in pain, *and* thirsty. Had her outrage over his supposed insult been part of an act?

"And what are you doing with that tray?" Boswick asked. "Here, let me help."

Liam heard a small sigh in response, followed by a shuffled step and the clink and rattle of dishes.

"I managed to carry this all the way up from the kitchen," she said with a lilt of evident pride. "I'm certain I could have made it three more steps, Father."

An aroma filled the air. Something sweet and warm, with the barest hint of pear. Liam drew in a breath, feeling his chest expand more than before. He told himself that it had nothing to do with her presence, but more to do with the scent he caught. His stomach growled.

"Since you noticed that our guest was awake and still bustled in here without a word of greeting or to ask for an introduction," Boswick chided, "I can only assume you've already exchanged pleasantries."

That wry grin tugged at Liam's lips once more. Their *pleasantries* had been somewhat varied. He preferred the ones from the beginning of their acquaintance, rather than after their introduction. In fact, he would feel more at ease if he still thought she was a servant's daughter.

"Of sorts," she answered, her tone clipped. "The earl awoke briefly—only long enough for a drink of water. Since he seemed ill-suited for company, I did not want to wake you, Father."

Knowing that pain awaited him should he laugh, Liam fought the urge. Gentleman's daughter or not, he liked her razor wit.

Boswick cleared his throat. "Our guest might have required my assistance."

"I sent her away with a desire for solitude," Liam said in her defense. Though why he bothered, he didn't know. He should have let her be chastised by her father. After leaving Liam to suffer an unquenched thirst, she deserved it.

"Ah, that explains it then. I imagine you were in even more pain earlier, Wolford," Boswick said, the gruffness gone from his tone. "Which leads me to my errand. I'll send a missive to Rendell posthaste."

As Boswick's footsteps moved toward the door, Liam felt the ghost of an old manipulation rekindle his ire. Miss Pimm had not been told to leave the room. "Surely it would not be appro—"

"Father," she interrupted, her voice turning colder by degree. "His lordship is worried that he will be forced into marriage with me if we are left alone. I pray that you would ease his mind in that regard."

Boswick's footfalls stopped. He was quiet for a moment. "My apologies, Wolford. With a man in your condition, the thought had not occurred to me. Nor had it occurred to me that your experience might have been otherwise. And should that be true, I am sorry."

The fact that Boswick read him so easily and spoke so sincerely left Liam feeling exposed. He shifted against the brace of pillows at his back.

"I will tell you, however," Boswick continued, "that my daughter is too precious to give away to just any man. I would not use her either to gain an earl for the family or for any reason."

Liam suddenly felt like a speck of mud. While typically an excellent judge of character, Liam might have faltered in this circumstance. The past tended to blur one's vision, he supposed. "Forgive me, Boswick. I meant no insult. You have every right to call me out."

"No need," his host answered, his tone straightforward, forgiving. "It is good for men to have an understanding of each other. That is the place where trust begins."

Then Boswick's footfalls started again, echoing in the hall and down the stairs. All the while, Adeline said nothing. Liam knew she was still in the room because of the crisp scrape and clack of porcelain dishes moving from one place to the next.

It did not escape his notice that he'd insulted her as well. That was, *if* he chose to trust his host completely. He felt a sense that he ought to, and yet experience cautioned him from being too hasty. So for now, it would be best to pretend more faith than he could freely give.

"Are you as merciful as your father, Miss Pimm?"

"Perhaps." Her tone was bland, revealing nothing. Then she hesitated, and in the pause, he heard a chair groan across the floorboards near his bedside. "I will forgive you on one condition."

"What would that be?" he asked, wary. If he had a mirror as well as his eyesight, no doubt he would see that his complexion had gone pale.

"You must promise not to marry me."

Relief came out on a puff of air that was part laugh. "You are a debutante in London for the Season. Your goal can only be to capture a husband."

"I already explained that I will not have you. So please stop *volunteering*," she teased, issuing a huff of feigned exasperation. "Besides, some debutantes might want to visit London solely for the adventure."

"*Adventure?*" He knew she must have still been teasing. "What adventure could be gained from attending a few balls and parties?"

"Plenty, if you've never been." The playful note vanished, replaced by curtness.

But what debutante had never been to a ball? "Are there no assemblies in your village?"

"I have not had the inclination to dance at those assemblies."

He felt his brow furrow beneath the bandages. He thought every young woman enjoyed dancing. Then again, perhaps she'd had an inferior master to train her.

He pushed that puzzle aside for the time being. "If you do not dance, then why would you want to attend a ball?"

"To see what it's like, of course," she said as if he were a simpleton. "There is more than dancing at a ball, or so I've read."

"True. A courteous host will have a card room as well. Otherwise, I see no purpose in attending." His sardonic tone drew a small laugh from her.

"There is music, punch, terraces leading to garden strolls, and—"

"And scandal, if you're not too careful with that last one." At his own words, Liam felt a jolt of inspiration hit him. If this was her family's first trip to town, then perhaps they weren't aware of his despicable reputation. He set about amending that. "And I know a thing or two about the topic. Simply read any issue of the *Standard* and you will see."

"Are you a libertine?" The censure in her voice was a relief to him.

While his reputation was bad, he still possessed a shred of decency. "I do not prey upon the virtue of innocent young women, no."

"Then what has earned you a place in the newspaper?"

"Many depraved acts that are too salacious for a debutante's ears," he cautioned, dropping his voice a few notes. He sensed her utter revulsion of his character was only moments away. And then he would be safe from any designs she may possess.

"Hmm…" she murmured as if taking the matter under consideration. "Likely those include drinking to excess?"

He nearly laughed at her naivety. Getting foxed from time to time was the least of his sins. "Yes."

"Gambling?"

"As often as I am able."

"Horse races"—she breathed—"on Rotten Row?"

The alteration in her tone gave him pause. Her excitement was palpable, charging the air in the room. "Occasionally."

"I imagine it's quite thrilling to snap the reins, urging your horse faster and faster."

Liam frowned, not liking the turn of their conversation. "Precisely what do you hope to accomplish through these adventures?"

She didn't hesitate. "To prove myself capable of having them. Why else?"

Her answer puzzled him and caused him no small measure of concern. "Racing is a dangerous activity, even for a skilled rider. And for a woman, the scandal would ruin your reputation, resigning you to a life of spinsterhood."

There. He might have laid on the warning a bit thick but felt this country miss needed it.

"And?" She laughed, undaunted. "If I have no desire to marry, then why should I not take as much adventure as I can while I am here?"

"Because you would also sully the names of your parents." He cringed. That sounded far too similar to a quote from his harridan housekeeper, Mrs. Brasher.

"You are a veritable toller of death, Wolford," she huffed, "using your bell and rope in an attempt to mute my enthusiasm. I will not have it. Now I shall think twice before mentioning any more from my list of adventures to you."

He didn't like the sound of that. "You have a *list*?"

"For a man of questionable reputation, you know nothing of adventure," she grumbled.

He opened his mouth, intending to tell her about the people who'd lost their lives on Rotten Row, but before he could, he felt her finger against his lips. The shock of it rushed through him, disassembling every word he'd been about to say, turning them all into formless syllables without meaning.

"No more dire warnings from you. I am going to attempt to feed you porridge. I do not know how well this will turn out, considering the water debacle and the fact that your whiskers are rather..." She drew in a breath and lifted her finger simultaneously as if she only now realized what she'd done. "...rather thick."

Her voice dropped lower. Instantly, his attention and hunger dropped lower too.

"I'm not certain I like porridge," he said, clenching his jaw and trying to draw his focus northward.

She paid no heed to his concern and instead brought a spoon to his lips. That sweet, creamy aroma filled his nostrils. Against his misgivings, saliva pooled in his mouth.

Then, obeying her wordless command, he opened. And then closed. A contented breath escaped his nostrils as his tongue pushed the warm, silky porridge against his palate. Such humble, simple fare and yet sumptuous. He swallowed, already eager for another taste.

"I think you *do* like it," she said, her voice still low and now breathy.

It had an uncontrollably arousing effect on him. And considering their topic and current activity, it was peculiar to say the least. "More."

He couldn't help it. *More* was the only word that came to mind.

Each spoonful she gave him had the same effect. It was as if he'd never eaten in his life. The contrary was true—he had a healthy appetite. In *all* things.

Usually, however, his fare was of a rich, succulent, decadent variety. He broke his fast with a stack of meats, topped off with poached eggs and a heavy sauce. But nothing had ever satisfied him like this.

After another mouthful, he noticed that the spoon trembled against his bottom lip. Immediately, he lifted his hand to her wrist to stay her. His fingers inadvertently curled around the delicate bones. "Are you overtired?"

Her pulse quickened beneath his touch. The tiny thing rose up to beat against his fingertips like an excited puppy eager for affection. Unable to help himself, he stroked the pad of his middle finger in a circle over that spot.

"No. I—" she began, then slowly pulled free of his grasp. "The bowl is nearly empty. I had not thought you would be so…so…"

"Ravenous?" Neither had he. And for porridge, no less. Though perhaps it wasn't only the food that had incited his hunger.

"Yes." She breathed the word, making no other sound save for the clink of the spoon resting inside the bowl.

Strangely, his fingertips itched, causing the compulsion to locate her wrist once more. Feel her pulse react. Listen to her voice. Taste her breath…

Dangerous thoughts, all of them.

Neither of them moved, nor broke the silence that followed. Then, after a moment, he heard the rustle of fabric and felt the air stir, telling him that she'd left her place at his side. The rattle of dishes across the room confirmed it.

"My mother and I have planned an outing. I should find her and tell her that I'm ready."

Before he could comment, he heard her shuffled step scurry out of the room.

CHAPTER THREE

The Season Standard—the Daily Chronicle of Consequence

Whispers of the illicit variety are still abounding over Lady F—'s infamous masquerade. While no single person claims to have attended, the names of supposed guests increase each day.

It should come as no surprise, however, that the wolfish Earl of W— did indeed attend. One report even claims that he left his mask and cloak behind... and in the center of a garden maze! Scandalous!

As the ton awaits the news of the Season's Original, our readers know one name that will, most assuredly, not be on that list.

Of course, no one can have greater anticipation than the Marquess of Th—and our resident goddess Lady G—. Their rivalry keeps us all spellbound and...

Adeline looked up from the newspaper, her heart racing. She had little doubt that the *Earl of W* was Wolford. After all, hadn't he confessed to knowing *a thing or two* about scandal? Perhaps he knew a great deal more.

This was just the news that would help Adeline be rid of him. And after this morning, she was growing desperate for his removal.

She still did not understand how feeding a man porridge could have made her feel things she'd never felt before. *But oh, sweet Lord in heaven*, Wolford had a magnificent mouth. Even though the swelling had diminished, his lips were still full and broad and—if truth be told—wicked. They were the lips of a man who, she imagined, had great experience in indulging in activities of the *illicit variety*.

The way it moved when he'd eaten the porridge earlier had left Adeline warm and tingly. Each time his lips had parted, his tongue undulated forward between the rows of his straight white teeth, welcoming the bowl of the spoon. Watching him, the muscles of his jaw flexing, his Adam's apple rising, caused her own mouth to salivate. And when she slipped the silverware from his mouth, the slight tug of his lips caused a corresponding tug in the pit of her stomach.

She wanted to know how his lips would feel against her own. What he tasted like...

The carriage jostled, yanking Adeline away from her wanton musings. *No more of those!* she thought in a sharp self-reprimand. This was precisely why she needed him gone.

"It is a pity we could not find sturdier hairpins at any of the shops we visited," Mother said from across the carriage, absently skimming a list she withdrew from her reticule. "Though as you know, I've always preferred your hair down."

Distracted, Adeline shifted in her seat, but her braid caught and tugged her head back. She'd used more pins than ever before, attempting a style with greater height, like those she'd seen in the ladies quarterly. Yet, they'd all come free before she'd made it to the second shop. So she'd ended up purchasing a length of lavender ribbon to tie the end.

Adeline knew she would need to come up with a permanent solution before she attended her first party. "I noticed that there wasn't a single other woman wearing her hair down in public."

"Perhaps when Hester arrives with the other servants, she will make friends with other lady's maids who might know a trick or two," Mother conceded after a moment of consideration. "Anything of note in the newspaper you were so determined to purchase?"

Thankfully, the question brought Adeline back to her main focus—the removal of a certain earl from beneath their roof. The moment Mother learned of the news, she would send him away, if only for the purpose of protecting her daughter. Even though Adeline did not want to be cosseted any longer, in this particular instance, it should work to her advantage. "There is a fair amount of gossip."

Mother looked up from her list. Glancing at the *Standard*, she cleared her throat. "While your father and I frown upon the practice, I know it is the breadstuff of society."

Adeline nodded sagely. "Actually, this article—"

"Though I must confess that I find it all rather"—Mother interrupted, sitting forward, her voice falling to a whisper—"*thrilling*. To a certain extent."

Adeline's mouth dropped open. "Have *you* been reading society columns?"

Mother glanced upward to the roof as if worried that Gladwin might overhear. Then she nodded. "Mrs. Harvey has a niece who works in a bookshop here and sends a paper or two through the post. Sometimes we sit in the parlor and discuss the important events."

Her mother and their housekeeper gossiping in the parlor? It was something she never expected. And more than that…"I wish you'd invited me to these chats."

Then again, they were likely harboring the one man who could impart far more interesting gossip, and about himself.

What illicit tales might he tell? Surely, he could tell Adeline many things about which she had never experienced. Never even considered.

Of course, *illicit* was far from the word she would use to describe her own experiences with the opposite sex. Thus far, she had received only a single kiss—and a rather bland one at that—from Paul Wittingham, their parish curate.

A year ago, he'd professed a desire to marry her. Or more aptly—to care for her for the rest of her life. "*I would cherish you and never once overtax you or impose upon your limitations. Happily, I would shoulder the burden of the demands of a man in my position in order to keep you comfortable.*"

The offer had left a sour taste on her tongue. Clearly, he saw her as helpless and unable to care for herself, let alone him or even their fellow parishioners. Needless to say, she'd refused him. Adeline didn't want to marry a man who pitied her. One who only saw her shortened limb instead of seeing *her*. She'd already endured a lifetime of well-intentioned coddling from her parents. And she never intended to spend her entire life in the same cocoon. Though clearly that was the only life she could expect.

"Speaking of society gossip...this activity is not something about which I am proud—*oh* and you must promise not to tell your father," Mother said with an uncharacteristically sheepish expression. "I fear he would not understand. He might imagine that I have been discontented all these years in Boswickshire, when the contrary is true. I simply prefer a...*taste* of London from time to time."

"I will keep your secret," Adeline vowed. "However, I fear that our guest might very well be the prime focus of today's gossip."

Mother lifted her brows and took the folded edge. "Truly?"

As she handed over the *Standard*, a lack of confidence washed over Adeline. Moments ago she'd been certain of her mother's reaction. Such wasn't the case any longer. Would Mother be scandalized by the column...or intrigued?

Adeline feared it might be the latter. She also feared that the main trait she'd inherited from her mother was a penchant for news of the illicit variety.

"In all honesty," Mother said after skimming the page, "I had assumed as much about our guest. Especially considering how we'd found him. Obviously the man, or men, who'd abused Wolford so grievously was not his friend."

"Does it bother you that what the column says might be true? That Wolford is"—Adeline swallowed down a wayward thrill—"a rake?"

In response, Bunny Pimm's indigo eyes lifted from the paper and trained on her like a falcon eyeing a field mouse. "Hmm...does it bother you?"

Truth be told, it intrigued her. The stories he could tell her would be like an adventure on its own, and one that would not ruin her reputation, just offer her things to ponder once she returned to Boswickshire as the different version of herself.

Though if he was hers…the news might have made her a trifle jealous. Thank goodness she needn't worry over that possibility. "I see no reason why it should."

Liam didn't need his eyesight in order to know how harried his steward was at the moment. Then again, an afternoon drizzle would rattle Rendell, with him feeling the need to count each and every drop. The reason Liam could tell was because—whenever something went wrong—Rendell used a copious number of *my lords*. He'd surpassed a dozen already and he'd just arrived.

"Had I known, my lord, that you were injured, my lord, I would have searched each one of your residences, sent word to your hunting boxes, inquired at Arborcrest—"

Liam interrupted Rendell's obsequious servility. "And should I ever go missing again, I would appreciate your thoroughness. Although I will spare you one errand, as you are not likely to find me at Arborcrest for another thirty years."

Arborcrest was Liam's boyhood home and ancestral estate. More than that, however, it was a pastoral, quiet place, full of fond memories. One day, he would take a wife and live with her there. Though not until he was sixty years old or so, as his father had been. Liam knew all too well that it was a fool's errand to entertain the notion of matrimony as a young man.

In the meantime, Liam was determined to live a full life before settling down and begetting an heir. He did everything he could to avoid Arborcrest and left Mr. Ipley in charge of the estate.

"Yes, my lord. I'll make a note of it, my lord."

Liam's head was beginning to throb again, directly behind his eyes. He lifted a hand to his bandages where pale light seemed to illuminate the jagged veins beneath the flesh of his eyelids. He hoped it was a good sign—that he could see anything at all—but he could not be certain. "Rendell, I would appreciate it if you would spare me the additional *my lords* for the remainder of our meeting today."

"Yes, of course, my l—" The steward cleared his throat. "My apologies, my l—"

"All I ask is that you do your best." Liam breathed through his clenched teeth. "Now, what business have we to discuss?"

Again the steward cleared this throat, the rapid staccato *hemming* just as grating as the *my lords*, if not more. The rustle of papers followed. "I brought the invoices for your latest acquisitions from the Continent. Where would you like me to send them, my lord?"

"You're making excellent progress. Only one that time," Liam said patiently, if a bit mockingly. "As for the pair of Oriental vases, I should like them delivered to Brook Street. The Elbe urn should go to Wolford House. Send the French sofa next door. I will require it soon."

"There is one problem, my lord. Your housekeeper has threatened me with bodily harm should I send any more objects into what she calls her *domain*. According to Mrs. Brasher, there simply isn't any more room, my lord."

Liam exhaled. He'd been adding to his collection exceedingly as of late. The increase had begun during a recent trip to the Continent, shortly following Vale's wedding. The problem was there were too many interesting items that required further study. So many that he'd needed to buy another house in order to fit them all. "Fine. Then send the urn next door as well. I have a house that I can fill."

"Not entirely, my lord," Rendell said with a nervous sniff. "You purchased the furnishings within each of the terraced houses as well."

In other words, Liam's most recently acquired property might not hold enough of his collection either. "For our next meeting we'll talk about rearranging a few of the pieces in order to make the appropriate accommodations. There is also the possibility of filling the third property here instead of letting it."

"Begging your pardon, my lord, but Lord Caulfield has offered quite a substantial sum for the Roman pottery."

"And as I have explained before, I will not sell any part of it, regardless of the offer. After all, it isn't as if I require money." Liam had inherited a fortune that could not be spent in five lifetimes. Therefore he chose to live the way he pleased. This included buying whatever bric-a-brac took his fancy.

He considered himself a lifelong scholar, reminiscent of his father's tutelage. The late Callum Cavanaugh used a collection of artifacts to teach Liam about history, the native peoples who created the work in question—their methods, tools, and indigenous resources—the philosophic teachings of the time, and even mathematics, among other things. And with such a vast collection of his own, Liam would require decades to study each piece in depth.

"Very good, my lord." Rendell's words were accompanied by the scraping sound of a pencil scribbling over a page—likely indecipherable, as the man had abominable handwriting. "Once I received word of your situation, I took the liberty of having your valet pack a satchel of clothes for you while you remain here. Mr. Neville would have come himself, I'm sure, but he experienced a sudden bout of nausea when informed of your unfortunate accident. Also, for your convenience, I've begun interviewing candidates for the positions next door, to ready your rooms as soon as possible. If you prefer, I could send an order to your valet to assist you here."

"That won't be necessary." Liam wasn't going to have Neville here to look down his nose at Boswick's family. Besides, if they could survive without servants, then so could he. "I rather prefer no one fussing about. And if you are going to interview candidates for next door, begin with my current staff."

"Yes, my lord. And one more thing, I took the liberty of retrieving the key to the adjoining door. If you'll recall, it is located across the hall from this chamber. I thought it would be easier for you to manage if you did not have so many stairs to navigate." He scuffed his feet across the floor and placed something metal on the bedside table. "I'll just leave the key here, my lord."

Before Liam had purchased this terraced house, he'd learned where the adjoining doors were, all of them hidden either by panels or large paintings. Fortunately, he wouldn't have to traverse the stairs when the time came for him to leave. Yet, thinking of the eventuality, his headache intensified, throbbing and threatening to crack open his cranium.

"Brilliant, Rendell. I knew there was a reason I kept you." Liam waved a hand in the steward's general direction.

"However, that was the last *my lord* I can tolerate for one day, so see yourself out, if you please."

He wanted relief from the pain. Automatically, he found himself listening carefully to the sounds in the house. Rendell's lumbering steps down the stairs. Boswick's deep baritone. The door closing. He held his breath, listening intently. But there was no Miss Pimm.

Peculiarly, her voice served as a tonic that he already found himself requiring. Tonic? He nearly laughed at the notion. What idiocy! Exhaustion, that was all this was. And perhaps the blow to his head had rattled his good sense.

CHAPTER FOUR

Adeline couldn't sleep. So, as she brushed her hair in her bedchamber, she listened to the steady cadence of Father's snores from the far end of the hall, as well as the clamor of traffic outside the window. The sounds of two opposing worlds—country gentility and London society. The latter were just now beginning their evenings.

Tomorrow evening, that would be her as well.

Setting down her brush, her cheeks lifted in a grin. Father had sent Gladwin to the opera house to procure tickets. The opera! Adeline had never attended one before. She had, however, heard a few performances over the years. Father hosted various musicians, singers, and play actors, inviting them to stay in Boswickshire. He had wanted to give the best of the world to his wife and daughter.

During the first years of her life, Adeline had felt rather spoiled in that regard. This lasted until she was eight years old, when a village girl revealed the truth that had changed everything.

According to Miss Georgiana Hatch, coming over to play with Adeline was part of the weekly chores that all the village girls their age had to endure. But they were told never to say anything about her leg. That was when Adeline had begun to feel secluded instead of pampered. From that moment on, she'd feigned a stomachache whenever her assigned playmate was scheduled to arrive.

She'd always wanted a friend, someone with whom she could feel comfortable, not pitied. In fact, part of her hoped she might find that here. Perhaps she would meet such a person at the op—

A sudden *thunk* startled Adeline. The low oath *"Bloody hell!"* followed. She looked to her open door, the sound coming from across the hall.

Alarmed, she snatched the lamp from her side table and rushed to their guest's door. She paused at the threshold for the barest moment. When she heard Wolford cursing under his breath again, she entered the room without knocking.

Then she stopped short, halting so abruptly that the lamp sputtered.

The greenest eyes she'd ever seen stared back her, the enigmatic clover color holding her transfixed for a moment. Liam did not move either. He was sitting up in bed, his legs draped over the side, and—more importantly—with the length of his bandage curled in his hand.

After speaking to him and sitting at his bedside for hours on end—with nothing to do but memorize the features exposed to her view—she already knew he was handsome. She'd gone to sleep thinking about the angular line of his jaw, the tendons on his throat that shifted when he swallowed, the shape of his mouth…She just never expected him to be *this* handsome.

How could she have guessed that the slope of his forehead was utter perfection? That his dark brows were so thick and tapered? That the length of his lashes served as a frame for those eyes, making it nearly impossible to look away? And that with the natural contour of his beard that he would look like a veritable pirate?

"You removed your bandage," she said, dumbstruck and unable to state anything other than the obvious.

He closed his eyes briefly and exhaled. Then when he opened them again, he grinned. "Miss Pimm."

The warmth of those two syllables caused her to blush, but the unbidden effect helped her to break eye contact. Pulling herself together, she stepped into the room and set her lamp on his bedside table. She knew in an instant that she shouldn't have dared to stand so close to him. Her skin tingled all over, from her scalp to the soles of her feet. Her fingertips pulsed as if yearning to glide over his brow, to trace those chiseled features, to memorize the texture of his skin.

Drawing in a steadying breath, she reached down and took his bandage from his grasp. "You shouldn't have done so."

"I was tired of the constant darkness," he said, his gaze unwavering. He studied every minute activity she did— winding the gauze, brushing it free of the ruffles down the center of her night rail when it started to cling, pulling a wayward length of her light brown hair free of the bundle, tossing that hair over her shoulder—and missed nothing.

Neither did she. Once the alarm faded, she realized she was standing before him in her night rail. She hadn't even thought to grab a wrapper. Thankfully, the garment was layered, thereby offering a measure of modesty. Or at least, that's what she told herself as she moved toward the sideboard to set the bandage down and pour him a glass of water.

"You're limping," he accused. "Did you hurt yourself on the way to my room?"

Adeline tensed. The question felt like a poke at a bruise that would not heal. While she would rather no one learn of her secret, there was no hiding it now.

Drawing in a breath, she prepared for the pity that would inevitably come. "I'm lame, Wolford. I always limp, unless I wear my corrective half-boots."

He pressed his lips together and nodded, his gaze dropping to her feet. "Ah. That explains the shuffled step."

While her left foot was planted cleanly on the floor, her right was on tiptoe. With the length of her night rail nearly reaching the floor, she was sure he couldn't see much of her feet, but she felt the need to flare her hem wider for concealment, nonetheless. "Pardon?"

"Whenever you walked into the room, your steps would shuffle," he said matter-of-factly. "Your father's footfall is crisp and heavy. Your mother's is steady and light. And yours..."

"Shuffles," she finished for him, feeling more ungainly than usual.

"Those are things I'd never noticed before. All sorts of sounds. While I'd always thought I was an astute observer of people, I never knew how much I'd relied on my eyes to assist me. Hearing only the cadence of a voice and not seeing their stance or expressions was difficult to overcome." His gaze lifted, and there appeared to be a question in his eyes.

She braced herself. Usually, along with the pity, people wanted to know exactly how she became lame. And she hated telling that story.

"You did not come to me again after your outing with your mother."

Surprise stuttered out of her lungs. Was that all he had to say about her leg, just a mere observation and nothing more? She doubted that was the end of it.

"How did you know when I returned?" Likely, he'd heard the sound of her ungainly, doddering footfalls.

Yet he surprised her again with his next words.

"Your voice has a certain…quality to it that is easy to recognize," he explained with the hint of a grin. The upward tilt of his mouth caused a curved, narrow fissure to line one cheek. "And I heard you return early this afternoon."

A certain quality? What could that mean? She wondered whether it was good or bad.

"You were asleep. I didn't want to wake you," she said, stating a partial truth. "Father believes sleep is important for healing."

"He is a wise man, for I do feel better. Certainly relieved." He lifted a long-fingered hand, gesturing to his eyes.

She noticed that his breathing was less labored than before, but not entirely easy. Holding the water glass, she moved toward the bed. Without thinking, she lifted it to his lips. When she realized how pointless her effort was, she stammered, "F-forgive me. I did not mean to—"

Yet before she finished or even lowered the glass, he stopped her by curling his hand around hers. Then, tipping the glass, he drank every drop. And his eyes stayed with hers the entire time.

She felt her cheeks heat once more. In fact, they might have caught fire because she had the distinct impression that she was glowing like an ember.

When he finished, she withdrew the glass and turned to face the table. Placing the glass beside the lamp sent rows of diamond-shaped shadows against the burgundy silk-covered wall. It brought her attention to the size of the room. It seemed a trifle smaller, more intimate, now that his bandages were gone.

She swallowed and tried to keep her head about her. Though when she turned back to him and noted that he was still looking directly at her, it proved difficult. She feigned a sudden interest in a key on the floor. Likely, it had fallen during his struggles to remove the bandage.

"What is this?" Picking up the key, she glanced over to the similar cloverleaf bow protruding from the lock in his door.

"Rendell left that for when I am well enough to leave. It opens an adjoining door between our houses," he said, his gaze pinning hers once more. "As soon as your father believes I am out of danger, I'll be gone."

"Your swelling has diminished completely," she said, feeling a strange fluttering in the pit of her stomach. Then she gripped the key tightly as if it were her life's purpose. "Your flesh is somewhat bruised, however, and purplish in places. When you arrived, we weren't even able to see that you had eyes."

"And now that you are able?" There was an edge of mockery to his tone and—yes—to his lips too. Now there were appealing fissures on both sides of his mouth.

"Are you seeking a compliment? I had not taken you for a vain peacock," she chided, feeling comfortable enough to tease him in return. Yet, that quickly altered when he reached up and closed his hand over hers.

He tugged her closer. "Your expression reveals little. And there are no mirrors nearby to show me whether I am merely bruised or disfigured. That pretty blush upon your cheeks could be because you are here in your nightdress and shy about it, not necessarily because you think I am handsome."

Were all the gentlemen in London this bold? She held her breath, trying not to move and wanting to absorb every sensation caused by her hand in his grasp. Her skin rejoiced, sending shivers of warmth through her like sparks from flint and steel. His thumb swept back and forth over the mound of her thumb. Then his fingers curled casually as if touches such as these were commonplace. At least, for him.

Adeline was not wholly unfamiliar to the touch of a man's hand. Mr. Wittingham had taken her hand…even if only to aid her into a carriage or up the steps to the parish church.

This felt far different. Wolford wasn't offering assistance. In fact, she might even presume that his only aim was to touch her, to feel her hand in his. It awakened parts of her that made her feel womanly. Not at all like a lame girl.

"I like the look of you," she confessed, holding his gaze. A man who'd suffered such a beating deserved that, at least. Yet when she noticed another grin at his lips—one clearly stating that he'd known her answer the whole time and was merely teasing her—her ire sparked. She slipped free of his grasp, leaving the key with him. "I'm sure you've heard as much from many women."

Not denying it, he flashed a full smile. Then winced a bit. Her gaze fell to the cut at the corner of his mouth.

Automatically, she reached for the jar of salve from the table. Before she gave a thought to her action, she dipped her fingertip into the silken jelly and brought it to his lips.

"You'll need to—" She stopped in near mortification. This time she hadn't been trying to anticipate a need but had simply reacted. And as if she had the right to touch him whenever she pleased. She would never have been this forward with anyone else.

It was her skin's fault, she decided. That sensation-greedy part of her enjoyed manipulating her into acting too familiar with him.

Pushing the jar into his hand, she pretended that she'd meant to do that. "And now you know exactly how to apply the salve."

"I never would have accomplished it without your assistance." He winked at her and then pressed his lips together. "Mmm…I enjoy the cool bite of the mint."

It was a favorite of hers as well. In fact, this was her jar. She usually applied it right before bedtime. All it took was the barest scent to cause her lips to tingle. Not only that, but the tip of her finger did as well, pulsing beneath the silky residue. She wanted to wipe it over her own lips, but such an action would be far too intimate.

She needed a distraction. And some distance would be preferable too. "There is also beeswax in the salve."

"Is that so?" He grinned, apparently amused as he placed the jar and the key on the bedside table.

"Boswickshire boasts the finest honey. In fact, we might have a jar in the larder. I could assemble a tray, if you have the appetite."

The instant she made the offer, she expected him to look down at her foot and shake his head in polite rejection. No matter where she went in the village, everyone knew of her limb and believed her incapable of so much as carrying her own ribbons to the carriage. And Father had never once let her walk there. It had taken him years to allow her to venture as far as the stables.

Liam, however, surprised her by accepting without hesitation. "A hearty appetite, in fact."

Her cheeks heated once more at the low timbre of his voice. His gaze dipped but not to her foot. To her mouth instead. And then drifted down her throat.

Suddenly, her offer seemed more intimate than a cheese plate.

Liam was ravenous. He devoured slice after slice of dark, grainy bread smeared with soft, salty cheese and drizzled with sweet, golden honey. "Miss Pimm, how did you ever discover such a delicious combination of flavors?"

Her gaze slid down to his mouth as he licked at a stray drop of honey. Actually, her gaze dipped often. He doubted that she realized how obvious her aroused state was. The signs were there. Now that he could see, he didn't miss a thing. Her dark pupils expanded, nearly eclipsing the acorn brown of her irises. All that remained was a ring of golden brown in between those mirrors and a blue rim along the outside.

Whenever he pressed his lips together, so did she. Whenever he swallowed, she did the same. And whenever their eyes met, she would look furtively down to the plate. Then she would cut into the end of the loaf.

And because it aroused him to watch her watching him, he'd already eaten six slices. At this rate, he would gain twenty stone by tomorrow.

"Miss Pimm?" he asked, when his previous question went unanswered.

She blinked at him and licked her lips. "Pardon?"

Even that single word tunneled through him. That lush, brushed-velvet voice could set a man aflame. Liam should have guessed she would have a mouth to match it—ever so slightly plumped and with the barest of indentions in the center of her bottom lip. The perfect spot for a dab of honey and the tip of a tongue. *His.*

But *no*, he should not think those things. He reminded himself that he did not tamper with debutantes. No matter how tempting they were.

He repeated the question, asking her about the food she'd chosen.

"Quite honestly, the pantry was not as full as I'd hoped. I had thought to find a wheel of the sharp, veined cheese that one of our tenants makes. It pairs rather splendidly with our honey," she said, busily slathering another slice of bread with creamy white cheese. "Unfortunately, the majority of our foodstuffs are packed and traveling with our cook and the rest of the servants. They should arrive on the morrow."

After adding a drizzle of honey, she lifted the slice to him. He wondered what she would do if he asked her to feed it to him. Likely she would grow still, as she had earlier when she'd smoothed salve over his cut. It was puzzling to see her so at ease with him one moment and then as skittish as a sparrow the next. Then again, he was rarely in the company of debutantes and did not know if they were all like this—seeming to flirt and then afraid of the results.

He liked to tease her, though. "Then tomorrow I shall look forward to another taste of your Boswickshire honey."

And yes, he intended the double entendre. He couldn't help it.

He took a greedy bite, paying more attention to the way she watched him rather than how hungry he was. Even so, he thoroughly enjoyed this coverlet picnic, the simple yet flavorful fare, and also the company.

When he swallowed, she swallowed too, a tantalizing undulation. And before he could stop his naughty mind, he thought of the soft, wet inner tissue of her throat, her tongue, her lips...

He shifted on the bed. While his main hunger was satisfied, another part of him...wasn't. It didn't help matters that she was sitting across from him wearing only her ruffled nightclothes and her unbound mass of fawn-colored hair. It was so long and thick that she was practically sitting on it. She was a veritable Rapunzel or Lady Godiva. He couldn't decide. Though the fact that she'd grabbed her wrapper before she'd returned with the tray forced him to stick with the former. In fact, he wished she were locked away in a tower, far from him.

Abruptly, the sharp hitch in his side returned, cinching like a vise around his lungs. With such pleasant distractions, he'd almost forgotten the reason he was here.

He closed his eyes and lowered the last bite of bread, exhaling through clenched teeth. "Miss Pimm, I require the sound of your voice."

"Oh," she said, the syllable too brief to offer much relief.

He felt the air stir beside him, and a shadow cross his closed lids. His eyes squinted open to see her standing beside him. "Don't go."

"I'm not. I'm merely removing the tray so that you can lie back." And she did, even slipping the half-eaten bread from his fingers. Then she returned from the sideboard in quick order, reclaiming her place on the chair. "Shall I recite poetry, do you think? But no, I do not take you for either the maudlin or romantic sort. Perhaps I should quote from *Fordyce's Sermons?* While they were written for the proper behavior of young women, I'm certain they would suit a man who finds himself in the gossip pages quite well."

He made an effort not to cringe as he settled back against the pillows and headboard, still mostly sitting. "Ah. Then you have read the *Standard*."

"The author spoke of a masquerade you had apparently attended. You are the only confirmed guest because they found your cloak and mask in the center of a maze. What was it that you were doing in the center of the maze?"

"Scandalous things, I'm sure. I've earned my place in the gossip pages," he admitted.

"As I've been warned," she responded, unmoved. "Though it sounds to me as if you do not remember. *Did* you attend the masquerade?"

"I believe so. I do recall a rather lively party and walking through the maze with a masked woman with an enticing decolle—" He stopped. "Well, that part doesn't matter. However, then my memory goes rather hazy. That must have been when I met up with a rather jealous protector or husband."

"She was *married*?"

"I could not tell you for certain. However, I usually avoid married women—and their jealous husbands—for the obvious reasons." He gestured with a sweep of his hand over his face and torso. "I am afraid to inform you, Miss Pimm, but we live in a world of debauchery."

"You're mocking me. And not only that, but you're mocking the union of two souls who will forever be united."

He marveled at her complexion. Her face was not the pale perfection of milk that so many women powdered themselves to oblivion in order to achieve. Instead, her skin had a faint but healthy pinkish glow that made her look sun-kissed, even in the light of a single taper. So innocent and pure. *Pity*.

"Hmm…I keep forgetting that this is your first experience with society. Your naivety is somewhat refreshing. It allows me to see this wicked society with fresh eyes, eager for corruption all over again." And when she narrowed her eyes at him and huffed at his smirk, he continued. "Most men and women marry for status and property. There is no 'union of two souls.' "

"I understand that many marriages take place for convenience, but is there never an exception in London?"

"Here? Absolutely not. Waiting for the banns to be read, signing contracts, and negotiating dowries—*that* is a London wedding. Never fear, however, as there are many foolish souls who rush off to Gretna Greene. In fact, a friend of mine was married only a week past in that manner. Not to mention, my cousin was married on his country estate over Christmastime. He even rode out in the dead of night to procure a special license."

She smiled. "Quite romantic."

"But not a London wedding," he said pointedly, not comfortable with the wistful tilt of her lips. "See here, weren't you supposed to be talking to me as part of my recuperation?"

She settled back against the chair and hid a yawn in the cup of her hand. "I think I'm more interested in hearing about the reason you don't seem to care that your name will be in the *Standard* for the rest of your life."

"I'm certain they'll tire of me eventually. Besides, in twenty years or so, I'll begin mending my ways by becoming completely boring to atone for my misguided escapades so that I can marry when I am sixty and in need of an heir."

At his last word, her brows lifted. "A marriage for *status and property*? I would not have guessed that for such as you."

He frowned. "And why ever not?"

"Because you were so afraid that I was trying to trap you into marriage. Yet that is precisely what you intend for your future—put your foot in the snare as bait to lure a bride young enough to produce an heir in exchange for your title." She gave him a grin that was sleepy near the corners of her eyes and soft on her lips. "It is rather comical, is it not?"

"I would not need to *lure* any bride. Once the word is out, they'll flock to my doorstep," he grumbled in his own defense. Though, while her mocking tone and sharp wit cut him to the core, he was not cross. Instead, he found himself oddly contented and wanted to continue this joust for hours to come.

"You'll be old. Not only that, but the woman you plan on marrying hasn't even been born yet." She feigned a shudder. "I suppose in ten years you'll be eyeing the sleeping inhabitants of perambulators and making a list."

A small giggle escaped. Then she closed her eyes, shifting in the chair as if trying to make herself comfortable.

Liam knew it would only be a minute before she left him to his solitude, so he tried to find a reason for her to linger awhile. "Tell me about your outing today. Did you drive through the park, visit shops, find adventure?"

She shook her head and slowly opened her eyes. "No park. Mother worried that after the shops, I would be too tired. In fact, the most adventurous thing that happened was losing my hairpins. It has a mind of its own."

"Your hair is magnificent," he said, distracted by the tuft she absently twirled around her finger.

"Thank you, Wolford." She released a soft sigh. "I know it is wrong to be prideful, but I rather like my hair too. Oh, certainly it is a bother when it will not stay put, yet I consider it my one remarkable feature that has nothing to do with my—" She broke off with a glance down to her foot. "Well, never mind. I do have a question for you that I've wondered since my outing. Perhaps you could tell me what a Season's *Original* is."

He could tell her that it was a bunch of foolishness, but it would be better for her to decide for herself. "An *Original* is a man or a woman who has earned the *ton*'s approval, so much so that he or she can do no wrong. The way they dress becomes en vogue. The debutante *Originals* are sought after by the upper echelon of the peerage. They can marry whomever they please. Whereas their male counterparts are cast upon the rocks as waves of manipulative, marriage-minded misses seek to drown them."

"It seems a far better reward for the debutantes." She battled another yawn and glanced over her shoulder to the door.

"Come here," he said on impulse. "That chair looks so uncomfortable that it's causing me pain." Drawing in a breath, he braced himself for another sharp twinge as he moved away from the edge of the bed. When he made a suitable space, he patted the coverlet.

She blinked, struggling to open her eyes as if her lids were filled with heavy sand. "I cannot lie beside you. Think of your reputation."

He chuckled. She should be thinking of hers. Yet even Liam could hear her father snoring down the hall. "I am in no condition to ravish you." Not properly, at any rate. And he was feeling rather selfish at the moment. He wanted the company. Unfortunately, he'd slept all day and was fully alert, his inner clock set to society's late hours. "Besides, it will be just for a minute. I want to hear all about the London adventure you have planned for tomorrow."

"Only for a minute," she said, eyeing the pillow with longing. She settled beside him. "We are attending the opera in the evening, and I need to be well rested."

"You must use my box."

She shook her head. "Father already has tickets. It matters not where we sit. I'm simply happy to go to the performance, instead of the performance coming to me."

Even though her answer puzzled him, he did not ask her to clarify. Instead, he continued to insist. "Then accept, as a favor or form of repayment for all you've done."

"Pimms do not require repayment for doing only what was right. Besides, I was ready to send you away—for your own people to care for you—almost immediately."

This made him laugh. "Why? Afraid of the sight of me?"

"No. Just afraid of my own"—her voice faded, garbled on a yawn—"I wasn't prepared. Still not. Need you to…leave." She snuggled in beside him.

"Afraid of your own *what?*" he prodded.

But she did not answer. Instead, she drifted off to sleep, her head on his shoulder.

The unfortunate thing of it all was that this had been his own bright idea. Now, with Adeline in his bed, his curiosity wasn't the only thing aroused. And here he was, finally awake, and lying next to a soft, warm woman whom he dare not touch.

CHAPTER FIVE

Adeline's pillow was much firmer than usual. Much warmer too.

Normally, she would simply flip it over to feel the cool side against her cheek, but this side smelled too nice to abandon. Pressing her nose against it, she drew in a deep breath. A familiar mélange of scents filled her nostrils, something oaky with hints of leather, vanillin, and musk. She exhaled contentedly.

Curling her hand over the coverlet, her fingers delved into soft, springy fur. Mmm…quite decadent. If given the opportunity, she would stay right here forev—

Wait a minute…*fur?* The last she knew, there were no furs on her bed.

Then perhaps this is a dream, she thought and summarily agreed with herself.

Inhaling again, she stroked her fingers against the fur. Coincidentally, she felt a similar movement against the small of her back. *Odd.* Her sleepy self, however, accepted this occurrence as logical. Each time she rubbed her fingers against the fur, the corresponding sensation brushed her back. And in the center of her palm, her pulse beat hard and steady.

She snuggled deeper into this dream, sliding her leg over the coverlet that—*apparently*—had bunched up against her. Strange, but even the coverlet was firm, thick, and far warmer than she remembered.

"Mind your knee, Miss Pimm."

Hmm…that was unexpected. She'd heard Liam's voice in a dream prior to this one, but he hadn't sounded so hoarse. Then perhaps in this dream, he had a head cold. It seemed possible.

She burrowed closer.

Liam chuckled. "I do not have a cold. Besides, if either of us were plagued with fever, you would likely be the victim. You are a veritable ember when you sleep."

Dream-Liam professed to know a great deal about her. Even for a dream, he was rather presumptuous, considering they'd only just met.

The sound of his amusement was so real it vibrated against her cheek. She rubbed against the pillow. When she discovered a spot of drool, she shifted further inward until she could hear the steady beat of her own pulse inside her ear. She liked that sound.

"Darling, as much as I enjoy hearing your sleep ramblings, it is time for you to rise and return to your own bed."

Darling…she liked that too. It was much pleasanter than the formality of *Miss Pimm*. After all, *Miss Pimm* was a stone wall between neighbors. *Darling*, on the other hand, was a lovely carved path through the thicket.

"That was almost naughty. There will be no path carving for us, however. No matter how tempted I might be." His voice came out in a low, rumbled breath as something warm pressed against the top of her head. A kiss, perhaps?

Even dreaming, she felt her cheeks grow warm. It was no use. She would have to flip over her pillow for the cool side. Drawing in one more breath, she lifted her head and—

Her hair caught, yanking her to a stop. Eyes closed, she reached her arm over her head to pull it free. Yet even then, it wouldn't come. *Drat this heavy pillow.*

"Careful," Liam said as the pillow shifted beside her.

Now she was just awake enough to realize that the pillow couldn't shift without her. Not only that, but why was she hearing Liam's voice so clearly when she wasn't fully asleep?

Adeline opened her eyes. Green irises glinted at her with mischief as a pair of dark eyebrows rose. Within a bed of whiskers, his mouth curved into a slow, knowing grin. A decidedly wicked grin.

She blinked, trying to make sense of what she saw. Her eyes drifted lower to her hand where it lay against a mat of soft, springy curls. Not fur. And the steady throb beneath her palm was not her own pulse but his heartbeat. Moreover, her leg was not draped over a bunched-up coverlet. It was draped over *him*—her knee, lower leg, and foot all nestled between his legs.

She reared back only to be halted by her trapped hair again.

"You said it would only be a minute," she accused, as if her falling asleep was his fault.

"And I believe it took even less time for you to fall asleep. You are a decidedly sound sleeper. It must run in your family.

I have been listening to your breathing as well as your father's snores for hours."

"Hours?" She struggled to free herself, lifting up on her side to free her hair. Liam issued a grunt. That was when she realized that her maneuvering had brought her half atop him. "I apologize. Have I hurt you?"

"As long as you do not lift...your knee another inch...then nothing vital." He turned slightly toward her, trapping her leg between his. This entire episode contained more intimacy than she'd ever shared with another person. And certainly not a man.

When his hand moved to her nape, she thought he would kiss her. Her lips tingled in response. Apparently, spending hours—*hours?*—locked in his embrace had still left her skin greedy for more. "What time is it?"

"I heard the clock chime five times a short while ago." His breath caressed her lips, and his sleepy gaze dropped to her mouth. He went still, lingering, neither moving closer nor retreating.

During this moment, she felt as if some sort of clock began to chime inside of her. Every strike of the bell said, "Now. Please. Kiss. Me. Now."

Instead of kissing her, however, he freed her hair and summarily rolled onto his back, breathing hard, as if winded. "Well beyond the time for you to go and for me to sleep."

She swallowed down her disappointment. "You haven't slept?"

"Not a wink. Your father might have been understanding before, but I'm not certain he would feel the same if he found you in your nightclothes and in my bed."

"There is a coverlet between us," she pointed out, blushing. "Besides, you are in pain. I'm sure my father would know that nothing transpired."

Liam issued a low, derisive chuckle. "And as a man, your father would also know that men are capable of enduring pain in order to reap certain pleasures. In fact, a man would walk through fire in order to—"

"Say no more. I understand what you are saying without elaboration," she interrupted, scurrying off the bed so quickly she nearly tripped on the hem of her night rail. "While I may be new to London, I am not a rusticated simpleton."

"No?"

She crossed her arms. "I know what happens after men and women marry, or—in your case—when men behave as if they are married to every woman they meet."

"Well, not *every* woman," he said, gesturing with a sweep of his hand to her.

Her mouth opened, but she was too stunned to gasp. The insult took her off guard. Over the years, she'd learned that men looked at her in two ways. They either saw her as something frail and wounded. Or they saw her as wholly undesirable.

She told herself that it did not bother her that Liam Cavanaugh felt the latter. Obviously last night, Wolford's ready manners had prevented him from betraying his true feelings. This morning, however, the truth was evident.

Averting her face, she prepared to leave him and lifted her lamp from the table. That was when she noticed that the taper that had burned down to the wick. Only the amber light of the glowing embers lit the chamber. There was a chill in the room as well. While she was tempted to walk out without another word, she knew that he needed a few logs on the grate.

She moved over to the basket near the hearth. As she kneeled down to see to her task, she wondered—if he'd been disgusted by her lameness, then why had he encouraged her to stay so long in his company? It made no sense to her.

The question began to needle her. He truly hadn't seemed bothered last night. In fact, he'd said everything to encourage her to stay. He could have easily dismissed her at any point. But instead, he'd invited her to close her eyes for a moment. He'd been rather insistent that she not leave him. And she'd stayed, because she understood what it was like to be…lonely.

Suspicion filled her. Perhaps this wasn't about her limb at all. If he'd been repulsed, then he wouldn't have made a space for her, wouldn't have held her all night. More likely, he would have nudged her rudely until she awoke.

"I know what you are doing," Adeline said when it dawned on her. Holding onto the mantel, she stood and turned away from the low fire. "You're trying to make sure that I believe you were doing me a favor by letting me fall asleep here."

"It *was* a favor. Nothing more," he said, his lips pressed together in a grim line.

She continued as if she hadn't heard him, went to the sideboard to refill his water glass. "When I was a child, I spent many a day tethered to my bed, enduring leg treatments— various braces, hot baths, cold baths—one after another. Other than the occasional performances from play actors or traveling acrobats, I had nothing to do but while away the hours. Sometimes my greatest entertainment was in seeing how many dolls I could knock off the foot of my bed with the lash of ribbon-stick. By the time I was ten years old, I became rather good at it too."

Without offering him the glass, she merely set it down on his bedside table and collected the items left over from his midnight supper as she continued. "Of course, my parents invited village children to come up to my chamber to play with me, but I grew tired of their pity and became surly, pushing them away so they wouldn't accept another invitation. And much to my disappointment, my efforts succeeded. I'd managed to erect a barrier between us, which left me all the lonelier in the end."

At the door, she paused long enough for him to interject. After all, she'd given him plenty of ammunition to fire a blow at her.

Meeting his cool, scrutinizing gaze, she found that his expression was impossible to read. And silence was his only reply.

"For you, however," she went on, "you'll soon be fit enough to leave this bed and return to your own life. And when you are in the bosom of your dear friends and family, who have been worrying over your absence, then you'll be free to forget all about your moment of weakness when *you* asked *me* to stay for 'just a minute.'"

Adeline closed the door, feeling somewhat vindicated. But more than that, she would always remember—for a short while—that the eighth Earl of Wolford had craved her company.

Liam did not sleep at all, not in the hour after she left his room or during the time when he heard her parents awaken.

He told himself that it was because he was on a different schedule. That he was used to coming home at dawn. That he would sleep soon enough.

But then a sliver of light bled in through the part in the curtain. Blindingly bright. So much so, that his head throbbed, spinning with dizziness even as he lay in bed. The sounds were deafening too. He heard his host and hostess rise and move about in their usual early-morning manner. Yet each footfall echoed inside his skull like the bang of a drum.

When Boswick came into his room, he offered a good-natured greeting, as well as gladness over Liam's reduced swelling, healthy bruising, and apparent unimpeded vision. Though, with his sensitivity to light, along with the dizziness, Boswick recommended that Liam remain abed. According to a missive from Uncle Peirce, Liam could easily fall into a worse state if he pushed recovery too quickly.

"However," Boswick added, "speaking as a man who abhors a sickbed, I've found that a hot bath seems to help many an illness make a hasty retreat. If you care to give it a go, I'm certain we could arrange it."

Ever grateful, Liam nodded. "I would, indeed."

Shortly after Boswick's departure, the cheerful Lady Boswick arrived with a bowl of porridge and pot of warm tea. Graciously, he thanked her as she propped the tray over his lap before bustling out when she heard the servants' arrival, at long last.

Within the hour, the butler and a footman introduced themselves. Finmore and Jones, respectively, offered their services should Liam require anything. Without deliberating, Liam sent a missive to his aunt.

Even the Pimms' housekeeper, Mrs. Harvey, dropped in to collect his tray and offered a friendly greeting.

But while he waited for the portable wooden tub to be lined with oil-slicked canvas and filled with steaming water, it did not escape his notice that there was one person who did not stop by to wish him a good day or even to wish him to hell.

At first, he'd been angry, ready to shout a command for her to return to his chamber at once. At that time, he would have told her that he had plenty of friends and family who were, no doubt, missing him. Therefore, she could take her pity elsewhere. He neither deserved nor desired it.

Yet during his long soak, he'd had ample time to ruminate over her parting words. Gradually, his temper cooled with the water, and he thought of her as a little girl sequestered in her bedchamber while physicians poked and prodded her for days on end. Not only that, but he knew from his own experiences that children tended to be cruel and imagined that the ones who visited her had not always been kind.

After his father's death, Mr. Ipley had *hired* suitable friends for Liam, paying them in sweets and trinkets. Even though Liam and his cousin, North, were close in age, they'd barely known each other in those early years. The reason was mainly due to their elders trying to prove which one of them had the right to inherit their uncle's dukedom. Having been born a month prior to Liam, North had become the Duke of Vale. Liam had taken his father's title, and all was as it should be. There were still those, however, who had frowned upon North's half-commoner blood and strove to keep the cousins apart.

Once Liam had been sent to Eton, however, he'd made his own friends—Vale, of course; Jack Marlowe, recently named Viscount Locke; and Max Harwick, the Marquess of Thayne. Though if truth be told, Liam wasn't certain he trusted Thayne at the moment.

That thought aside, however, Liam had mulled over Adeline's words at length, and he'd come to one conclusion. He'd been an arse.

At first, he hadn't understood why he'd become cross with her. All he knew was that one minute her body had been next to his, warm and sleepy, and eliciting the strongest desire for a good, thorough tupping that he'd ever felt in his life. And in the next, she was gone.

Instantly, that had felt wrong. His arms were too empty. The bed too cold. He'd wanted her back. His body ached for her. Then she'd just *had* to mention marriage and ruin a perfectly pleasant morning.

"I know what happens after men and women marry."

Those words had caused an icy deluge to wash through him, reminding him of the carefully crafted deception he'd once fallen for. He'd felt like that foolish seventeen-year-old all over again. He didn't like it—or his peculiarly intense reaction to her.

Summarily, he'd concluded that this entire episode—the coverlet picnic, her pretense of exhaustion—had been a scheme. After all, what kind of young woman would willingly accept an invitation to lie beside a man with his reputation? A naïve one, to be sure. Perhaps even one fresh from the country…

Now the reason for his surliness sounded like an excuse. He knew he'd been a despicable cad, and he intended to make amends. As soon as Aunt Edith arrived, he would.

Knowing that she would come soon, he knew he should shave, but the truth of the matter was he was exhausted. It had taken every ounce of strength he possessed to get in and out of the tub and then to dress. Thankfully though, Jones filled in for Boswick's valet from time to time and assisted Liam. Jones tied a fine cravat as well. He even trimmed the stray thread from the button of Liam's gray waistcoat and helped him into the blue paisley banyan that Neville had packed.

Liam would have liked nothing more than to doze off for eight hours or so, but he knew he needed to build his strength in order to leave. After last night and this morning, it was clear to him that he should not have stayed this long. Living amongst the Pimm family was beginning to affect his sense of reason. There was no other way to explain his lapse in judgment.

Of course, Adeline would be quick to call him a lonely soul. Why, she intimated that he would miss their company—and hers in particular—when he left. All the more reason to prove her wrong.

Therefore, he forced himself to sit up with a brace of pillows behind him, no matter how dizzy or nauseous it made him. He was thankful that he hadn't eaten more than one mouthful of porridge this morning, for he feared he might cast up his accounts all over the burgundy and blue rug on the floor beside him.

Trying to catch his breath, he closed his eyes as another wave of pain and sickness swept through him. All he could do was listen for Miss Pimm's familiar tone. Before Jones left, Liam should have told him to send her. But what reason would he have given? He couldn't very well confess that the sound of her voice was the remedy he required. No doubt, the footman would have wondered if the blows to his head had scrambled his brain. Liam knew this because he wondered the same thing.

He caught the faintest trace somewhere far off, as if she was not one but two floors separated from him. Hearing her, Liam was quick to forgive her incorrect assumptions. He wasn't lonely. Far from it.

He must have dozed off, because the next thing he heard was a gasp at the door. Looking past the foot of the bed, he saw the Dowager Duchess of Vale. Beneath her elegantly coiffed silver hair, her penciled brows furrowed in concern and her faded blue eyes turned luminous.

Then with a sniff, she stormed into the room and began scolding him. He couldn't help but smile.

"Three days," she chided, plucking her gloves from each finger before she settled her hand over his forehead. "Three days and the only mention of you is from the *Standard*, and all this time, you've been hurt and in a stranger's home."

He didn't bother to correct her on who owned the property since the results were the same. He was beneath Boswick's roof when he should have been beneath his own next door. If he had managed to stumble over his own threshold, he was sure Rendell would have found him…eventually.

"I am well." Though, he supposed, the only reason he was on the mend was due to the Pimms.

"Liam, don't you dare. I have eyes, young man. You are bruised, your complexion has a greenish cast to it, and heaven knows what else is hiding beneath that ghastly display of whiskers. But the fact that you did not rise to greet me tells me that you cannot." She turned to Lady Boswick, who was just now coming into view. "I hope he has been a good guest."

"Perfectly agreeable, Your Grace. He has made no fuss, nor any demands. I dare say, he has also been generously forgiving of our familiarity," Lady Boswick—*Bunny*, as he was asked to call her—said before she inclined her head and left them to their privacy.

Some of Aunt Edith's ruffled feathers smoothed upon hearing this. "Thankfully, your manners are impeccable, even when you're being a scoundrel and your name is all over the scandal sheets."

His aunt had a wonderful way of focusing on what *truly* mattered. Yet, with a bit of charm, she would soon see his transgressions as trivialities. "But you always forgive me, and that is how I know that I am your favorite nephew. Under the circumstances, admitting it would be acceptable. Fear not; I won't tell Vale."

She shushed him but fought a smile as she settled into the vacant chair that had been left at his bedside. "You know very well that I do not hold favorites of my nephews and niece. All I desire is your happiness. Though perhaps one day you will find it *without* causing gossip."

"I have managed to remain free of scandal for these past few days, Aunt."

"Yes, but at what cost to your hosts? They have a daughter."

"I am well aware of Miss Pimm's existence," he said with a wry laugh that died the moment he caught his aunt's expression. "Why does this statement of fact earn your curiosity?

You said yourself that Lord and Lady Boswick have a daughter, and I merely confirmed it."

"But it is not often that a debutante earns your notice," she said with a peculiar smile that made Liam shift against the pillows.

The movement caused a sharp hitch in his side once more. The pain knifed straight through his ribs, to his stomach, and to the center of his skull, but he made every effort to conceal his discomfort. Thankfully, a maid entered the room with a fresh pot of tea, allowing him a moment to recover. After placing the tray within the fluted edge of the side table, the maid took a step back and curtsied.

When Aunt Edith hesitated to dismiss the maid immediately, a sense of wariness filled Liam. He studied his aunt. Her brow was still lifted in curiosity, her eyes narrowed slightly. Damn. Liam knew that look. It was the same one that warned him she was up to mischief. And since they had just been speaking of Adeline, he could just about guess that she was deciding whether or not to ask the maid to fetch Miss Pimm.

Liam steeled himself, not revealing the frisson of alarm spiking his pulse. He didn't know why, but he didn't want his aunt to see both him and Adeline in this room together.

Thankfully, after a watchful moment, Edith inclined her head and dismissed the maid.

Once they were alone again, Liam made a point of setting the record straight. "No notice was taken of Miss Pimm, I assure you. Other than my mistaken assumption that she was a servant."

She pursed her lips as she poured the tea. "Come now, her manner, features, even her hands are far too delicate."

"Until a few hours ago, my head was bandaged, including my eyes. I saw no one. I had to take their word that they were who they said they were." He was determined to refute whatever notion his aunt possessed. Yet now that he said it aloud, it seemed odd that he had trusted them at all. Again, he wondered at the state of his gray matter.

"Bandaged…" she said, her voice broke, her expression fretful. "And not one of your own family to know the worst of it."

Ignoring the pain, he reached out and laid his hand over hers. "I did not want to worry you needlessly. My hosts have done everything for me that my own family would have done, of that I am certain."

She offered him a tremulous smile and patted the back of his hand. Since their own was not the warmest of families, they both knew this was an overstatement. He could never imagine Edith carrying a breakfast tray to his room and then feeding him. She would have, however, penned a marvelous letter to a physician and assigned the best servants to his care.

"For a man with such a razor wit, you rarely give such high praise. Perhaps I should add them to the guest list for the dinner I'm hosting at Vale's, in honor of your Uncle Albert and Cousin Gemma's return from abroad in a fortnight."

Liam settled back into the chair, battling another wave of dizziness. "Just as long as Uncle Albert does not try to sell Lord Boswick any of the artifacts from his travels."

It was known only between Liam, Aunt Edith, and Vale that most of Uncle Albert's supposed artifacts were forgeries. Not even Uncle Albert knew. In order to keep Albert from being embarrassed, they'd all agreed to keep the secret. Apparently, the poor man had been swindled by whoever had sold to him.

"Though perhaps a mere dinner would not be enough to repay them," Edith said.

And now was his chance to make amends. He hadn't wanted to make his reason for sending the letter to her obvious. Knowing his aunt's desire to see him settled, he didn't want to give her any amount of chain to see him shackled. Therefore, the invitation needed to be her idea.

"It just so happens that they are attending the opera this evening," he said with a practiced air of disinterest. "Though, I must warn you, Miss Pimm is a rather proud creature and has refused the use of my box."

Curiously, his statement caused her to grow still, her cup paused mid-lift, and he didn't understand why.

"You asked Miss Pimm and not her parents?"

Shrill alarm bells began pinging inside of his skull. Realizing his mistake, he made a quick amendment. "All the Pimms are quite proud. Worse, they believe that any member of our society would have come to my aid as they did and likely would have refused any form of repayment. Therefore, I thought appealing to their daughter first would garner their excitement and willingness to accept."

Edith nodded as if in perfect understanding, and not even a hint of mischief marked her expression. "And so you offered your box?"

"Of course," he said, relieved that she did not see every slip of his tongue as a prelude to nuptials. "Surely, you would agree that it is the very least I could do."

"But if you knew that you were not well enough and planned on asking me to assist you, then why not offer Vale's box instead?"

To him, the answer was obvious. "Because mine is better. It has the best vantage point for the performance, and I would like to repay them with...a London adventure.

"And yet, Miss Pimm refused an invitation from an earl." She tsked. "When I met her moments ago, she seemed perfectly sensible and agreeable. Whatever did you do to make her spurn you?"

"Spurn me? Ha!" Since he had dealt out plenty of teasing to his aunt over the years, he supposed it only right that he allow her to mock him this once. "It was an invitation refused, nothing more. Regardless, none of that matters."

"And why ever not?"

This time he didn't bother to conceal his grin. "Because Miss Pimm will not refuse you."

"Dear Liam," she laughed. "I believe you've been spoiled for too long. You're used to getting precisely what you want."

With everything settled, he released a satisfied breath, closed his eyes, and rested his head. "I see nothing wrong with that at all."

CHAPTER SIX

"*The opera,*" Adeline breathed, crossing the threshold behind her parents.

It was like stepping into another world. Everything appeared glittering and bright, with walls adorned with intricate plaster moldings, statues tucked into alcoves, and crystal chandeliers hanging overhead. And all of this was accompanied by the animated chatter of hundreds of people rising to the domed ceiling.

"Unfortunately, the only tickets available were for *Seville*, which we have already heard." Father shook his head, disappointed.

But this was far different from their home. It was common to have their house open during the day with dozens of villagers filling the foyer and main hall. They lined up to talk to father about important issues or sometimes bringing wares to sell or bestowing gifts. Yet even then, their home was never as crowded as the opera house was tonight. And certainly none of the villagers were as well dressed.

Adeline looked down at her pale-pink satin gown. She'd worn her new rose-and-ivory striped half boots this evening, having saved them for this special occasion.

Mother patted Father's forearm absently as she too looked around in wonder. "Though this particular venue makes it seem new to me, and I haven't even heard the players."

Mother wore a lovely bronze satin gown, her hair in a twist. Unfortunately, Adeline's hair had not cooperated with combs, pins, or any manner that Hester could fashion. She'd even given the maid permission to cut some of the length, but Hester had wanted to get Mother's approval first. It seemed that her parents' efforts of treating her as a fully grown, capable woman were more successful than those of the servants.

Frustrated, Adeline had settled on a herringbone braid, tucked under and interwoven into a weighty and out-of-fashion chignon. Even with the failure, she still felt rather pretty. In fact, she'd almost given in to an impulse to show herself to Wolford, but then thought better of it. After their last encounter, she hadn't quite decided whether or not to forgive him. She would see how the night progressed before making her decision.

A footman asked for their ticket and Father also gave him the dowager duchess's card. Then they were escorted up the stairs, down a carpeted hall, and past archways draped in heavy brocade.

The dowager duchess greeted them with a smile, reaching out a gloved hand to press Mother's while nodding to Father. "Lord and Lady Boswick, I am so very pleased and honored to have you as my guests this evening. For the generosity and kindness you have bestowed on my nephew, I cannot thank you enough. Each of you," she said, her gaze alighting on Adeline. "And Miss Pimm, how lovely you look this evening. I believe Liam intimated that this is your first opera."

When the dowager duchess initially extended an invitation to join her at the opera, Adeline had wondered how much Liam had divulged. Had he asked his aunt for this favor out of pity for the Lord and Lady and their lame daughter who'd helped him?

Like earlier, however, the dowager displayed no outward sign of sympathy, revulsion, or even cast the barest glance down at Adeline's feet. Could it be that Wolford was too much of a gentleman to mention her limb?

Wanting it to be true and leaning ever so slightly toward the side of forgiving him, Adeline nodded. "It is, Your Grace."

She decided not to go into the details of how she'd seen operas in her home. The last thing she wanted to do was arouse questions regarding the reason. She wanted her London life to be different, and without people pitying her or seeing her as helpless. Thankfully, her parents did not elaborate either. Adeline gave them a quick smile of appreciation before she spoke again. "I'm overwhelmed by Your Grace's generosity. The view from your box is positively stunning!"

The dowager duchess smiled. "It is quite exceptional, isn't it? But I must confess that I usually sit in the Duke of Vale's box, my other nephew," she explained and then pointed with her fan to the shadowed one across the way, on the corner. "This belongs to—"

And even before the dowager duchess spoke his name, Adeline knew. Wolford seemed to be here with them, his own smirk in the faces of the sculpted cherubs in the molding.

"Liam," the dowager duchess confirmed.

Oh, that man! Even after she had refused his offer to sit here, he'd found a way to get exactly what he wanted. He deserved to be scolded for this manipulation. After all, she could have enjoyed the opera from the floor just as well.

Perhaps.

Feeling cross with Liam once again and with those smirking cherubs, she was thankful that her parents interjected their astonishment and praise, promising to pass on a word of gratitude to their houseguest when they returned home.

During their small exchange, two more guests arrived. The dowager duchess introduced the two women as Zinnia, Lady Cosgrove, and her cousin, Juliet, Lady Granworth.

Adeline forced herself not to stare in awe at Lady Granworth. She was beautiful. Flaxen hair, flawless complexion, and enigmatic eyes that were even bluer than Mother's. There was something incandescent about her too. Like gold shimmered from within, coming out through every strand of her hair. A veritable goddess walking amongst mere mortals. Goddess...

Instantly the column in the *Standard* came to mind. Could this be the one and only *Lady G*?

Lady Cosgrove was similar in appearance, though perhaps Lady Granworth's senior by twenty years. Her hair was neatly coiffed and threaded with silver, her posture refined. Adeline felt dowdy by comparison and subtly straightened her shoulders. Then she made sure to plant her corrective half boot firmly down so that she did not get tangled in her skirts as she curtsied.

Once the introductions commenced, Adeline stepped over toward the edge and rested her hands on the brass railing. While she took in the sights before her, the dowager duchess drew Lady Cosgrove and Adeline's parents into the hall for more introductions.

The view from the balcony was breathtaking, not only of the stage, but of all the other boxes and the floor as well. A sea of people churned below them. In the boxes opposite, the audience held their lorgnettes to study everyone...including her.

Her first inclination was to ensure that her half boot was hidden beneath her skirts. Which was silly, since a short plaster wall blocked their view of her lower half. She fidgeted all the same but stopped when Lady Granworth came up beside her.

"I have found that if you smile and tilt your head just so, they train their glasses on another quarry." Lady Granworth offered a demonstration. Soon enough, several heads and lorgnettes turned in unison, their focus on the box next door. "Clever trick, is it not?"

Adeline nearly laughed. "There is much I need to learn about living amongst the *haute ton*, my lady. Having arrived late for the start of this Season and having lived in the country, Father warned me that I'd likely be a curiosity."

A warning she had not taken lightly.

"Indeed, you are, though perhaps there is one other reason why." Lady Granworth hesitated long enough for Adeline to feel her heart lunge up into her throat before continuing. "You have gained favor with the Dowager Duchess of Vale, and there are not many who have accomplished such a feat."

Too relieved to form a response, Adeline swallowed and smiled.

"Is society much different from where you live?" Lady Granworth asked.

"Somewhat, though not entirely. Since my village is small, everyone knows everything. There are no secrets."

"Then I am certain you will adjust quite easily to London society, for it is the same here. I cannot fan myself when the room is overly warm without it appearing in the *Standard* the following morning, accused of using my wiles."

Adeline thought of the edition she'd read this very day. "Then it is true. You are, indeed, *Lady G*." The moment the words tumbled forth, she cupped her hand over her mouth. "Forgive me, please, my lady. That was incomparably rude."

"Please, you must call me Juliet," she said with a musical laugh. "You see, London is not so very different from your village. I dare say, however, that the frequent appearances of my name may have something to do with a scandalous wager I made with the Marquess of Thayne. Even I knew better than to incite their interest. I do not know how else to explain it, other than Max brings out the worst in me."

In that moment, a dark-haired gentleman joined them near the edge of the box. He flashed Juliet a daring grin that seemed to simmer in his brown eyes. "The feeling is most definitely mutual, Lady Granworth."

"Do try to be civil, Max. Miss Pimm and her parents are new to town and I would like for her to have a good impression, if you can help it. Adeline, this is Maxwell Harwick, the Marquess of Thayne."

"Pleased to meet you, my lord."

"Thayne, please," he said with a nod, his hand splayed over the center of a black satin waistcoat beneath a brushed pewter-colored tailcoat. "After all, from what I understand, you saved Wolford's life, or very near it."

"Not I, but my father. We are thankful that we found him when we did." For the most part anyway. There was still part of Adeline that wished she'd never met him.

"I see that calculated gleam in your eyes," Juliet interjected, closing her fan with a snap and pointing it at Thayne. "You should be ashamed of yourself."

He lifted his brows in innocence and darted a glance to Adeline. "I do not know what you could mean."

"That Wolford's injury will soften the hearts of the *ton*." Then Juliet directed her next comment to Adeline. "Max believes that Wolford is the perfect candidate for this Season's *Original*."

Adeline fought a laugh. "When Wolford explained this contest to me, I'd assumed the person named would have to be…well…someone the *ton* admired, not reviled in the *Standard*."

"I couldn't agree more," Juliet said.

Thayne's grin never faltered. "Then you will be doubly surprised when he is named at month's end."

"You believe that Wolford plans on reforming?" Adeline tried to hide her amusement. It would be rude to laugh aloud, even at such a ridiculous notion.

The marquess did not seem too bothered by the question. He merely shrugged. "It is all a matter of perception. I have already heard the whispers this evening about Wolford's daring escape from Death's clutches. About the Samaritans that saved him, took him in, and earned favor with his aunt."

"Rumors certainly do travel quickly. We have not been present for a quarter hour," Adeline murmured. Her gaze skimmed over the boxes of voyeurs, who once again trained their glasses on Wolford's box.

Juliet seemed to notice as well. Though instead of smiling as she was a moment ago, her delicate brow furrowed with fine worry lines. "If that is true, then a certain *Miss P* will make a first appearance in the *Standard* tomorrow morning. For your sake, Adeline, I hope not. Sweet whispers often turn sour when one least expects it."

Adeline drew in a breath as understanding hit her. Hadn't Juliet already warned her that society was similar to a small village? A frisson of fear hit her next as she thought about her only secret. She shifted from one foot to the other, taking the weight away from her corrective half boot. She would hate for people to discover her deformity, to treat her the way she'd been treated all her life.

Then again, how would they discover it? The family's servants were loyal. And, thus far, she had no indication that Wolford would speak of it.

"Forgive me for mentioning this, Miss Pimm, but it would be a disservice to you otherwise." Thayne's dark eyes softened apologetically. "A moment ago, as I made my way over to make your acquaintance, I witnessed Lady Falksworth refuse an introduction to Lord and Lady Boswick."

Adeline waited for him to continue. This couldn't be too terrible, could it? A refusal for an introduction was so trite compared to what she most feared.

"*Refuse*? Of all the—" Juliet scoffed and then reached out to curl her hand over Adeline's arm. "I never liked her. She has far too many birds caged up in her solarium. Hundreds of them kept from flying. Anyone who can be so cruel ought to be banished from society."

Thayne's mouth slanted in a small grin as he offered Juliet a nod. "I'll see what I can do. After all, this title ought to offer some sort of compensation. The banishment of harridans should top the list."

The cold flash of vehemence in Juliet's gaze suddenly warmed as she looked at Thayne. It only lasted a moment, however, before she turned toward Adeline once more. "Unfortunately for us, those harridans carry a great deal of influence over society."

Adeline secured the soles of her half-boots to the floor and squared her shoulders. "The *ton* can speculate all they like. If my name appears in the *Standard*, then I shall consider it an adventure."

"You will do quite well in London, Miss Pimm," Thayne remarked with apparent approval. "You are so matter-of-fact that you remind me of Wolford. His name appears so often that he hardly notices."

The thought gave Adeline pause. Liam admitted to a rather hedonistic lifestyle that garnered attention. Yet she would hate for him to endure any more rumors in his condition. "If the *haute ton* could actually see how much Wolford is hurt, they would think kinder of him."

Thayne and Juliet exchanged a glance.

"Perhaps in that, there would be a way to ensure that the gossip was favorable," Juliet said, as if to an unspoken question between her and the marquess. "But make no mistake, Max, this would not mean I am helping you win our wager. I still mean to defeat you."

"I wouldn't expect anything less, Lady Granworth." Thayne grinned and inclined his head before taking his leave.

Then Juliet faced Adeline once more. "You must forgive my rudeness. How can I speak of a wager and not explain it?"

Adeline's curiosity must have been obvious in her expression. Her cheeks heated in embarrassment. "Please. You do not have to explain anything to me."

Juliet waved off her concerns before she continued. "From your comment earlier, I gather that you have an understanding of the Season's *Original?*"

Adeline recalled what Wolford had told her. "When the *Original* is named, heads turn in their favor?"

"Quite." Juliet nodded succinctly. "Without too long of a story, one day, Max declared that anyone could be named an *Original.* I believed otherwise. And thus, a challenge ensued, resulting in our wager."

"And this has earned you a place in the *Standard?*"

"Among other things." Two nearly imperceptible spots of color tinged Juliet's cheeks before she looked down to adjust the fan chain at her wrist. When she looked up in the next instant, she was perfectly composed once more. Elegance personified. "As for you, we are going to make certain that the gossip is as gentle as goose down by procuring your invitation to the most coveted event of the Season. What do you think of that?"

Adeline's head was spinning. All of her earlier concerns were gone now. There was so much drama and excitement to feast upon, and this was only her first night in society. "I believe that this is the most exciting opera I've ever attended, and it hasn't even begun yet!"

Liam heard the moment that the door opened below. Three pairs of footsteps followed, Lady Boswick's, Lord Boswick's, and then Adeline's. Mr. Finmore had gone off to bed some time ago, but not before checking in on Liam one last time.

Liam knew he shouldn't still be here. Earlier, however, Boswick had urged him not to overtax himself in a rush to leave, repeating his concerns over the dizzy spells. Too exhausted to argue at the time, Liam had remained here.

When he'd awoken a short while ago, however, he'd felt more refreshed. With the help of Finmore and Jones, he could have made it next door. Yet the truth was, he stayed because he wanted to hear Adeline tell him about her night at the opera.

And now, a surge of anticipation filled him as those footsteps came up the stairs and to his room.

After a quiet knock, Serge and Bunny entered, overflowing with appreciation for the use of his box. Apparently, Aunt Edith had let the matter slip. He assured his hosts that it was the least he could do in return for all they had done for him. Yet all the while, he wondered what Adeline had thought. But hers was the only face that did not greet him.

His hosts soon bid him good night. A short while later, Boswick's familiar snoring began, and the house fell into relative silence. At least, until he heard a muffled click of the door latch across the hall.

Or rather, he *thought* it was a door. His ears perked, straining to capture the faintest sound of a shuffled step, the swish of a skirt, a breath, anything. But in his eagerness all he could hear was the quick drum of his heart and the whoosh of each weighted breath. He stared hard at the door, willing it to swing open.

Then it did, and Adeline stepped inside without even knocking first.

She was radiant. Her eyes sparkled in the low lamplight, emitting a brightness of their own. The pink satin of her gown matched the glow of her cheeks. Long, curling tendrils of glorious hair snaked down, brushing her cheeks.

His breath stalled, caught beneath his solar plexus as if he'd taken a center blow. "How was your opera adventure?"

"Divine, Wolford." She began to buzz around the room, telling him about his aunt and meeting Lady Cosgrove, Juliet, Thayne, and Mrs. Harwick. A lengthy description of the scenery, costumes and the *magnificence of a real opera* followed. Then at last, she stopped by his side. "And I just wanted to thank you."

He had the startling urge to take her hand just now. With his resting on the mattress by her hip, only scant inches separated their fingers. Seeing her so happy made him greedy, he supposed. He wanted to feel the effervescence that bubbled through her. He wanted to be part of it. And suddenly, he wished that he had been with her this evening, watching delight gleam in her eyes.

"Would you like another cheese plate?" she asked, all eagerness.

"I am content for the moment." Besides, he did not think he could survive another coverlet picnic. And yet, he didn't want her to leave either. "However, perhaps if my pillow were fluffed."

She looked at him as if he were teasing her, but played along nonetheless, chafing her hands together. "I must have an innate talent for pillow fluffing."

If one could possess a talent for such a thing, she certainly did not. Not that he would tell her. Because if he did, he already knew the result. She would leave his side, and he would lose the relief—or whatever this was—he found in her presence. And he had never been one to deny himself necessary comforts.

Then, as she had done before, she leaned over him. Her hands went to either side of his face, pressing into the pillow, the inviting plumpness of her breasts resting on his chest. Enjoying the moment, he closed his eyes and drew in a deep breath that hinted at pear blossoms.

She went still. "Why are your hands at my waist?"

Were they? He squeezed his hands and found that, yes, they most definitely were. He also discovered that the satin gown was warm from the heat of her body and fine enough that there was little barrier between his hands and the slender curve of her waist and the slight flare of her hips.

"I'm merely aiding in your efforts by offering stability," he said, by way of an excuse. Of course, he hadn't intended to touch her—*gentleman's daughter and all that*. Given his pleasure-seeking nature, however, he wasn't entirely surprised by his wayward hands. Perhaps he should think about removing them before he found them cupped around her breasts. Inadvertently, of course.

"Afraid that I will crush you?" she said with a laugh against his lips. "Well, do not worry, because I have finished. Your pillow is sufficiently plump."

More than. And lumpy as well, but he did not mind in the least. Especially when he felt her lips against his cheek.

"Thank you, Wolford. I had a delightful evening."

In the next instant, he didn't know what came over him. Suddenly, he found his hand at her nape, pulling her mouth to his.

The kiss took him by surprise. It was lips and teeth, fierce and needy. Unexplainable. Apparently he was weak-willed from his injuries. At least that was what he told himself. The only proof belying that was that his grip at her nape and the hand at her waist felt strong and certain. Every drop of blood in his body told him that this was right. Essential. And so he continued to kiss her.

The innocent press of her lips told him that he should take his time, tutor her, ease her lips apart with the gentle sweep of his tongue. Instead, he schooled her quickly, thrusting, tasting, consuming her as if he'd been held captive by monks all his life, and she was the first woman he'd ever seen.

But not just any woman. This woman. Adeline Pimm, whose lips tasted like they were brushed with fine Boswick-shire honey and whose flesh had the faintest scent of pear blossoms. Especially on her throat and more still here, in this tender spot just beneath her jaw.

Her inexperience made him feel all the more primitive. He wanted more of her lips. More of the tender exploration of her tongue against his. More of her low, decadent murmurs.

As she kissed him back, he knew there was something different about it. He had a hard time controlling himself. He couldn't get enough of her. They should not be in a bed, he knew. This was the most dangerous place to kiss her. He could easily seduce her. Already, she lay atop him, the delicious feminine weight of her causing no pain. Her body molded perfectly to his. The softness of her stomach cradled the turgid length of him, and all he could think about was how good it would feel inside of her. He might be too weak to resist…

Thankfully, she was strong.

She pulled away and stood beside the bed. He saw what his whiskers had done to her. He'd been a savage. He should feel chagrinned for marking her. Instead, he felt satisfied. He had an animalistic desire to pinken her flesh everywhere. To make her skin tender, as a reminder of where his mouth had been.

"Two adventures in one night," she said, breathless.

He was having a difficult time breathing too. "What do you mean?"

"I've just been kissed by a man with a questionable reputation. I'd call that an adventure, wouldn't you?"

But before he could answer, she slipped away, exiting the room and leaving him to answer it alone. "No, darling, there is no question regarding my reputation."

One touch of her lips, and he'd lost his head. Not that he'd minded. He often chose the path of pleasure. But this was different—she was unspoiled.

No matter what her professions might be against marriage, Liam could not entirely believe her. One taste of her passion had proven that much.

Someday she would want to explore that side of her nature. A keen and peculiar sense of certainty filled him with the notion that she would marry. And the bastard she chose wouldn't deserve her or her family...

Liam stilled. Every vein in his body seemed to boil at the thought. Not because he knew Adeline would marry. No. Because, if he didn't know better, he might believe that he was jealous.

CHAPTER SEVEN

"Pardon me, my lord, but there is a Mr. Rendell to see you," Jones said from the doorway.

From the bed, Liam looked over at the rosewood clock on the mantel and noted that it was well before time for business matters. In fact, it was well before his usual time for waking. "Send him up, please. Thank you, Jones."

The truth was, Liam had not slept last night either. Not after what he'd done.

He could no longer remain under Boswick's roof. And given Liam's past experience with debutantes, he should have been wary of spending any time alone with Adeline. After all, if he possessed strength enough to kiss her the way he had, then he likely would have found strength enough to seduce her completely. Irrevocably.

Minutes later, Rendell knocked and entered the room with his head bent, spouting several *my lords* and begging forgiveness for the disturbance. Already Liam knew that whatever news brought him thither was not good.

Soon enough, Rendell managed to calm himself.

"It appears, my lord, that your house was burgled sometime in the night."

"On Brook Street again?" A month ago, the same thing had occurred. Yet for all the destruction of the main floor study and the strewing about of papers, the only thing that had gone missing was a pair of silver candlesticks.

Rendell shook his head. "Wolford House, my lord. Like the previous instance, the study was the primary focus, much of it in disarray. I sent word to Bow Street immediately. An investigator by the name of Hollycott is here now, my lord, waiting below."

Liam thought instantly of his collection, of what pieces were in jeopardy.

"Lord Boswick ordered a breakfast tray for your lordship. He was also kind enough to do the same for Mr. Hollycott and for me."

At this, Liam emerged from the list he was making in his mind. He thought of his host. Even besieged by visitors shortly after dawn, his inclination was to see to the comfort of his guests. Boswick was a purely altruistic creature. Knowing this, Liam felt ashamed that his own first thoughts, upon hearing Rendell's news, had not been on the well-being of the servants who resided in his house.

He tried to make amends with himself by asking after them now. "Was anyone in the house injured?"

Apparently, Rendell hadn't expected as much from him either because his mouth remained agape for a few moments before he collected himself. Then he cleared his throat. "No, my lord. As before, no one was aware of the burglary until this morning."

"Very good." Liam waved him off. "You may go and break your fast. I will be downstairs presently."

With the help of Jones, Liam managed to dress and make his way down the stairs after a quarter of an hour had passed. He soon found Boswick, Rendell, and a stout, auburn-haired man in a brown coat and trousers. Hollycott, Liam presumed.

There were no breakfast dishes in sight, but the aroma of tea and honey lingered. Liam's stomach growled.

Boswick introduced him to the newcomer. Hollycott had the rough, square face of a man who'd had a scrape or two in his life and a keen, careful gaze, as if he suspected everyone he met were guilty of a crime. After scrutinizing Liam, he began directly.

"There were several burgled houses near yours, Lord Wolford." Hollycott spoke with a Welsh accent, baring his upper teeth as he enunciated. "The culprit likely knew the house would be empty and the servants asleep. I understand that this happened not long ago at another of your houses."

"You must find that circumstance quite frequent. A house in a fine neighborhood burglarized in the middle of the night cannot be a rarity."

Hollycott's shoulders twitched in a shrug. "Usually more in the summer when these properties are empty. But what was strange is that the burglar didn't try to disguise his presence. He left clutter behind at each location. Of course, in your house, that fact was much more difficult to ascertain."

"No doubt you are referring to my collection." Though to Liam it was more disturbing than merely losing an object. He truly enjoyed the pieces in his collection. They were like scholars he could talk to, revealing their history in conversations whenever they met.

"Do you recall what was stolen from the previous burglary?" Hollycott asked. Since he didn't seem like a man who would have come unprepared without that information, Liam suspected he was being tested.

Rendell began to sort through a stack of ledgers that listed all of Liam's goods.

"A pair of silver candlesticks," Liam answered, feeling a measure of satisfaction at Hollycott's eventual nod. "I'd found it odd at the time that such a mess had been left behind for something that had been in plain sight all along. I'd also heard similar reports from my neighbors—a candelabra, an ormolu clock, a gold snuff box—all inconsequential items."

"Inconsequential to you, perhaps, but easy to sell and less likely to raise alarms than a fancy painting." Even though Hollycott kept his tone measured, the cold snap of censure laced his wording. It was sharp enough to lift Boswick's brows.

"Still, the question remains," Liam added, "if you were the burglar, why ransack and let it be known? Why not merely take the bauble and disappear with no one the wiser? These houses are not likely to notice immediately otherwise."

Again, Hollycott offered a nod. "That is one of the inconsistencies I'm investigating."

"And the other?"

"It has to do with part of your collection. There appears to have been damage to a sketch, along with a shattered glass case."

Rendell cleared his throat. "I didn't want to alarm you, my lord. The Turkish dagger above your mantel…Someone used it to stab your sketch of the Elgin Marbles. And left it displayed on your desk."

Liam reeled at the news as if *he'd* been stabbed. His hand gripped the edge of the desk. It wasn't that he was fond of that sketch or even the dagger. No, instead he was alarmed. That sketch usually hung in an upstairs parlor, *not* in his study. He said as much to Hollycott, then made up his mind to go to Wolford House and sort out this mystery.

"With your injuries, are you certain that is wise, Wolford?" Boswick asked.

"While I am still on my feet, I should like to make use of them." Liam appreciated the concern but felt guilt over it at the same time. "Besides, it is time that I leave, regardless. Your family has been more than generous. One day, I should like the opportunity to repay you."

"As I have said before," Boswick began, "it is not necessary. We were glad to be of service."

This time Liam would not concede so easily. He was determined to make amends, even if his host—at least, he dearly hoped—was ignorant of the reason. "I should like to, all the same."

After a moment, Boswick inclined his head. "As you will."

"Then it is settled." And so final. Part of Liam already felt the absence of their company. "If you have no other engagements, I would be honored if you would join us at Wolford House."

Boswick inclined his head in agreement, then stepped apart to have a word with Mr. Finmore and Rendell.

As they made their way to the foyer, Hollycott studied the left side of Liam's face more closely. "Was this the result of an attack or a pugilism exercise?"

"The former," Liam answered, "but I don't think it has any bearing on the burglaries."

"It might surprise you. If I may, what happened?"

"I still don't recall everything, but I believe it must have transpired around the time I was leaving a masquerade. It was likely a jealous man because all I remember is one of the men saying, '*If you let her go, we could end this. Your choice, guvna.*' But since I do not possess any woman, I do not know of whom they were speaking. I'm certain the matter has sorted out itself."

"How so?"

"Let's just say that I haven't been well enough to make any man jealous since." Just then Liam spotted Adeline on the stairs. Even though he'd never concealed his nature from her, in that moment, he regretted speaking of it with his usual cavalier air.

Their gazes connected, and a pink blush slowly crept to her cheeks. Undeservedly, he felt the warmth of it burrow beneath his skin.

Boswick stepped forward. "My dear, would you please inform your mother that I am going out?"

"Yes, Father," she said with a nod. Then her gaze alighted on Liam, her delicately arched brows drawing together. "Are *all* of you leaving?"

If he didn't know better, he'd swear he felt a tug of pleasure at the concern in her expression, in the soft rounding of her slender brows, the subtle pout of her lips. "Your father has been kind enough to accompany me to Wolford House this morning, Miss Pimm."

"I will return shortly," Boswick answered, ending their discussion as they walked out the door.

Liam, however, would not return. He almost said as much to Adeline, but he found he suddenly lacked the energy to bid her farewell. So he merely tipped his hat to her and walked out the door.

"You'll wear a path on the carpet, dear," Mother said, when the sound of a carriage drew Adeline to the window. Again. "I would not expect their return so soon."

Adeline peered out at the street, searching for the family landau from amongst a dozen others passing by. Ever since she learned of the burglary and saw her father and Liam walk out the door, she'd had a feeling that Liam would not return.

Of course, she knew he would leave eventually, when he was fully healed. But this was different. And drat it all, she was worried about him.

She didn't want to care about him. In fact, she'd been trying to keep her distance from him.

And look how well you've managed thus far, she mocked. She nearly laughed aloud at the thought. Had she truly been trying when her lips were pressed against his? She certainly hadn't attempted to stop his kiss. *Their* kiss, she corrected. After all, she'd been as much a participant as he.

And then all night long, she told herself that she was glad to have gotten that out of her system. She could go through the rest of her life knowing exactly what kisses were meant to feel like. She would no longer be curious.

Then why was she so eager to kiss him again? Why was the pull to him even stronger than before?

It would be best not to ponder the answer, she was sure.

"*Their return?* Oh, you must mean father and Wolford. No, I thought perhaps that Juliet would pay a call this morning. She mentioned something to that effect last evening," Adeline said, pretending to have another purpose for rising so frequently. She also didn't want her mother to think that she knew every thought in Adeline's head.

Mother did not look up from her sewing with any sort of speculation or surprise by this announcement. The least she could do was to fake believing her. "Then perhaps you should send word to the kitchen. See if Mrs. Simmons could prepare a tray. You might suggest the spiced scones."

Adeline wished she'd have thought of that beforehand. It would have made her excuse more plausible. Nevertheless, she took the opportunity to ring the bell and alert Mrs. Simmons of their potential guests. Though, in part, Adeline felt rather foolish for her charade, as if she were ordering a full tea for her imaginary friends.

Then, the moment she sat down to study the ladies quarterly, someone rapped on the lion's head knocker on the outer door. Startled, she looked up so sharply that she felt a crick in her neck. Mother looked surprised as well.

Adeline recovered and said, "This must be Juliet now," and sincerely hoped she was correct.

Mr. Finmore arrived at the parlor door, announcing the Duchess of Vale and Lady Granworth. Believing that their butler had misspoken, Adeline expected to see Wolford's aunt, the dowager duchess, arrive with Juliet. Instead, she was surprised to see Juliet accompanied by a young woman near her age, with white-blonde hair, winter-blue eyes, and flawless skin that glowed with her smile. In short, they were introduced to Ivy Bromley, the Duchess of Vale and wife of Wolford's cousin.

Shortly thereafter, they sat together, chatting amiably as if they were old acquaintances instead of new. And when the tray arrived from the kitchen, Adeline could have kissed Mrs. Simmons for how well it looked. Resting upon it sat a flowered teapot and tiered tray, laden with spiced scones, mincemeat tarts, and a walnut cake. To others it might have seemed ordinary, but to Adeline, it was the most splendid tea tray ever assembled. Because this was her first London tea and there wasn't a single guest present who had been forced to attend as part of a chore.

"The dowager duchess spoke highly of you and your family upon her return from the opera," Ivy said, kindly pouring their tea. "Had it not been for a previous engagement, I would have insisted upon meeting you last night."

"The generosity of the dowager duchess made the opera a wondrous experience. I am grateful beyond words," Adeline said and then passed a cup and saucer to Juliet, secretly reveling in this simple act of hospitality. "And Lady Cosgrove is elegance personified."

"Zinnia said the same of you," Juliet added. "I believe her description of you was of an *easy grace and warmth* that charmed her from the start."

Adeline blushed. She had not realized she made such a positive impression, but she was glad of it. More than that, she was relieved. Apparently no one had noticed her shuffled step.

"My husband planned to join me today to meet you and to visit Wolford. However, he stayed behind when he learned his cousin was no longer here. You see, our house is not too far from Wolford's in St. James," Ivy said and frowned. "Terrible business. The house across from ours was burgled as well."

Juliet reached across and squeezed Ivy's hand. "Thankfully you did not have to endure this trial. Though I do feel for Wolford. I'd heard that he had been burgled before."

"How awful." The news shocked Adeline and only added to growing concern she had for him. He already suffered such a violent attack and now this? "Though I am glad he wasn't present for it. And it is good to know that Wolford has family he can depend upon."

"And the kindness of strangers," Ivy said with a smile as she handed Adeline a cup.

"I wouldn't say that we're strangers any longer. Serge and I think of him as one of the family." Mother began slicing into the cake, oblivious to the three teacups that stalled mid-sip.

Adeline nearly choked in her rush to swallow. "But only because my parents feel that way about *everyone*, our servants and the villagers alike."

She would have glared at Mother if she wasn't so busy pretending to be unaffected.

"Forgive me," Juliet began, her tone tinged with gravity. "I wonder how much you know about Wolford's reputation amongst the *ton*."

Mother nodded solemnly. "He did warn us. Though things like that do not concern us when a man is injured."

"Which only confirms your goodness," Ivy said with a warm smile.

"Unfortunately, there are certain persons in society who do not bother to take that into account." Juliet placed her cup and saucer on the table. "As you likely realized last evening with Lady Falksworth. Her actions were just shy of a cut direct."

Adeline hadn't realized it was that serious, but Mother nodded as if she'd known all along. "Mother, you didn't say a word."

"I didn't want to worry you. The night was so full of promise."

Truer words had never been spoken. Adeline felt another blush when she thought of how last night had ended.

But a cut direct—or a gesture just shy of it—was serious. If Lady Falksworth treated her parents so abominably, and in front of the dowager duchess and Lady Cosgrove, the situation was dire, indeed. A woman's reputation was all she had.

"That means I won't gain society's acceptance." When Adeline noticed the slight rattle of her cup, she set hers down as well. "Does it not matter that he was bedridden for the entirety of his stay up until today?"

Adeline felt a rush of guilt. Had she taken advantage of him last night? Had he been unable to push her away from him? During the kiss, it certainly hadn't seemed that he'd lacked any strength, but now she felt rather wanton and lecherous. Poor Wolford! She felt her cheeks heat.

When both Juliet and Ivy nodded solemnly, Mother rose from her chair and stood at Adeline's side, resting her hand on her shoulder. "Dear heavens, what did Lady Falksworth suppose? That we are such simpletons that we left our daughter unchaperoned in the lair of a libertine?"

"Knowing Lady Falksworth, that is precisely what she thinks. Her *ladyship* prefers the company of finches so much that, I do believe, she shares the same size brain." Juliet huffed, her eyes flashing daggers.

Adeline was overwhelmed by the support of her new friend, if a little awed by her. Even scowling did not mar Juliet's beauty. She could tease, laugh, and also rant but always remain refined.

Then Juliet straightened, sitting at the edge of her chair. "But that will be a trifling matter soon enough, for we"—she gestured to Ivy—"have procured an invitation."

"And not just any invitation," Ivy added, a lively grin dancing on her lips and in her eyes, "but the Select Seventy."

Adeline had read about the Select Seventy in this morning's *Standard*. Apparently, this was a big to-do that caused speculation to run rampant over which guests would be invited.

Mother's grip on Adeline's shoulder eased. "However did you manage it?"

Juliet beamed. "It turns out that Lady Strandfellow, while having her own reservations, absolutely abhors the idea of agreeing with Lady Falksworth."

"But, I presume, she still has reservations," Mother said.

Ivy and Juliet exchanged a look before the latter spoke. "Wolford's reputation has been so…*unwashed* for so long that nearly every woman who speaks to him at social engagements must deal with speculation of some sort. As you might imagine, he is not often invited to attend proper engagements. Although, since he has such an esteemed title and great wealth, there are some who make an exception."

Adeline was beginning to see a clearer picture of what Liam's life was like. Shunned from part of society through his own actions but welcomed by another and solely because of his wealth and title. It was no wonder he had little trust in people.

"North tells me that the *ton* has always been enthralled by his cousin. Sadly, they are eager for any errant whisper," Ivy said. "I see a different side of him, however. Though I suppose my fondness for him began the day he brought a toad to my wedding."

Ivy proceeded to tell the story, and as Adeline listened, she felt a reluctant surge of affection for him. Then she sighed in dismay. It would be so much easier for her to forget about him if he wasn't so appealing.

Juliet slowly shook her head. "Wolford has far more substance than anyone realizes. That was my own mistake as well. Had I known, I never would have made that wager with Max." Then she turned her attention to Adeline and Mother. "This was the wager I spoke of at the opera. While it was initially a private battle between Max and me, it is now a rather public war. You see, Max and I have had this ongoing animosity, ever since we were engaged in a small"—she paused to take a sip of her tea—"kissing scandal, over five years ago."

Adeline sat up a little straighter. "Between you and Lord Thayne?"

Juliet offered a succinct nod and then took another sip. At first, Adeline was surprised by the news and then, recalling the exchange between the pair at the opera, it made perfect sense. Mother too seemed to nod as if the history between Juliet and Thayne were obvious.

Yet, for Adeline, one question remained…"How did you survive the scandal?"

"I ran off and married the first man who would have me. Needless to say, mine is not an example to be followed," Juliet remarked gravely, apparently forgetting the fact that the *ton* was enthralled by her as well. "Back to the matter at hand—the wager.

"A month or so ago, when I returned to London, I had planned to buy the house that had once belonged to my parents. Unfortunately, upon learning the news, Max went out that very day and purchased the house out from under my nose."

"No!" Mother gasped. "What a wretched thing to do!"

Adeline and Ivy agreed.

"I was livid but quickly decided to get even instead of angry. I was determined to take back my house by whatever means necessary. It just so happens that Max provided the perfect opportunity that same day. So, when Max began spouting nonsense about how anyone could become the Season's *Original*, I challenged him to prove it." Juliet drew in a breath. "After all, I had the advantage of studying those who were named in the past. I know that it takes a special quality. So, with the help of my dear cousin, Lilah—whom I cannot wait for you to meet once she returns from her honeymoon—I was certain of our success."

"And she would have been named too," Ivy said with undeniable certainty.

"But when the end of the month came—that is when the name of the *Original* is posted in *Standard*," Juliet explained, "there was no announcement, other than to say that the *Original* would be named at the end of this month instead."

Adeline was putting the pieces together. "So, while you were helping your cousin become the *Original*, Max was helping Wolford?"

Juliet offered a small laugh. "Max believes he can win the wager without any effort."

"But at the opera, you made a suggestion to help Max," Adeline said, confused.

Juliet held her gaze and then Mother's. "It was not for Max. I simply abhor what gossip can do. And with the help of my gracious friend"—Juliet gestured to Ivy—"the duke and duchess will also attend the Select Seventy. Soon thereafter, your name will be linked to all of us, respectably separated from Wolford's reputation without quitting his circle of friends."

"It is a great honor to be invited and also quite clever of you to secure an invitation which—one can assume—would not be extended to Wolford," Adeline said. She'd gained an understanding of society's intricate workings in the last hour.

"Certainly, Max is welcome to try to garner an invitation on Wolford's behalf," Juliet said with a slow smile. "However...this is a wager after all."

CHAPTER EIGHT

A headache assaulted Liam. Closing the door of his dressing chamber, he leaned against it, trying to catch his breath. Apparently, he'd grown used to the barest light in Boswick's guest chamber, because here, it felt like his eyes were about to explode.

This windowless room was the only place in Wolford House that was dark enough and blissfully free of the sounds of servants going about their tasks. Not only that, but it was the only place to escape Rendell's constant queries and *my lords*.

Hollycott had left a short while ago but not before asking Liam a series of questions concerning the attack. The inspector was determined to prove that the theft and the assault were related.

What concerned Liam more was the fact that the burglars had been in the parlor. That reason alone demanded a thorough examination of his entire house. Given the amount of items in Liam's collection, he needed as much help as he could get. Therefore, he postponed the reassignment of servants to

Sudgrave Terrace. Which meant that he would not be staying next door to the Pimms until this matter was settled. And perhaps not even then.

Dizziness caused his stomach to roil suddenly. His *empty* stomach, he reminded himself, pressing a fist there. What he wouldn't give to have just one more coverlet picnic with Adeline.

A succinct knock sounded on his bedchamber door. The absence of any nervous throat clearing told him that it wasn't Rendell. When he heard the sure, steady footfalls heading in his direction without having asked permission to enter, Liam knew precisely who it was.

"Vale, I thought you were giving Boswick a tour," Liam said, pressing a hand over the latch and debating whether or not to open the dressing chamber door.

During the final leg of the tour of Wolford House, Vale and Boswick had begun a discussion on honeybees. Since Vale was a scientist by nature, he was no doubt thrilled to have found a fellow beehive enthusiast. The only interest Liam had in honey was how it would taste on Adeline's lips. And that was certainly not an appropriate topic to discuss in front of her father.

Liam wanted to linger here, hoping that the mere thought of her would soothe him as much as her voice seemed to have done thus far. Instead of a moment of solitude, however, Vale found him.

Nevertheless, his cousin had a way of taking charge that was not invasive. Not usually, at least.

Although, Liam had been relieved to find Vale here this morning. It had allowed Liam the opportunity to see to business matters and not neglect Boswick. Not only that, but Liam was moved by Vale's response upon seeing his injuries. His stoic, analytical cousin rarely allowed his countenance to reveal his thoughts, but the shock and concern had been evident in his gruff manner.

"Your housekeeper is giving Boswick a tour of the gallery instead," Vale said. "I wanted to speak to you privately."

"You sound rather ominous, Cousin. What is there to speak of that you do not already know? I have informed you and Hollycott everything I remember from the attack."

"I wish you had informed me sooner. Though perhaps the reason you did not is partly my fault. I should have done something to breech the barrier that our family set in place during our boyhoods. I thought the matter had sorted itself over the years."

Liam had not made an attempt either. The truth was, it was difficult for him to form attachments. After his father's death, he'd been so lonely and broken that he'd feared loss more than he desired companionship. That all changed when he was seventeen, when a debutante and her family seemed to see right through him and welcomed him as one of their own.

Yet after the deception, he found it difficult to trust anyone enough to close the distance he kept between himself and others. Though he should have made an exception for his own family.

Right now, it was too much to think about. Liam felt pain stab at his temples. And damn it all, he missed the quietude of Boswick's residence.

"Stop this, Vale. I insist." Yanking open the door, he squinted and wished he'd closed the drapes in his bedchamber.

"I never cared that you became the duke. The title was right-fully yours to begin with, and so there was never a need to speak of it. There. Now that we've settled things, please tell me why you've suddenly become a loquacious ninny who cares a farthing what I think."

"Ivy mentioned that my"—Vale straightened his shoulders and tugged at the hem of his waistcoat—"regard for the people closest to me is not always evident."

Shaking his head in pity, Liam crossed the room to close one of the drapes. Sadly, it seemed as if he and Vale had this in common as well. But at least Liam held himself together with a measure of dignity. In contrast, his cousin was utterly henpecked.

"Well, you may inform your wife that I am rather percep-tive." Then Liam paused, thinking that there might also be another reason his cousin was not behaving as usual. Vale had been married nearly four months now. "Congratulations on the expected arrival of your heir."

"How did you—"

When his cousin's brows lifted, Liam shrugged. "I've seen that look of terror in the eyes of other men when their wives were in confinement."

Vale's shoulders relaxed and he offered a nod, not disput-ing Liam's observation. "The physician confirmed our own suspicions yesterday. By my calculations, the child should arrive—Why did you laugh just now?"

Liam couldn't help himself. It was so typical of Vale to put everything into an equation. He'd even come up with a mathematical equation for marriage. The *ton* was still talk-ing about Vale's *Marriage Formula* and how he'd used it to find his own bride. What most people did not understand was that it hadn't happened like that at all. After all, it was obvious that Vale had been smitten with Ivy from the first moment he'd met her. He never needed a formula.

Liam shook his head. "Oh, nothing. I just had a glimpse of young Northcliff's life, scribbling calculations over the nursery walls."

His mocking prediction made Vale grin broadly before he remembered himself and resumed his more typical austere expression. "Regardless of the turn our conversation has taken, I sought you out for a reason." He straightened his shoulders once more. "I am here to inquire what you intend to do about Miss Pimm."

At the unexpected mention of her, a jolt shot through Liam. "I *intend* to do nothing."

"Surely, being the rather *perceptive individual* that you are, you realize the harm you caused Lord and Lady Boswick and Miss Pimm. While I have not met his wife and daughter, Boswick seems unconcerned about your reputation. He is an intelligent, amiable fellow, but I fear he is unused to the ways of the *ton*." Vale released a slow exhale, laden with disappointment. "As it stands, Miss Pimm will have no chance of being accepted into society or in finding a husband."

Liam gritted his teeth against the bitter tang of guilt at the back of his throat. "That is why I asked Aunt Edith for assistance. She invited them to the opera the last evening."

"Considering your reputation, it should not surprise you to learn that, even after our aunt's intervention, speculation is running rampant, and none of it favorable for Miss Pimm."

Damn. "Society is full of fools. We both know that."

"There are whispers that the family is full of gullible, naïve country folk," Vale said. "Because they have never visited London before or entered—what many believe to be—*proper* society, they are seen as easily seduced."

Liam swallowed, remembering last night. "I have been injured. Let's just say that I haven't been up to the task of seducing an entire family. Give me a few more days and then perhaps—"

"The *ton* does not know the extent of your injuries. Many are already whispering that there never was an attack upon you. They believe that you are holed up in a den of iniquity."

"Which would be preferable to whatever you have planned for me, no doubt." Liam cast a gaze of longing to his bed. He needed sleep. He needed quiet. He needed just one more taste of Adeline's lips...He shook his head to dislodge that errant thought. "I can only assume that is the reason you are here. You want me to make an appearance."

"It so happens that I'm not the only one," Vale said, withdrawing a silver emblazoned invitation from his inside pocket. "Thayne sent this. The messenger explained that our friend had the audacity to wait for Lady Strandfellow's steward to finish it before he would leave."

Liam stared down at the card, feeling nauseous once more. *The Select Seventy.* "No doubt at an event so full of respectable, pious members of our society that I will burst into flames upon crossing the threshold."

Vale smirked. "I don't imagine it will be spontaneous combustions, but you might be singed."

Splendid. Liam was already looking forward to this evening.

CHAPTER NINE

Liam arrived late. Since a prompt arrival at any of the events he typically attended was considered bad form, this should not have mattered. Tonight, however, he was supposed to make a favorable impression on his hostess—a Sisyphean task, if ever there was one.

Lady Strandfellow did not like him. She'd been coerced into extending an invitation, and she did not bother to hide her displeasure at his tardiness, his appearance, and likely his reputation. Though, if Liam were to rate his own appearance, he'd say he looked acceptable under the circumstances.

It couldn't be helped that part of his face was a mottled blend of violet, green, and yellow. But at least he was clean-shaven, though with no help from Neville. After enduring three solid minutes of his squeamish valet's choking sounds and open-mouthed gagging, Liam had done the job himself. A fine effort, if he did say so himself. Not a single nick. And more than that, it had felt satisfying, slicing off the old and uncovering the fresh, unmarred flesh beneath.

He was beginning to understand Boswick's simpler practices. There was nothing he expected of his servants that he would not do himself. For too many years, Liam relied on his servants to see to everyday tasks without thought. Now he found that it was good to step away from what he'd always done and take a new approach.

Perhaps relying on his servants, as he had done since his father's death, had kept him from seeing things in a new light. His encounter with Vale earlier today had told him that he required a closer look at his familial relationships as well. But all in good time.

Tonight was for Adeline.

At the edge of the hall near the archway to the ballroom, Liam cast a cursory glance at his own reflection in the glass front of a curio cabinet. Since there was nothing he could do about his face, he paid closer attention to his attire. Thankfully, Neville had been able to hold his stomach long enough to tie a proper cravat and help Liam into his tailored black coat, or else he would have arrived even later.

Straightening his shoulders, he stepped into the ballroom. As luck would have it, a footman toting a tray of wine glasses passed by in the same moment. Liam snatched one for himself and immediately took a fortifying swallow. Then he cringed and glared down at the offensive vintage. It was wine-colored water, and nothing more. This would not do. How did Lady Strandfellow expect her guests to survive this insipid gathering without assistance?

In answer to that question, Liam's gaze quickly scanned the room for a glimpse of Adeline. The instant he found her, he felt the wine begin to work, relaxing him in subtle doses.

This evening, she wore a sheath of white netting over a yellow petticoat that brought out threads of gold in her light brown hair. She possessed an honest beauty. Her complexion had that scrubbed-clean pink that made her all the lovelier. And when she looked at him in return, he felt his lungs expand, as if the air he breathed was somehow fresh and untainted.

The upward lift of her brows indicated her surprise at seeing him, but there was something almost beseeching in her gaze, calling to some slumbering part of him that he'd never awakened.

Adeline stood beside her parents and Juliet. Not far separated, Aunt Edith chatted with Lady Strandfellow, the latter glancing at the Pimms sourly. That was when Liam realized something was amiss.

Only now did he notice that Adeline's eyes were too wide, her smile more brittle than bright. She should be laughing, her eyes shimmering with gaiety. This was her adventure, after all.

He had the impulse to cross the room immediately and stand by her side. Yet he also knew such behavior, amongst such *pious* company, would only make matters worse for her.

Liam loathed these types of events. Here, propriety was paramount…at least on the surface. Everyone looked the part—styled and coiffed to perfection, their finery without flaw, their gloves gleaming white. He smirked at this pretense. The utter hypocrisy.

Several familiar faces amongst this lot had not only attended a few gatherings hosted by the infamous Lady

Reynolds but were also members of an elite gentleman's club run by Lady Hudson. And when Liam caught their gazes, each one in turn would startle and dart a nervous glance at their wives.

What? Did they imagine that he was the bringer of sin and that theirs would be exposed in his presence? At least he had the decency to wear his misdeeds in the open.

"You look like the devil," Thayne remarked, sidling up to him.

"Then it is fitting, considering that I am now standing in hell." Liam cast a baleful look over the length of the ballroom. The paneled ceiling, walls, and dark wood floors might have set the perfect stage for an illicit encounter behind one of the potted trees in the corners. Instead, wall sconces, chandeliers, and tapers lit every nook and cranny and made the room overly warm. He tugged at his cravat. "Should have known you'd make the cut for the Select Seventy."

Only gentlemen who were highly regarded and married, or highly regarded, unmarried, but searching for a bride received invitations. The only qualification Liam fit was being unmarried. Likely, Lady Strandfellow was reciting a constant litany of prayers under her breath to be saved from such an unworthy guest as he.

"Ah, yes. Quite the achievement, considering I've done nothing other than become a marquess by happenstance," Thayne mocked. Though the truth was, the moment he'd inherited the title from a distant relative, he'd turned downright respectable. *Traitor.*

"You did not have to force such a fate upon me," Liam insisted.

Thayne was doing all that was expected of a titled nobleman, attending teas and soirees, riding through the park at a fashionable hour, and refusing invitations deemed *improper* by the *ton*'s matrons. In contrast, and because nature abhorred a void, Liam typically accepted more than his usual share of improper invitations. At least until now.

Though it did not escape his notice that soon enough, Liam would not have any of his real friends left. He'd be the only one of their foursome without a family. Not that he needed one.

"What are friends for?" Thayne remarked a bit too brightly.

Liam grumbled. "All I require now is a decent drink. Yet there are no spirits to be had. At least, nothing stronger than this watered-down wine and cups of tepid green tea."

"Yes, unfortunate that." Thayne frowned as he looked down into his empty glass. "Apparently, Lady Strandfellow has recently taken to believe that even black tea causes too much stimulation and therefore leads to uninhibited behavior."

"Not a single card game in sight either."

Thayne chuckled. "This is *polite* society. The only attraction this evening is the event itself. Conversation is acceptable, and dancing—"

"As long as it does not allow for too much contact between partners," Liam added with a sardonic laugh.

Their hostess needed to turn her quizzing glass on Vale and his bride. They appeared engrossed in their study of a clock stand's pendulum, but Liam wasn't fooled. He noticed how Vale discreetly toyed with Ivy's glove, and how she smiled coyly in response, her cheeks flooded with color. Even though they were married, everyone knew that their hostess disapproved of any open sign of affection.

Such familiar touches from an unmarried gentleman to a debutante would cause a scandal. In fact, if Liam were to stop beside Miss Pimm and explore the flesh beneath *her* glove, their hostess would likely gasp and faint on the spot.

And it was just shocking enough that it made Liam itch to do it. His fingertips, and other parts, pulsed with yearning as he looked at the narrow expanse of skin exposed above her glove and beneath the gathered sleeve. More than that, he wanted to hold her against him, to brush away the curling tendrils from her cheeks. And he was weak-willed, already imagining how soft they would feel against his own.

Then again, he didn't have to imagine it. He knew exactly how it felt to have her hair brush his face. To have her lips upon his. Her sweet breath on his tongue...

He issued an involuntary groan. *Bollocks.* He never should have kissed her.

"Are your injuries paining you?" Thayne asked, interrupting Liam's dangerous thoughts. "I can procure a chair..."

Liam shook his head and dragged his attention away from Adeline before he caused a spectacle.

"Had I known, I would have asked you to stay with me for your recuperation."

"Think nothing of it. I was not even conscious the first day, and following that, I was not capable of leaving the bed."

Even now, Liam did not want to admit how exhausted he felt.

"Ah. So then you were *unable* to leave Lord Boswick and his family," Thayne said blandly as if this was all a matter of curiosity. Nothing more. "That is a relief. I thought you'd chosen to stay. There are rumors abounding, you know."

"So I am told." Liam felt his hackles rise. He knew where this was going and cast Thayne a look of warning. "I'm certain that did not bode well for your wager."

"Wager?" Thayne scoffed, feigning innocence. Then he shifted from one foot to the next, and his gaze shot across the room to where Adeline stood with Juliet.

"I've always known. You must have forgotten how fond of me your mother is." Liam drained the last of his watered wine with a shudder and gave the empty glass to a passing footman before turning back to Thayne. "What I can't fathom is why you would do such a thing? Wagering to transform me into an *Original* is like trying to lose."

Thayne said nothing in response, but his knuckles turned white as he gripped his own glass.

"But wait! Have I hit the mark?" Liam asked with a waggle of his brows. "Are you trying to lose in order to make Juliet stay in London?"

"You are an arse."

"Do try to be more original with your insults." When Adeline had said the same words, at least she had a wealth of emotion behind them.

Thinking of her automatically drew his attention to her. Again. Yet, as he looked across the ballroom, the vivaciousness and determination that marked her character were still absent. In place of it was an air of uncertainty in her wide eyes as she stared at the dancers.

Only now did he think of her limb, recalling what she had confessed to him about not dancing. Though he guessed she'd never had the opportunity. After all, Adeline was not one to permit anything from stopping her. She'd proven her bravery by attending this gathering.

As if sensing his careful study, she looked in his direction. For two beats, they shared a knowledge to which only he was privy—her secret and his admiration. Slowly, he inclined his head, still holding her gaze. In response, her mouth tilted up at each corner before she turned back to her parents.

Lord and Lady Boswick hovered protectively by her side until Aunt Edith called them away, apparently, to speak with Lady Strandfellow. Liam wondered how that encounter would fare. For Adeline's sake, he hoped for the best.

"All right, then," Thayne said curtly, stepping in front of Liam, his dark brows lowered in obvious irritation. "I wagered on you because you have the makings of being an *Original*. You fascinate the *ton*."

"My title and wealth garner their interest. That is all," Liam corrected, beginning to feel his own ire climbing. This was not a topic he liked to discuss, and Thayne knew it.

"It is more than that. Even those who disapprove of you love to whisper about your escapades. But what they don't realize is that I know that there is something worthy buried beneath that unscrupulous façade. I've seen it."

Liam winced from the attack. "Are you threatening me?"

Thayne scoffed, and after a minute of glaring back at him, barked out a laugh. "Only you would take those words as a threat. Anyone else would know that he'd been complimented."

Not Liam. He needed his reputation to stay as it was. If the *ton* saw him as respectable, then they would start to imagine him as a genuine candidate for the marriage mart. The last thing he needed was another brush with a conniving family who used deception to gain his favor and affection. He preferred knowing exactly where he stood. He would never be tricked again.

For Adeline's very first London soiree, this was not much of an adventure. In fact, it was downright unpleasant.

Upon arriving, Lady Strandfellow had been cordial, but only just. She received Adeline and her parents with a curt nod and a sniff that wrinkled her nose. And then she'd made it perfectly clear that they'd been invited only as a favor to the Dowager Duchess of Vale.

Then she was introduced to a few young women and their mothers. Well, Adeline supposed that *introduced* was not quite the correct word. Perhaps *identified* or *classified*—as one would a certain species of garden weed—was more fitting. *And this is* Adeline Pimm…*in Latin we refer to her as* debutantus most unwelcomus.

Having spent her life in Boswickshire with everyone knowing about her limb, she had become accustomed to pity or revulsion. But she hadn't been prepared for censure.

More than anything, Adeline had wanted to turn up her nose at them in return, but displaying rude manners was no way to thank the dowager duchess, Ivy, and Juliet for this great favor. So instead, Adeline kept with the lessons she'd learned from her parents—to smile at those who would disparage her.

She wasn't the only one who earned scorn from this sanctimonious gathering either. Whispers began the moment Liam entered the room. *A rake invited to the Select Seventy? What could Lady Strandfellow have been thinking?*

Adeline had been surprised as well, and beside her, Juliet's silence spoke volumes. She was positively fuming, albeit beneath a cool exterior.

Among the guests, speculation ran rampant. Sometimes Adeline heard her own name, other times Liam's, but mostly both together. It was hard to discern what was being said, as it sounded very much like the hiss of a bellows over smoldering embers. One thing was for certain—something or *someone* was bound to catch fire.

Though even with the censure of so many, Adeline could see the effect Liam had on the guests. Men and women alike skirted sideways glances at him, outwardly scandalized but with greedy interest.

Adeline couldn't blame them one bit. This had been a dull, tiresome affair until he walked through the door. But the moment he had, the air vibrated, turning charged and heated. She still felt the effects of it cover her skin in sensitized gooseflesh.

"With those bruises, Wolford appears positively grizzly," Juliet said with a glance to where Liam and Thayne stood.

Adeline followed her gaze. From this angle, she had a full view of his bruises. But also of the clean line of his jaw, the broad mouth, the sensual lips that—whenever she closed her eyes—she could still feel against her own. Would kissing him now, without those dark whiskers, be different?

Though perhaps, now was not the time to wonder such things.

Juliet faced her. "Nonetheless, it is good that he has made an appearance. That should lessen the rumors at least."

Adeline frowned. "True. However, it isn't fair that he should be made to venture out when he isn't fully recovered."

"If not, my dear, it likely would have been far too late to save your reputation."

"Society is forcing him to come to my aid." The entire episode bothered Adeline. She'd wanted to come to London to prove herself, not to need rescuing.

Even so, as sour as this entire episode made her feel, there was a certain sweetness as well. After all, Liam was here…because of her. And her heart beat in undisguised pleasure over that simple fact.

"It is rather gallant. I knew Wolford was charming, but this is almost heroic." Juliet closed her fan and tapped it against her lips as if in thought. "Of course, once the whispers spread about this evening, Thayne's task will be all the easier. By week's end, Wolford might be named as a contender for the *Original*."

As realization dawned, Adeline stopped and turned to Juliet. "And you would lose your house."

Stomach-churning guilt assailed Adeline. It was all her fault that Thayne thought of this. Not only was Liam here when he clearly needed bed rest, but now Juliet's hopes were in jeopardy.

Juliet lifted her shoulders in a delicate shrug, fanning herself once more. "Well, I've already lost my house. But if he wins, our game will end, and I won't have the chance to buy it back."

"Is there a great deal of animosity between you and Lord Thayne—" Adeline gasped, her hand rising to cover her mouth. "Oh dear. That was rather impertinent of me. Pray, forgive my lapse in decorum."

Juliet shook her head. "There is no such thing as impertinence amongst friends. To answer your question, I would not call it animosity, per se. Not on my part. I have accepted what happened long ago." She closed her fan with a snap. "It isn't my fault that he hasn't."

Adeline admired her new friend's strength. It took a great deal of courage to encounter Thayne each day. After all, it was obvious to Adeline that something other than a kissing scandal stood between them. No wonder the *ton* was enraptured. She didn't say that aloud, however. Impertinence, even amongst friends, had its limitations.

"Hmm…" Juliet murmured, her gaze flitting across the ballroom. "Adeline, a peculiar sort of restlessness has overtaken me. If it wouldn't be a bother, would you like to take a turn about the room?"

Was it a coincidence that Thayne and Liam began heading in their direction at the same moment? Adeline thought not.

"I would love to," she answered, her gaze following the gentlemen's progression along the outer rim of the ballroom.

"But let us stroll toward the opposite corner," Juliet suggested, slipping her arm through Adeline's. Then she turned her head to whisper. "It would not be wise for us to seem eager for their attention or conversation. There are too many who would assume improper things."

Adeline nodded. Since the moment she first saw him tonight, she'd tried to school her reaction, mentally cooling her own cheeks and chiding herself for every errant thought related to their kiss. She only hoped she would be able to continue once they were in closer proximity.

Aside from that, walking was a relief. If she had to stand still a moment longer, she feared her foot and corrective half boot would merge into one. She'd tied the laces a little tighter than usual as a matter of defense against any mishap. Now she was starting to lose feeling in her toes.

"Until I arrived, my biggest fear was what would happen if a gentleman asked me to dance," Adeline confessed. "I know that I am to make a favorable impression, but I am only adept at a country dance. I worried about what to say, should I be asked for a quadrille."

She heard a faint gasp from a pair of young women they passed. From their earlier introductions, she knew they were Miss Ashbury and Miss Leeds. When Adeline glanced at them and saw that they were not looking at her, she knew that her nerves were getting the better of her. After all, what harm or interest could stem from such information?

Other than Liam and her parents, no one here knew about her leg. No one here knew that the footwork in quadrilles— not to mention cotillions, reels, and the minuet—caused her no end of misery and embarrassing missteps. And they would never find out if she could help it.

Juliet tapped her fan against her lips. "Then we will need to avoid any awkwardness in the future. After all, once a young woman declines to dance with a gentleman, she cannot dance at all. Therefore, we must be clever."

Adeline had not known that rule. Of course, she hadn't needed to know it this evening because no one had bothered to approach her or ask her to dance. Nonetheless, she was glad that she had not made a terrible faux pas and was ever grateful for Juliet's advice.

"First of all," Juliet continued, "you must always acquaint yourself with the hostess in order to discover the list of dances for the evening."

Adeline tried not to laugh. "I do not believe Lady Strandfellow would have divulged her list to me."

"Yes, well, sometimes this proves more difficult than others. In that circumstance, you would find a mutual friend. In this case, the dowager duchess. However, if even she does not know because the hostess has not been particularly friendly"—Juliet tsked—"that is when you must bat your lashes at the musicians and claim to have lost your dance card. Make up a story about needing to know when the next country dance is because you promised it to Lord So-and-So."

Flirt with the musicians? Her? Adeline appreciated Juliet's confidence but did not possess it herself. Nor was she practiced in the art. She imagined that batting her lashes at the musicians would only inspire concern for whatever object must have become fixed in her eye.

"Now this requires a measure of subtlety," Juliet said with a surreptitious glance upward toward the minstrels' gallery. "Do you see the handsome man playing the viola? The one with the rakish gleam in his eye?"

Both she and Juliet lingered near an arched alcove and surveyed the room. Beside them stood a cherub sculpture, balancing on one foot as he held an amphora filled with drooping flowers. Adeline pretended to study it while lifting her gaze to the quintet. In the next instant, she ducked her head and moved closer to the cherub. Then quietly she answered Juliet. "I think he...winked at you."

"No, indeed, for I was not looking in his direction. He must have winked at you." Juliet tsked and then laughed. "My, what a flirt you are, Miss Pimm. Adept with a single look."

Adeline blushed, her face overly warm. "I did nothing more than lift my gaze."

"Sometimes that is all it takes." Juliet pursed her lips but only to hide a saucy grin, Adeline was sure. "As for our quarry, his name is Maurice, and he was ever so helpful at offering a set list." Juliet paused long enough to withdraw her own card from beneath her glove. "Once you have that, then you simply scribble a few lines beside the dances you do not want to endure, thereby eliminating any awkwardness."

Adeline noticed that the card revealed names beside every dance. Mortified, she felt her cheeks grow cold. "I've kept you from dancing all evening."

Juliet shook her head. "That is my secret. I've been doing this since I was a debutante. If I don't feel like dancing, I'll fill up my entire card with illegible scrawls. One trick I've learned is to switch the pencil from one hand to the other."

Oh! Now Adeline understood. "You are incomparably clever."

In answer, Juliet slyly tucked her card away and opened her fan with a flourish to hide her smile.

"You are quite skilled with your fan," Adeline said. "I've read about the practice, but I've never employed it myself. As you might imagine, there is little need for such arts in Boswickshire."

Juliet demonstrated a few turns before passing the fan to Adeline. "Now, it is time for your next lesson in flirtation, but first, we must choose new quarry."

Forgetting about the censorious glances cast her way, Adeline was finally enjoying herself. She toyed with a bead that hung suspended from the blue ribbon dangling from the fan. "Are you certain? After all, I would hate for Maurice to become jealous."

"Your loyalty does you credit," Juliet quipped with a thoughtful nod. "Though in all seriousness, your hands are quite graceful. You have a certain way of flicking your wrist that draws the eye. It is quite unique, in the best possible sense, of course."

Adeline smiled at the compliment and was about to respond when the air around her stirred, and gooseflesh covered her skin.

She felt Liam come near before he uttered a word.

"Is this what gently bred ladies talk about when they whisper behind their fans? I must say, I'm rather disappointed," Liam said, his gaze resting on Adeline. She was even lovelier than he recalled, her blue-rimmed gaze brighter, her complexion glowing, her lips all the more irresistible. "I'd hoped to overhear something scandalous regarding Thayne. Although since he became a marquess, he does nothing interesting."

Even though neither Liam nor Thayne acknowledged a destination when they'd begun their tour of the ballroom, apparently they were both pleased to linger here. And while it was in Adeline's best interest for Liam to bow his head and move on, he couldn't seem to find the will to leave just yet.

"I do not agree, Wolford," Juliet added with a challenging lift of her brow to Thayne. "He's taken quite an interest in real estate. I have even heard that the construction happening in my house is coming along quite nicely."

Thayne answered with a grin. "You might want to rethink what you say in a public sphere. You wouldn't want to look foolish at the end of the month when the *Original* is announced."

"The same could be said of you," Juliet said sweetly.

Liam grinned, enjoying this far too much. After all, Thayne deserved to have his hackles raised. This was only a small dose of the reprisal that he would get for wagering on Liam.

More than his desire for retribution, however, was his distraction from Adeline's nearness. It seemed wrong to stand so close and not touch her. Unfortunately, there was no way he could without causing a scandal. Unless…

He glanced down at the fan and had an idea. "Come now, children. Let us return to the safer topic of fans and Miss Pimm's extraordinary wrist flicking. I sense there might be a secret lurking at the cause of it."

He tossed Adeline a wink.

"A secret?" Juliet asked. "I must hear it, Adeline. After all, you are privy to one of mine."

Thayne scoffed. "Secrets? Hardly. The entire *ton* holds you beneath their quizzing glass. You could have no secret."

Juliet smiled sweetly. "How little you know of me, Max."

During this little tête-à-tête, Liam liberated the fan from Adeline. Their fingers tangled for an instant. That was all it took. Not even two seconds of time, and his heart was thudding hard in his chest, his breathing labored. She looked up at him, her pupils expanding, darkening. Her lips parted as she glanced at his mouth, her breasts straining against the line of her bodice with each breath.

His gaze darted around the room, locating shadowed archways leading off to dimly lit rooms where they might find a moment—

Adeline shook her head as if reading his thoughts. "You are not overtaxing yourself, are you?"

Then again, perhaps she didn't know where his thoughts were. "No. I am well." *And all the better for seeing you*, he thought but quickly wondered how the voice of a foolish romantic had entered his mind.

After a moment, her breaths became even, relaxed. He felt himself do the same. The purpose of his presence was to repair her reputation, not ruin it further. Why did he continue to forget?

Sliding the ribbon free, he knotted it closer to the end of the fan, lengthening the silk. Then, without a word, he returned the fan to Adeline, upside down so that she would grasp the handle, like that of a whip. She swished the dangling ribbon, as if testing the weight of the jewel on the end. Then her gaze met his, and he witnessed a trace of uncertainty.

He offered a nod of reassurance. "Are you up for an adventure?"

"Indeed." She grinned.

He looked over his shoulder to the guests, noting they were all immersed in the dancers performing the minuet. Turning back, he saw the vase of flowers in the cherub statue's grasp. "It is a sad sight, Miss Pimm, when a dog rose wilts, is it not?"

Adeline looked over her shoulder too. Apparently satisfied, she gripped the fan and flicked the ribbon toward the flowers.

It happened so fast, he barely caught a glimpse. Yet in the next instant, that single blossom erupted in a sudden scattering of pink.

Liam was impressed. But more than that, something inside of him shifted, like a loadstone fracturing beneath a heavy weight. Adeline Pimm was positively lethal. He would do well to remember that.

By this point, Juliet and Thayne returned their attention to the group. "That was simply marvelous!" Juliet exclaimed but then lowered her voice and clapped softly.

Thayne's mouth opened and then closed, like a fish. "However did you learn to do that?"

"When I was a child," Adeline began, "I used to stave off boredom by flicking my dolls off the end of my bed." The full story she kept to herself but with a glance to Liam. The rest remained shared only between them.

Juliet sidled up to Adeline and linked arms with her. "I must learn how you do that. I have a mind to take you for a ride through the park one day this week, so that we may practice on trees with low-hanging leaves."

Adeline beamed. "I would like that very much."

"I am an early riser and prefer the park when it is quiet. Would it be too much to ask if I called upon you earlier than what is good form? The day after tomorrow?"

"Being from the country, we are early risers as well."

As the pair of them walked away, Liam forced his feet to remain fixed to the floor.

Somehow this was turning into more than simply coming to her aid to protect her from the gossips. Much more.

Chapter Ten

The Season Standard—the Daily Chronicle of Consequence

The highly anticipated Select Seventy gathered last night at Lady St—'s elegant home. In a surprise to many, this most coveted event transformed into the Seventy-Seven instead! The last-minute guests included the Duke and Duchess of V—, not to mention the shocking appearance of a certain earl. While rumors about an attack on W— were earlier refuted, the ghastly evidence speaks for itself. For the time being, however, we withhold judgment on our wolfish earl. For as we know of all canines, there are some you simply do not invite into your home, or else risk being bitten.

"**A**ugh!" Adeline shouted as she threw the paper down onto the secretaire in her bedchamber. That last line was clearly a jab at her family. It seemed no matter what they did, they could not alter the *ton*'s opinion of them.

She'd come to London to prove herself capable of being just like any other debutante, but she could not find the opportunity to do so. And more than that, it was no longer solely about her. Liam was involved.

It truly angered her that society portrayed Liam as a man without any morals, especially when he'd sacrificed his own recovery for her. Did these society people have no eyes? Couldn't they see how much he'd struggled; how exertion shortened his breaths and flared his nostrils; how his dark pupils expanded as his gaze searched for a place to rest and find comfort?

No, of course they had not. They were more concerned with her reputation and her parents' supposed gullibility. Which was likely the reason they had received no invitations to any party or ball this evening.

She sincerely hoped that her new friends were not looked upon as fools for assisting her. And even more so, that the dowager duchess would not suffer spiteful whispers for having invited the Pimms as her special guests to the dinner ball she was hosting for Liam's Uncle Albert and Cousin Gemma.

Staring down at the letters she'd written to each of them this morning, she wondered if they showed the abundance of her appreciation, or if she should pen new letters instead.

Before she came to a conclusion, Hester tapped quietly on the open door. "Pardon me, miss, but I found this key on the side table of the room across the hall. It does not fit into that door, and so I wondered if you knew where it belonged."

Instantly, Adeline recognized the cloverleaf bow. It was the key to the hidden door between this house and the next.

Liam's house. A shiver of excitement rushed through her, but she did her best to conceal it. Holding out her hand, she said, "Not to worry. I will find its proper place."

The maid frowned. "I shouldn't want to overtax you. In fact, I can ask Mr. Finley—"

"I am perfectly capable of completing this task," Adeline interrupted, her tone more forceful than she'd used before.

Hester blinked, taken aback. Then she curtsied and summarily opened her hand. "Thank you, miss."

As Hester left the chamber, Adeline curled the key into her palm so tightly that it made an instant impression. She would find the *proper place* for this key. And if that particular door should open by accident…

Well, how could she resist such an adventure?

The second floor hall at Sudgrave Terrace was crowded with statues, urns, marble busts, and an assortment of bric-a-brac. There were also dozens of crates that had yet to be opened, and not one single servant within sight. The house was pleasantly dark, the curtains still closed, the air a bit dusty.

Liam knew it would take some time to arrange the house so that it was livable, but this wasn't even close yet. He thought when he'd asked Rendell to find tenants for one part of the house—as Liam had always despised an empty house—that his steward would have arranged to have all three properties readied.

Standing at the top of the stairs, Liam heard no sound from below either, which meant no footmen to finish uncrating his collection. He was completely alone—a state he should have become used to by now. Yet for some reason, he was more aware of it than ever before.

"How clever!" a familiar lush voice exclaimed from the opposite end of the hall.

Liam turned his head to see Adeline emerge through the adjoining door. The tension he felt a moment ago suddenly evaporated, the emptiness no longer pressing upon him. He told himself that he would have felt the same way had it been a servant who'd entered just then, but he knew better. He wasn't at all certain that he liked the realization either.

"Have you come to spy on me, Miss Pimm?"

She gasped and turned quickly in his direction. "I was not aware you'd returned. I thought you'd left us."

Still accustomed to lower lighting, he could see her fidget with the end of the plaited hair drawn over her shoulder. She blinked as if to see the vague silhouette of him at the far end of the hall. "I have only come to check on a few objects here, nothing more."

She did not pout, as he'd expected, but flicked her hair back and dusted her hands together. "I don't suppose we could be rid of you even if we wanted. You are, after all, our landlord for as long as we remain in town."

He took pleasure in knowing that he could smile without a witness. That he could reveal how much he liked the way she teased him. "Whatever length of time it is, I'm certain it will seem an eternity."

"Especially now," she agreed with a nod.

Her sudden lack of humor made him question, "Why now, precisely?"

"I've had two days to ponder, and I've come to the conclusion that you should not have kissed me."

Liam was just about to agree. He even decided to ignore the fact that she'd been thinking about their kiss for two days. But then she continued, and all thought instantly left his brain. All the blood too, for it rushed south.

"But I enjoyed what you did with your tongue. It was quite...enlightening." She ended with a dreamy smile.

He was glad she stood twenty paces from him or else he would have given her a reason to smile again. All day. *Hell,* all year.

"In what way?" he asked because, well, apparently he was an idiot.

She paid no heed, turning her attention to an urn instead. "Only that I can imagine what a morsel of food feels like inside your mouth."

Bollocks. He was as hard as a marble Priapus. *But wait,* his scholarly instruction chimed in to save him, Priapus was the god of fertility, among other things. And fertility meant offspring, and offspring meant marriage—*or rather one before the other*—and he wasn't going to marry anyone. Not for another thirty years. Therefore, he needed to stop thinking with his marble protrusion.

He cleared his throat, deciding that a complete change in topic was in order. "That urn is a recent addition to my collection."

With hands clasped behind her back, she bent to study the mosaic pattern. "It is quite interesting. Though it does not resemble the black Grecian urns I've seen."

"This was unearthed along the Elbe. The rough texture of the clay and the distinct grayish hue indicate that it was made by an ancient people. I do believe that is volcanic glass, though I am not certain. Nor have I determined the era."

Normally, he wasn't so free in speaking about his studies. There were only a few people he trusted with his secret—his aunt; his cousin; a fellow scholar, Lord Caulfield; and now, apparently, Adeline.

A measure of trepidation shivered down his spine like the touch of a ghost from his past. *Did* Liam trust her? As much as he'd tried thus far, he'd been unable to find a reason not to do.

He let out a breath. The weight of it leaving his lungs made him somewhat lighter.

"You speak as if you enjoy the puzzle it presents," she said.

He nodded, strangely pleased by her understanding of his nature. "In fact, I am presenting a lecture at the Royal Society on ancient marbles and forgeries."

There. He'd done it again, offering her another secret, and this time without a cold chill.

She straightened, facing him, her eyes bright. "How thrilling!"

"Vale was appointed a fellowship recently and asked me to speak." Distracted, he didn't even realize he'd begun walking toward her. "That was after I became aware of a surprising number of forgeries finding their way into private collections, and Vale thought I could use my knowledge to shed some light on the issue."

"Have you any forgeries in your collection?"

"A few, yes. I like to compare them to the originals." He told her of the head of Aphrodite that his uncle had sold him and how it differed from the one his own father had purchased—though it had been considered "lost" from the collection that Elgin had brought to London more than fifteen years ago. "Not many people know about the traces of blue paint left on the original sculpture."

And other than Vale, no one else knew that he had the original in his collection as well.

She tilted her head up at him. Only then did he realize that he'd stopped within arm's reach of her. "I would love to see it and hear your lecture. I find this all fascinating."

And he would love nothing more than to show her, but…"I'm afraid it is not here." He hated seeing her disappointment in the subtle shrug of her shoulders, the fade of her smile. "But I will open any crate here that you wish."

And then her lips curved again as she laughed softly. "Thank you for humoring me, but perhaps we can talk about this one." She turned again to the urn. "I cannot decide if the women are holding spears, planting trees, or…"

"I'm not certain I remember. This is a new acquisition for my collection," he said, using it as an excuse to move closer. He was drawn by her complete absorption of the mosaic. He remembered feeling that way—still felt it—the awe and wonder. "Ah, yes. They are gathering sheaves of wheat, symbolizing…"

He coughed on the final word. He couldn't seem to escape it.

"Fertility," she supplied for him. "And prosperity, I believe."

Now it was his turn to be impressed. "Very good."

"As I mentioned before, I've had time to read at length. However, it is a joy to see something like this, to be able to touch it and feel what the person who created it must have felt." She studied the figures, stroking her fingertips along the obsidian. "Hmm…In looking closely at the women, I see different hues of glass used for their abdomens. It is a shade lighter."

It was? He looked again, angling closer.

"Remarkable. I had not noticed this before," he admitted, somewhat enthralled. But not by the mosaic. By *her*. He bent so that his head was at her level, examining the urn as if for the first time. He traced the glass with his fingertip, following the path hers had taken.

"You have to be in just the right light."

He felt her breath against his cheek, and a shudder tumbled through him, tripping over every nerve on its way. If he turned his head, he knew he would kiss her. Hell, if he turned his head, he knew he would do *more* than kiss her. And it was only because he wanted to so badly that he didn't. The intensity of his desire frightened him.

"I've found such symbolic imagery on other pieces before," he said, his voice so hoarse that it wavered slightly. He wanted to stand erect and move apart from her, but there was no way for him to disguise the effect she had on him. So he remained uncomfortably hunched over and tried to distract himself with a more scholarly approach. "Historically, such symbols came during times of blight that destroyed the harvests. People starved. Populations dwindled. Which would mean that you are correct. They were asking for an abundance of food *and* births. Their survival depended upon it."

"Oh," she said, her voice oddly strained. Then she turned pale suddenly, straightened, and backed away. "Of course it did."

He stopped her before she could leave. "What is the matter, Adeline? Did I say something to offend you?" Never before had he worried over offending anyone.

"No. You know very well that you did not. I enjoyed your lesson. It's just that…" She frowned. "My own guilt began to creep upon me like a blight of its own."

"I don't understand what you mean."

Adeline pressed her lips together and touched them with her fingertips, her discomfiture apparent. For her sake, he was about to alter their topic, when, after a small hesitation, she drew in a deep breath and began.

"My mother had wanted a large family. As you've likely noticed, she has the nature for it. However, because of me, she was unable to bear any more children. I was a difficult birth. Breech, I was told. Anyway, my leg was broken during the process, but it went unnoticed because Father and Uncle Peirce were busy trying to save her life, as they ought to have done." Tears shimmered in her eyes. "And the worst part of it all is the fact that my father and my mother have carried the burden of guilt over my leg all these years."

His hands skimmed down her arms as realization dawned. "And you carry guilt over theirs."

She nodded. "Always. Even more so since I've decided not to marry. Which leaves them without grandchildren as well. I am truly a horrible and selfish child."

"Then why not marry to ease the burden for everyone?"

She looked up at him with those clear, luminous eyes. "I cannot."

"Why not?" He wondered if there was a man who had once spurned her. Had her heart been broken? Set on a gentleman who did not fancy her?

She averted her gaze. "I don't want to be coddled for the rest of my life. I want to be seen as someone who is capable of doing everything that any other woman can do. That is why I am here. I want to prove myself to my parents that I am just like all the other young women of society. And by the time we return to Boswickshire, they will rely upon me so that I can begin to repay them for all they've sacrificed."

Then, without warning, she gave him the key to the adjoining door, their hands clasping for an instant before she pulled away.

"You are the most peculiar and selfless family I have ever met. I fear the *ton* will make a meal of you." And he didn't want to see that happen. Nor did he want her London adventure to end.

Suddenly, he knew that his sojourn into polite society wasn't over. Not yet.

CHAPTER ELEVEN

"Normally, I would have the driver let us out here so that we could walk," Juliet said once the carriage reached the park the following day. "This morning, however, I fear that the clouds are threatening more than a drizzle."

Adeline peered through the open carriage window. The soot-gray sky hung overhead rather ominously. Father always said, *good sense is its own reward*. Though at the moment, good sense did nothing to abate the possibility of a missed adventure. "There will be time for another tour of the park, I'm sure."

"Walking here is one of my great pleasures. I'd missed this park after being away in Bath for so many years." Juliet's voice turned quiet as she looked out the window. An instant later, she drew her gaze back to Adeline. "Now that my cousin Lilah has married, I have no walking companion and would greatly welcome your company as often as you are able."

"I should like that," Adeline said with a smile. But it faltered when a thought occurred to her. "I'm not sure it would be wise for you to be seen with me...considering the opinion society holds."

Two days had passed since the soiree at Lady Strandfellow's, and still there were no invitations.

"I only look to my own opinion. I find that you and your parents are far better people than the *ton* deserves." Juliet gracefully waved her hand through the air as if that matter was part of ancient myth. "However, I'm certain I will be unable to keep you to myself for long. Have you not read the *Standard* this morning?"

"No. I was too excited to see Hyde Park." *And Rotten Row.* Adeline watched as Juliet unfolded the paper and angled it toward the light.

"Our Earl of W— made a miraculous showing at Lord and Lady Kn—'s dinner of most distinguished guests. While a little worse for wear, he was no less dashing. Great hopes abound that this will only be one of many more appearances in polite society."

Adeline frowned. "I don't see how that has anything to do with my acceptance, or lack thereof, into society."

"You will see. If Wolford holds favor, then so will you. After all, your family has brought the wolf back into the fold."

"Heaven help the fold," Adeline said with a lift of her eyes to the carriage roof.

Juliet laughed. "That is likely a truer statement than either of us dare to think about."

And yet there was so much more to Liam than most people gave him credit. The *ton* would believe that he was on this earth for the sake of debauchery alone. Yet he wasn't simply a charming, devilishly handsome rake. He was also a scholar with a love for history. His collection held an amazing assortment of artifacts, to which he made a point of studying each and every one.

Then, as if her thoughts had the power to conjure him, she glanced through the carriage window and saw a dashing figure approach. Her heart's rhythm altered tempo, quickening. The sound of it seemed to match the happy trot of his horse's hooves.

Liam drove up in an open crimson gig, drawn by an eager gray high-stepper. Once he reached Juliet's carriage, he lifted his hat. "Lady Granworth. Miss Pimm. What a serendipitous meeting."

"*Serendipitous?*" Juliet tsked. "I do believe you were present when I'd asked Adeline to join me in the park the evening before last."

"Was I?" With the mischievous gleam in his green gaze, he wasn't fooling anyone. He tapped his gloved fingertips against his temple. "I fear that the wounds I received may have affected my memory."

"A sudden case of amnesia?" Adeline issued a single *ha* in challenge but smiled. "I hope your horse knows the way home."

"But you see, Miss Pimm, my horse is holding me captive at the moment. He has no compassion for me and longs to race. Of course, I prefer a long, steady canter, but what am I to do?" His innocent expression altered when he tossed them a wink and reclined back, draping his arm across the wooden rail along the back. His green coat parted as he shifted, widening his legs in a way that caused the buckskin to tighten over his muscled thighs. In the other hand, he held the reins loosely, stroking the strip of leather beneath his thumb. "With no seat companions, I fear that I might fall off this perch. Surely the pair of you could offer a stricter hand on the reins."

The more Liam spoke, the deeper, more suggestive his voice became, and all the while he held Adeline's gaze. It was all she could do not to leap out of the carriage and onto his lap.

Juliet cleared her throat. "Wolford, you would do better to hie yourself back to one of your houses to break your fast."

"What makes you think I have not broken my fast already?"

Juliet glanced from Wolford to Adeline and back again. "Because you look positively ravenous."

He grinned, and rather wickedly too.

When he made no denial, Adeline's cheeks flamed. Oh, why did she not want to look away? "It must be a trick of the light."

"A trick of some sort, to be sure," Juliet muttered. "I am convinced you came this way to lure my friend into scandal. Then our efforts would be for naught."

"What scandal can be had in an open curricle?" His eyebrows lifted in innocence, but the tilt of his mouth suggested he knew quite a few ways. "There would be none at all if you joined us."

He spoke as if Adeline had already agreed. Likely she should be offended by his presumption. But who was she fooling? She wanted to go more than anything. She could be cross with him later.

"There is hardly room for you, let alone two or three. Besides, it looks like rain."

"I do not mind the rain," Adeline said, unable to help herself. "And the moment the first drop hits, we could return to your carriage."

Juliet peered around them, considering. "Hmm…There is no one about. Most sensible people are still abed, and the gossips too, I imagine. Very well. However, I will remain here. Quite honestly, Adeline, I'm a little frightened of that contraption. I've seen them here before, and they go dreadfully fast."

Adeline's heart raced. She could barely contain her excitement. Her hand reached for the door at the same time that Wolford opened it. With a backward wave, she said, "I won't be a minute."

Liam secured her beside him and felt his mistake immediately. A shudder wracked through him at their close press of bodies. It was so powerful that he had to close his eyes against it…or to savor it. He wasn't quite sure.

"Hold on, Miss Pimm. This is going to be only a short jaunt but fast." He enjoyed taking his time in most activities that brought him pleasure. Unfortunately, he wasn't certain he could trust himself beside her for too long. Yesterday had drained his resistance.

"I don't know what to hold on to. There is nothing but a frail bend of metal along the side of this seat."

"Then hold on to me." He snapped the reins, leaving her without much choice. Unfortunately for him, she settled her arm along the back of the seat instead. But the view her position provided—the modestly cut blue muslin pulling taut against the inviting swells of her breasts—made the sacrifice worth it.

She let out a lush laugh as the horse sprinted away and down the length of the track. "I'm so happy I could burst. If

it wouldn't ruin my reputation, I would kiss you again, Wolford. Right here."

"Don't burst, or you'll frighten my horse."

After the turn, the first sprinkles of rain began. *Hell.*
"We should head back." Since they were the only ones on the
track, they could. A distant rumble of thunder warned him
to slow.

"No, please." Adeline set her hand over his on the reins.

"You'll be wet through," he warned, his wicked mind
veering slightly when he saw the beads were already clinging to her lips. And when she licked the rain away, he nearly
groaned. "Then so be it. I want to be wet through. I want this
adventure, Wolford."

Now it was his turn to tilt his head back and laugh at the
heavens above them. But his was far more sardonic. "Promise
me one thing first, Miss Pimm."

"Of course." She said, far too eager, far too naïve.

"Say those words to me once more."

She looked at him peculiarly, tilting her head. Then in no
time at all, she released his hand, and a deeper color bloomed
on her cheeks. "I don't know why I am blushing but have a
feeling that I should not repeat what I said."

He grinned at her and snapped the reins. "Likely not, for I
am greedy and would ask you to say it again and again."

Adeline stared out the carriage window and watched Liam
drive his gig away. Even though both Juliet and she had
offered to share the carriage, he'd insisted on driving himself, stating that he'd been abed too long and that the rain

would do him good. Before he left, however, he withdrew a dry handkerchief and gave it to Adeline.

Thankfully, there was nothing more than a drizzle or else she would worry about him. But who was she kidding? She would worry about him all the same.

"I hope you can forgive me," Adeline said, blotting her face. "It was impossibly rude of me to leave you here."

"There is nothing to forgive, silly. I believe we should seize moments of daring whenever we are able. Otherwise, how can we know what lives inside of us?" Juliet spoke with undeniable certainty, while her smile was somewhat wistful. "Besides, if it had not been for the rain, I surely would have gone. Wolford is rather persuasive, after all. Not only that, but he seemed...determined to make it happen. I have never seen him thusly."

Adeline couldn't imagine him any other way. "I have no knowledge of him other than who he is now. What was he like before?"

Juliet pursed her lips in thought. "I did not know him well, mind you. There had only been a handful of parties and dinners we'd attended together. Most of the time, the esteemed host would have invited Wolford because of his title and not necessarily for his charm. As you can imagine, he was always an incorrigible flirt, which seldom earned him favor. And many held his excessive wealth against him. He was known for being spoiled, his focus on buying whatever object he wanted.

"Yet since the evening of Strandfellow's soiree, I've noticed a marked alteration in him. I daresay, he is almost noble in his bearing and no longer thinking of his own pursuits."

Hmm…yes. He was quite gallant this morning, Adeline mused pleasantly.

"Perhaps it is the result of the attack upon him." She noted the keen brightness in Juliet's gaze that reminded her of Mother's *knowing* look. Not wanting a blush to give her away further, she patted her cheeks with the handkerchief. "Though, since I have not known him long, it is a mere speculation."

"That is the stranger thing still. The pair of you seem…*familiar*, though not in a scandalous sense. More so like two people who have been acquainted for many years. After all, he seemed to know that you would not be able to resist a race this morning."

Was that what this was about? Adeline breathed in relief. "I might have mentioned such a desire. When he first awoke, his head was bandaged, his eyes covered, and I felt as if I could not leave him alone. So I talked with him, nattering on and on. I'm sure he was eager to be free of the sound of my voice."

"Ah. So that is how he knew about your ribbon trick."

Adeline nodded. The truth was, he knew a good deal more about her than anyone else. She'd told him her deepest secret. He knew her regrets. He knew her fears. And never once had he looked at her as if she deserved his pity.

Instead, he was understanding, and he shared his thoughts with her too. He didn't choose his words carefully, guarding her or coddling her. Because of this, they were connected, *bonded*. And to her it went deeper than a mere friendship ever could.

Chapter Twelve

After his race through the rain, Liam returned to Wolford House, feeling oddly invigorated at such an early hour. He'd spent years indulging in the pleasures of the night; he rarely awoke before noon most days. Now an entire day stretched before him, and he was eager to make the most of it.

His coterie would certainly laugh at him, if they were awake to witness the sight of him bounding up the stairs two at a time. Most of them were only now thinking of their own beds in matters of sleeping and asking their valets to dismiss whichever companions they'd brought home for the evening's entertainment.

Liam had had years of similar experiences—endless hours of pleasure, a sumptuous buffet of delights, women in various states of undress frolicking before him, over him, under him. He'd been content with his life, as one would be with a buffet laden with rich delicacies. Something different to dine upon each day, and very unlike the porridge he'd eaten two days in a row at Boswick's.

He thought of his own breakfast of ham and poached eggs drenched in buttery sauce that morning, how it had pooled on his plate and hadn't satisfied him for long. He felt his stomach rumble. Perhaps there was something to be said for a bowl of porridge. His palate missed the simplicity of it, the warmth that had lingered with him afterward.

And even though Liam knew that his desire for porridge had more to do with Adeline than his palate preferences, he instructed the kitchen to bring him porridge the following morning. And he would have porridge every single day until he grew tired of it. The only thing was, he didn't think he would.

Liam closed his chamber door. Even now, just thinking about her feeding him porridge that first morning, he was inexplicably aroused.

I want to be wet through… Damn. Those words were killing him too. In fact, everything she'd said played over and over in his mind, eliciting desires that he knew better than to entertain.

But who was he kidding? Desire was in his makeup. In the marrow of his bones. He lived for pleasure in all he saw, smelled, touched, and tasted. And presently, he had a craving for Adeline's face, the scent of her skin, the feel of his mouth on her flesh. He would lick porridge from her body and Boswickshire honey from her navel…

He groaned. This was not the thought to have while stripping out of his wet clothes. He was half tempted to take himself in hand—something he hadn't done since he was a lad. He hadn't needed to. There were always women aplenty seeking pleasure. Likely, he could call upon any number of them, even at this hour, to slake his lust. Yet the only one he wanted right now, the only one in this fantasy, was the one he could not have.

And with that thought, his lust turned to frustration.

As he donned dry clothes, his mood darkened. He felt as if he were under the spell of Aphrodite's girdle—unable to control this desire.

And as he was silently cursing Aphrodite, his thoughts suddenly veered to his collection. Since this was a safer line of thought, he trained his focus upon it, in order to keep from going mad.

The day before his attack, he'd left Rendell in charge of sending the Aphrodite crates to the Royal Society, but he hadn't bothered to make sure that they'd arrived safely and ready for display at the symposium. And with the burglary happening within days of the supposed move, he needed to know.

Striding out of his bedchamber and downstairs, he sought out Rendell. He found his steward in the library, using the room as his office since the one below stairs was likely filled with various bric-a-brac in need of accounting.

"It just occurred to me that both heads of Aphrodite are missing from the ballroom. Do you have that on your list of items you are cross-referencing for Hollycott?"

Rendell looked into the ledger, turning a few pages. "Accounted for, my lord. The forgery was crated and sent to the Royal Society two days prior to the robbery." He turned to another page and then pointed to a mark. "It appears that the original is listed amongst the crates sent to Sudgrave

Terrace, my lord. My apologies, my lord. I shall see to it that both are sent to the Society immediately, my lord."

The original had been there all this time? Considering how much Adeline had enjoyed viewing that vase, he saw this as an opportunity instead of Rendell's failing. "Actually, I have a mind to study it more closely. Leave it at Sudgrave Terrace for the time being. I'll have it sent before the symposium."

Yet even as he spoke, Liam knew the last thing he needed was an excuse to see Adeline.

"Yes, my lord."

In addition, Liam needed to leave the room before his steward *my lorded* him to death, but first he had to ask, "Any correspondence?"

"On your desk, my lord. I placed two correspondences from your lordship's most respected archeologists. A new collection of Chinese scrolls has arrived. And more Roman artifacts have been discovered at Lord Caulfield's country estate. They arrived at his townhouse yesterday, and he extends the courtesy of first viewing to you."

"Very good, Rendell." A pleasant distraction was exactly what he needed. Taking a rather elegant correspondence off his desk, he grabbed an umbrella and walked a few doors down.

"My, my, Wolford. You must be eager to see the latest additions to my collection," Caulfield said as Liam was escorted to the drawing room. Most people would expect an exquisitely furnished room, but here, long straw-packed crates filled the space, and tucked inside, a treasure trove of artifacts awaited.

Liam felt perfectly at home.

"I appreciate the invitation." Liam gripped Caulfield's hand.

When Caulfield nodded, fine particles of orange-colored dust sifted down from the hank of snow-white hair on his forehead and landed on the slight paunch beneath his gray waistcoat. "I thought the embossed invitation was a nice touch."

It had been a jest, Liam knew, because there weren't many days during the week when he did not drop by. Until recently. They'd known each other for years, a friendship born out of mutual appreciation and similarities in their natures. Though Caulfield was thirty years Liam's senior, they enjoyed a comparable lifestyle of indulgence. In Liam's opinion, Caulfield was confirmation that a man could have everything he wanted.

Taking in the collection at a glance, he focused on the disc resting in plain sight. "You've unearthed a pewter plate, I see."

Unlike some of the larger items that some men collected, Caulfield preferred the smaller, more intimate pieces that depicted the daily lives of the people who lived during that time. As for Liam, he enjoyed all of it.

"A dozen or more. My original estimation, that the *previous tenants* on my land were poor and few, is now changing." Caulfield went back to studying the piece, not out of disrespect for his company, but because he was absorbed and comfortable with a fellow collector.

Liam made himself comfortable, shrugging out of his coat and draping it over a crate. He passed up the pewter plates in favor of the pottery, picking up a vase here and a bowl there, murmuring various observations about each piece, and noting the figural designs carved into the terra cotta. "I'd have to agree. Evidence suggests that this family was quite prosperous."

They spoke at length about the new digging sight on Caulfield's property and the unearthed boundary markers that he intended to keep in place. Both of them moved down the rows, finding new treasures.

Liam wasn't even paying attention to how much time had passed until his body began to stiffen. His neck was sore, and a dull ache pinched his side. Most of his wounds were healing, and he was feeling stronger, but he'd done more today than he had in a week. Tomorrow he would think about sending for his sportsman.

"That vessel is not in ideal shape," Caulfield said about the broken jar Liam was holding gingerly. "However, I noticed the markings around the rim that suggested it was for honey. I thought perhaps it would be of some interest. There is even some sort of residue inside."

Liam drew a lamp closer and saw the marking for himself and felt a laugh rise up. Honey. He imagined Boswick would enjoy this find. In fact…"I have a friend who might be interested in this jar. What would you take for it?"

Caulfield was never one to take advantage of Liam's wealth and quoted a fair price.

"Done." Liam handed the jar to a footman before moving on to the final crate.

Caulfield joined him, pointing out various pottery and even wooden artifacts that had petrified to resemble marble.

"And now I will test the scholar," Caulfield said and handed Liam a piece of terra cotta. "What do you think this is?"

Liam studied it. The object was the size of his palm, roundish, and somewhat misshapen. There were still lingering traces of earth compacted into the creases that surrounded it. What he couldn't figure out was the small cone-shaped protrusion. "While the object is too irregular to be a ball, it appears to be a toy of sorts?"

"Yes. It is a rattle. In fact, there are two." Caulfield handed him one for his other hand, this one less round, but more in the shape of a dog or cat, the pointed ears giving it away. The animal tinkled faintly as it shifted.

Liam was oddly entranced by these two small objects. He did not remember finding such items like this in the attic crates at Arborcrest. Infant toys. Likely he'd once had them. He recalled a rocking horse in the nursery, a ball and cup, a stick and hoop, but they had not been preserved as Father's collection had been.

He thought of Adeline—though without cause, other than the fact that she might enjoy studying these small objects. And he would enjoy testing her to see if she made the discovery of what they were on her own. Then he thought of his cousin and his bride. What better gift for the new addition to the family than an artifact that once, long ago, another tiny hand had held?

Liam felt pleased by this. "Name your price, Caulfield."

"I'm not certain I want to sell that, Wolford. Though you may not have heard, as the news is so recent, but I am going to be married. This June, as a matter of fact, to Miss Poppy Tremaine." He puffed out his chest and grinned.

"Married?" Liam was stunned for a moment but wasn't sure why. "Well, congratulations. At long last, you won't have to roam these halls alone."

Caulfield wiped his dusty hands over his waistcoat. "You forget, young Wolford. Of the two of us, I've never been the one to complain about an empty house. I love my solitude." He sighed. "I shall miss it, I'm sure."

Never complain about…But Liam thought they both had objected to the idea of an empty house. Thinking about it now, however, he realized that it hadn't been Caulfield. It had been him.

How many times had he told that harridan of a house-keeper, Mrs. Brasher, that he purchased artifacts out of a need to fill his empty houses? Likely too many to count.

Pushing that aside, Liam collected himself. "I wish you every felicitation."

"She is the youngest of seven and the only girl amongst them," Caulfield said with a nod. "I went to school with her father and know him to be a smart fellow, so I am assured to have an heir with some sense at least."

Liam suddenly understood the peculiar sense of surprise. Caulfield was doing precisely what Liam planned to do—to live on his own terms until the time came for an heir. That was what his Father had done, as well.

But now that Liam saw it playing out, he couldn't help but feel sorry for Caulfield's heir, imagining that he would spend much of his life without a father and with nothing but a collection of things to fill the void.

Liam felt that shifting sensation once more. This time, he recognized the weight bearing down on the *loadstone* as his own. He felt heavy-hearted for Caulfield's future children, and also—strangely—for his own.

For the first time, Liam began to question the path he'd decided upon, so many years ago.

Outwardly, he had a smile at the ready for an old friend. "Then as a wedding gift to you, I'll offer that Roman pottery collection you've had your eye on for years as a fair trade."

Caulfield didn't hesitate. "Done."

CHAPTER THIRTEEN

The Season Standard—the Daily Chronicle of Consequence

Our infamous Earl of W— is making quite the recovery. Dashing as ever, he escorted the Dowager Duchess of V— to a dinner party of so little importance that it is hardly worth the mention. The fascination lies in the sudden emergence of whispers, naming W— as a potential candidate for the Original!

Of course, we must not forget our dear Lord E— who has been a favorite for many weeks…

Adeline marveled at the swift alteration in the *ton's* opinion of Wolford. Because of the daily accounts in the *Standard,* even her family had begun to receive invitations in the days that followed. Most surprisingly was one from Lady Falksworth, who'd slighted them at the opera. Apparently, Juliet had been correct. Society could now show favor to the family who had aided Wolford instead of branding them with the stamp of ruination.

Tonight, she attended a party at Lord Tarlston's. Adeline was pleased to be better received now that her reputation had been repaired. At least for the time. There was no telling what one unfavorable report of Wolford's activity might do. It was still odd to her that the collective thoughts of the *ton* were so eager to jump to conclusions, vacillating from one extreme to the other. If they vilified Wolford, then her reputation was sullied. And if they esteemed him, then she was a veritable vestal virgin.

Given her white satin gown, she certainly looked the part this evening.

Little did they know how scandalous her thoughts had become since she'd met Liam.

"Are you feeling warm, dear?" Mother asked, mistaking an errant blush for an illness. She plucked at the fingertips of her glove as if she meant to strip it off and press a hand to Adeline's forehead.

Adeline did not doubt that she would too. And while standing in the parlor with guests milling about.

She took Mother's hand in an affectionate squeeze and lowered it. "I am feeling perfectly content."

That motherly indigo gaze still scrutinized her. "I don't believe our host waters down his wine as he ought."

"I drank only one glass." *And a half*, she thought, remembering how efficiently the footman had refilled her goblet in between courses. She also had a wonderfully handsome table companion by the name of Lord Ellery. The viscount was affable as well, and there was a certain soulfulness in his eyes that spoke of a sincerity, which many of those she'd met lacked.

Even with his wonderful qualities, however, she had not felt drawn to him. Not even a little. Her skin did not tingle at the very thought of him. The study of his mouth while he ate did not stir her. She never once imagined her lips on his.

Her lips, so it seemed, were only eager for the press of one single gentleman. And he was not even in attendance.

"I wonder why Wolford did not attend," Mother said, mirroring Adeline's thoughts. "His aunt is here, so I imagine he received an invitation."

The dowager duchess was across the room, conversing with Juliet and Ivy. In the hall before dinner, Ivy explained that her husband had been distracted by one of his "brilliant inventions" and, therefore, did not attend. But that did not stop Ivy from glowing at the mere mention of him.

"Perhaps he is with his cousin, the duke," Adeline said, hoping that was correct. Yet a dark jealousy churned in her stomach. He could very well be at another party. Perhaps even like the masquerade he'd attended the night of his attack. Which shouldn't matter to her. She knew the type of man Liam was. He could very well be engaged in an assignation, his lips on someone else's mouth right this instant.

"Are you certain you are feeling well?"

Adeline realized she'd pressed her fingertips to her lips as if she were trying to capture the fleeting essence he'd left behind. She nodded to her mother. Noticing her probing stare, however, she quickly looked for a distraction. "Oh look, Father and the other gentlemen have finished their port."

Mother turned her head in his direction and smiled. "I wonder if anyone will play the pianoforte this evening. After all, one would assume the reason we gathered here with the instrument in the room would be for entertainment. Perhaps you should be the first. Your father would love to hear his favorite piece of music."

Adeline wasn't certain that was proper etiquette in this circumstance. Thinking of Juliet's prior instruction, she said, "Perhaps we should inquire with our hostess."

But before she could, Miss Ashbury sat down at the pianoforte, arranged her skirts, cleared her throat with a slight cough, and then began to play. Adeline felt her mood darken again. From her previous encounter with Miss Ashbury and her bosom companion, Miss Leeds, Adeline knew that both young women were all affectation and little substance. Even a young woman from the country could see the difference.

"She plays beautifully," Mother commented. "Perhaps we could sit near our friends. I do believe the settee across from the dowager duchess is now available."

Mother began walking, intercepting Father along the way, but when Adeline noticed that the hem of her gown was caught on the toe of her half boot, she paused to tug it free. By the time she lifted her gaze, Miss Leeds had stepped in front of her.

The fair-haired young woman offered a thin smile reminiscent of a snake in need of a charmer's flute to return to its basket. "Miss Pimm, I am told you hail from a small hamlet in the countryside."

Adeline nodded, both in answer and by way of greeting her cordially, if not carefully. "Yes. Boswickshire has been home to my family for generations."

"It is such a small world we live in, for my family has a scullery maid in our employ who also claims such a birthplace. Perhaps you know her." Miss Leeds clasped her hands before her and smugly pursed her lips. At the same time, Miss Ashbury offered a trilling of the keys. But to Adeline it was like the rattle of a snake's tail.

Alarm jolted through her, but she made every effort to conceal it. She fixed her own smile in place on an indrawn breath. "With fewer than two hundred villagers living there, I'm certain we have met."

"Are you not curious about her family name? Perhaps I could pass on a good word from you. Of course, under different circumstances I wouldn't think to inquire. However, rumor has it that your family is rather unconventional." Miss Leeds dropped her voice to a whisper and slithered closer. "Tell me—is it true that you arrived in London without your servants? And that you undertook Lord Wolford's care on your own?"

Adeline saw a trap yawning before her. If she answered any of the questions posed to her, others would likely arise; whispers would abound no matter how careful she was. Though, quite honestly, she didn't see that it was any business of Miss Leeds. "We are so new to town, I was not aware that you were introduced to my parents. I will be certain to *pass on a good word from you*. Unless you wish to tell them yourself. We could join them now."

"You are too kind, but I am needed at the pianoforte." Her smile thinned as she inclined her head and slithered away without another word.

Unfortunately, that was not the last encounter that Adeline had with Miss Leeds.

Later that evening, both Miss Leeds *and* Miss Ashbury ambushed her in the retiring room.

Adeline was adjusting the laces of her half boot, her back to the door, when they both walked into the room. Hurriedly, she tried to conceal the thick cork sole.

"Why, Miss Pimm, I would know the back of your head anywhere. I dare say I have never seen a braid on a woman in public past the age of her debut," Miss Leeds said with great hauteur.

"Perhaps Miss Pimm longs to cling to her girlhood years," Miss Ashbury said. "Is that the reason you waited so long to come to town for a Season?"

"Or perhaps she wears her hair styled so simply because she does not wish to strain her *friendship* with her maid. Assuming, of course, that you have a maid, Miss Pimm. Or does your mother style your hair?"

Adeline held her ground, though she had little experience dealing with mean-spirited people. Those who pitied her on sight usually never sought to degrade her character and for them, she employed a calm, assuring demeanor. Somehow, she doubted that would work in this circumstance.

"I have a maid," Adeline said, turning to face them. "She is most excellent in fashioning various hairstyles. Since we have only seen each other at two social events, I am certain you haven't had the opportunity to witness the wide variety of her skills."

"Oh yes, now that you mention it, I do notice that your hair is woven with baby's breath, whereas at Lady Strandfellow's it was interlaced with ribbons." She grinned with a look of *oh, yes, I noticed and found you lacking!* before continuing. "I also recall hearing a whisper about you only knowing one dance."

Miss Ashbury feigned a gasp, covering her mouth with her hand. "A country dance, no less, where the elegance of…footwork…is of little concern."

The pair of them glanced down to the hem of Adeline's skirts. She knew that her half boot was concealed, but all the same, she felt as if she were standing completely nude in the retiring room. It suddenly became clear that Miss Leeds had learned a great deal from the servant who hailed from Boswickshire.

Adeline stiffened, preparing for the worst.

Miss Leeds's eyes flashed in revulsion. "Once I learned of your singular skill, I did mention your name to my lady's maid for a laugh. She mentioned your name below stairs, and sure enough, one of our sculleries knew of you. All about you, in fact, *and* your deformity."

"It is no wonder your parents kept you hidden in the country." Miss Ashbury sneered. "I imagine they took great pains to ensure you appeared to be like all the other debutantes, but you cannot hide a deformity, can you?"

This was the moment Adeline had been dreading all along. Her worst fear coming to fruition. And as she stood there, taking their jabs, feeling more freakish by the moment, she realized that this was her moment. The one she'd been waiting for. The chance to prove that she was just like every other debutante.

But she wasn't like every other debutante. She was different. And quite unexpectedly, she was grateful for that fact.

"No, I cannot," she answered, straightening her shoulders. "While some deformities are only on the outside, I have just now discovered that the ugliest are those that lie beneath flesh and bone."

She was prepared to walk out of the room with her head held high. But Miss Leeds had a little more venom in her fangs. And unfortunately, poison hit the mark.

"Which only proves how little you understand your purpose," Miss Leeds hissed. "A debutante's goal is to secure a husband. The best you could hope for is to find a man who takes pity on you."

CHAPTER FOURTEEN

Liam sat in a wing-backed chair in Vale's study with his legs crossed at the ankle and the toe of his boot rocking a wooden cradle. This was not the usual way he spent his evenings.

"No. That won't do. It is too fast." Vale crossed his arms but with one fist propped beneath his chin as he stood over the contraption. "The persimmons are rolling over and colliding with the side walls."

"Yes, well, far be it from me to point out that your child will be neither as small nor as round." Liam's observation went unheard, as many words spoken in his cousin's study often did.

Whenever Vale was in the midst of a new invention, he rarely focused on anything else. Of course, being a duke, he'd learned to put on a good show of attentiveness. But Liam had seen through all of that long ago.

This evening, Liam had merely dropped by to deliver his gift to Vale and Ivy. But with the duchess, in addition to Aunt Edith, out for the evening, somehow Liam found himself enmeshed in his cousin's latest invention.

At first, when he saw how distracted Vale was, he intended to leave the gift with a note and be gone. However, the thought of returning to his collection at Wolford House, or even on Brook Street, didn't appeal to him. Neither did the notion of joining his usual crowd at Lady Reynolds's for one of her infamously wanton parties. While he might have the appetite for indulgence, he was not recuperated enough to take part in hours of debauchery, or so he told himself. He almost believed this excuse too.

"Perhaps a sack of barley would be more appropriate," Vale murmured as if to himself, reaching into the cradle to collect the fruits. "After all, what child is as small as a persimmon?"

Liam suppressed a laugh. "You have a brilliant mind, Cousin."

Vale glanced up with a start, proving that he'd forgotten he wasn't alone. Then when Liam offered a small wave, Vale shrugged and scrubbed a hand over the back of his neck, nearly losing a persimmon in the process. "I've been somewhat distracted since the news."

Liam lifted his brows in mock surprise.

"'Tis rather obvious, I gather."

"Only to the untrained eye," Liam teased and found a persimmon launched at him. He caught it handily and with only a slight hitch in his side from the sudden movement. He thought again of his reasons for being here instead of Lady Reynolds's, but he didn't like the answers that floated into his brain. His life of indulgence didn't satisfy him anymore. He wasn't sure if it ever had. So then why was he doing it?

He shrugged off another uncomfortable question that he did not want to answer and gestured to the box on the corner of

Vale's desk. He'd laid it on top of a stack of papers and a handful of ledgers. "I came bearing a gift, if that earns your forgiveness."

When Vale's hands were empty, he picked up the box and removed the lid. His brow furrowed slightly as he glanced over at Liam.

"An ancient Roman rattle, unearthed at Caulfield's excavation site. I thought it would make for the perfect gift, under the circumstances. You can tell little Northcliff that his uncle Liam will teach him all about the people who made it when he is old enough to understand." Liam shifted in his chair, suddenly uncomfortable. By the alteration of Vale's expression, Liam realized that his little speech had revealed more than the simple amusement he'd intended. "Of course, since we are merely cousins, your offspring would be another cousin, so referring to me as 'uncle' would not be appropriate."

Vale grinned and shook the tinkling rattle. "I think *Uncle Liam* has a nice ring to it."

With that settled and behind them, Liam stood and stared pointedly down at the contraption. On the outer foot of the cradle, Vale had attached a series of gears that resembled the inner workings of a clock, accompanied by a heavy weight that swung like a pendulum. "Let's try this out with a sack of grain, shall we?"

It shouldn't have surprised him that Vale had one at the ready, but it did. Vale withdrew a plump burlap sack from one of the many cluttered shelves that lined the walls. "Hmm...approximately eight pounds, I'd gather."

"I surely hope you are not suggesting that little Northcliff resembles his mother," Liam said as he watched Ivy step into the room behind her husband.

Vale hefted the grain to his shoulder and pretended to pat it fondly. "All the better for him, I should think."

"What are you talking about?" Ivy asked, stopping short when she saw Vale. "Are you *cradling* a sack of grain?"

To his credit, Vale did not even shift his stance or demure in the slightest. "An *eight-pound* sack of grain." As if that made all the difference.

Apparently, it did. Ivy beamed instantly and moved toward her husband and their barley child, offering a kiss to the former and a pat for the latter. "Did I hear Liam call him *little Northcliff?*"

"And he has asked to be called *Uncle Liam*," Vale said with a taunting smirk in his direction. "Not only that but he brought the first gift."

Discovering the rattle, Ivy gifted Liam with one of her smiles. "Thank you, Uncle Liam. It appears the two of you have been quite busy. I wish I'd remained here instead of living through the torture of the *ton*."

Vale's demeanor changed immediately. He lowered the burlap and lifted Ivy's chin to his gaze. "What happened?"

"Careful. We don't want to drop our little Northcliff," she said, curling her hand over Vale's.

Liam looked away from the intimate family scene, feeling a weight press against his chest. While he'd been privy to many forms of sexual touches and looks of hunger and satisfaction, none had been more intimate than this. Such moments kindled a longing that Liam had been ignoring for a lifetime—to be part of a family. His own. Yet if he were ever going to make a life with someone, it would have to be honest and true. Unfortunately, he'd learned years ago that deception came in many guises. And now, like always, he was nothing more than a voyeur.

"We left early. Aunt Edith pleaded a headache, though truth be told I was ready to do the same. Either that, or I would have doused Miss Leeds with punch."

Vale's countenance darkened. "Is Miss Leeds still antagonizing you?"

"Not me," Ivy said with a glance to Liam. "Miss Pimm."

Liam stepped forward. "What happened?"

Before she could answer, his gaze already veered to the door, and he thought of the quickest path to take to Lord Tarlston's.

"Miss Pimm is no longer at the party," Ivy said, a level of understanding in her pale blue eyes. "As is Miss Leeds's nature, she made certain that Miss Pimm felt most unwelcome. After their encounter, Aunt Edith and I offered to drive Juliet, Bunny, and Adeline to their homes."

"Bunny?" Vale asked while Liam contemplated the door.

"Oh yes, Lady Boswick insists upon it, just as I have asked her to call me Ivy. Aunt Edith, however, is not as modern. At least, not yet." Ivy stepped into Liam's field of vision and lifted her brows in question. "It is a late hour, to be sure, but perhaps you could stay awhile longer and tell me about this rattle. I could certainly use the distraction."

Likely Ivy saw that Liam was the one who needed the distraction, or else he might find himself making the wrong choice—leaving directly and seeking out Adeline. It would be improper to call at such a late hour. Therefore, with a nod, he remained in their company and told them of the dig at Caulfield's country estate.

For the next hour, however, he was still lost in thought. He might have tried to tell himself that he was debating whether or not to drive to Sudgrave Terrace, but the truth was he'd already made up his mind. He was merely biding his time.

Even after Mrs. Simmons had made her a glass of warm milk before turning in, Adeline couldn't sleep. The night had not ended as she'd hoped. Yet another misadventure. So far, the only time she felt as if she'd had a true adventure was when she was with Liam.

But her journey to London wasn't really about adventure. She'd wanted to prove herself capable of handling any situation. Tonight, she'd failed. Again.

She stared at her reflection in the small round mirror above her washstand. There was nothing she could do to alter her limb, but perhaps there was something else she could do to change her outward appearance…

And cutting her hair was the answer.

Even though it became tangled and caught under her from time to time, it was still a part of her. If it were merely a burden, her decision would have been simple. But how many hours had she brushed it and found comfort in the act? Too many to count. How often did she luxuriate in the feel of the heavy tresses gliding over her bare back after her bath? How many times had she pretended to be Lady Godiva, veiling herself with only her hair? Well…only in the privacy of her bedchamber. No one ever knew.

But the truth was, when she looked in the mirror, she saw a girl. Not a lady. Certainly not the woman she knew herself to be. At two and twenty, she had a mind of her own. She had determination to do whatever it took to prove herself.

Now, more than ever, she felt a need to see something different. Therefore, it was time to lose these yearling locks of hers and look every bit the woman.

She let out a breath, picked up a glass of the brandy she'd secreted from Father's study, took a hefty swallow, and then coughed as it burned all the way down.

Sweet heavens, how do men tolerate this spirit?

Once her coughing subsided, she took another swallow and hissed out a breath, wondering if flames would erupt from her throat. But gradually, it warmed her inside. Her breathing came easier, filling her with a modicum of confidence.

She picked up the razor she'd liberated from Father's shaving kit. When her hand trembled, she forced herself not to think about it too much.

Hefting her braid, she held it up above her head, and then…sliced through her hair.

Or she would have, if she'd had the strength. On the first pass, she only freed one-third and ended up sawing through the rest. And when it was done, she looked in the mirror and cried.

When Liam arrived at Sudgrave Terrace, he went directly to the connecting door from his place to Boswick's residence. Since Adeline had left the key behind, he used it now.

His conscience warred with him. Should he be here in the dead of night?

Likely not. Though Liam reasoned that his purpose was purely altruistic—he only wanted to ensure Adeline's well-being. Besides, Boswick had mentioned on several occasions that Liam was always welcome…

Yet Liam's conscience knew that even the affable Boswick would frown upon this visit.

Therefore, he was careful to listen to the sounds of the house to ensure no one was about. All he needed was one look at Adeline, and he would feel reassured.

Aside from the faint glow of the street lamps shining through the open drapes at the end of the hall, the house was silent and dark. Though having spent much of his time in the dark, Liam was able to maneuver quite easily.

Even from this distance, he could hear the steady cadence of Boswick's snores. It was as good as an invitation.

As he moved down the hall, he noticed another light as well. And it was coming from Adeline's bedchamber.

From the other side of the door, he heard a shocked gasp. "What have I done?"

Pain rasped in her voice, hitting him hard with worry and fear. He opened the door, propriety be damned. What he saw halted his steps.

Adeline stood across the room, her head bent as she stared down at her hands. One clutched an open razor. The other held a long rope of hair. Her hair.

His eyes darted up to see waves of fawn-colored tresses kissing the tops of her shoulders. But no, not fawn-colored any longer. This color was a shade deeper, a richer brown than before. And without the heavy weight, it curled in loops at each end. Tendrils now framed the face that he knew by heart— the winged brows, the gently sloped nose, the soft divot in her plump bottom lip. The same lip that trembled now.

Reaching behind him, he closed the door with a soft click. Adeline's gaze lifted, but she didn't startle. Her liquid eyes simply held his, beseeching.

"Shh…" he crooned. Then crossing the room to her, he gathered her in his arms, taking care to set the razor on the washstand first.

"What have I done?" she asked again, pressing her wet face against his coat.

He shrugged out of the garment, dropping it to the floor without letting her out of his arms. A single instant felt too long. "It looks as if you've cut your hair, darling."

She nodded and sniffed against his waistcoat, drawing the bundle of her lost tresses between them. "I have. I did this to myself. I am so—"

"Beautiful," he said with a certainty that no one could argue against. He always thought so, even before he'd been able to see her. He pressed a kiss to the top of her head and to her temple. Lifting his hands to smooth the riotous looping tendrils away from her face, he kissed her brow, her damp lashes, the bridge of her nose, the upper crest of her cheek, all the while repeating his declaration.

Adeline released a stuttered breath and shook her head. "You are being kind, pitying me for my impulsive foolishness."

"A harsh mark against my character, to be sure." Liam continued to press tender kisses to her face, blotting away each tear with his lips. Each salted droplet caused him agony. He couldn't understand this keen desperation to rid her of these. He'd seen other women cry, though mostly crocodile tears for attention. None had ever been true. And none had ever affected him this way. Her sadness crippled him, and he would do whatever it took to banish it. "You know me better than that. I am more prone to mockery than to pity."

"Perhaps, though I have my doubts." She scoffed quietly but did not retreat from his embrace. In fact, she swayed toward him, her body molding against his. Her arms settled around his waist. The supple yielding pressure of her breasts, the rise and fall of her stomach with each breath, brought her closer to him.

His body responded in kind, obliterating any distance between them. He knew he should step back. He'd come here out of concern for her, not to seduce her. But as he nuzzled the hollow on the underside of her jaw and tasted how warm and sweet her flesh was beneath his lips, he found himself pulling her even closer instead.

Gliding a hand down her spine, he settled it into the curve of her lower back, lifting her and aligning their hips in one motion. "This is not the hot, insistent weight of *pity* pressing against your sex."

Her eyes widened. "You…desire me? Even now, with my hair shorn like a lamb in spring?"

He chuckled. Her hair was hardly shorn, but even if it were…"Long hair, short, or with only whiskers on your scalp, I would still want you."

The truth of those words filled him with a modicum of panic. He knew he wasn't only speaking of filling her body with his flesh, but something more. Something deeper. And in that moment, the certainty of him wanting her—all of her—tunneled through him.

Warned of the dangerous ground shifting beneath his feet, he set her down and released her. The moment he did, however, she wavered, teetering to the side. Automatically, he reached out for her.

He'd forgotten about her leg.

Adeline stumbled away from him on a strained gasp. She covered her mouth with her empty hand, her face pale, her eyes haunted, bleak. "And lame too? How that part of me *must* inflame your passion."

Actually, it never entered his mind. Not even from the first moment that she'd told him. "You have never once seemed in want of wholeness or support." She was complete in every way imaginable.

"W-what did you say?" Adeline's voice trembled.

Had he spoken aloud? Damn it all. Those words—like the others he'd just spoken—were too true. He should never have said them. Should never have revealed so much.

His heart pounded in his chest, fierce and raw. Seeing the distress on her features stirred a terrifying helplessness in him. He would do anything to banish her insecurities, to prove that she was everything a man could desire and more. But her tears were causing his undoing.

Behind him, the door beckoned. Yet, how he could leave her like this? Especially when he wanted to be the one who stripped away her sadness?

"I said 'Lift your nightdress and I will tell you.' " He employed the practiced tone of seduction, wanting to return to where he felt more secure. When he earned a choked laugh from her, he finally felt some relief.

She looked askance at him. "Showing you my limb is not an adventure I care to have."

The distraction was working, for both of them. His own panic subsided as he settled back into a more familiar skin. "You've never thought about it? Not even once?"

"Baring myself to you? Of course not." Her blush deepened as she focused on the hair in her grasp.

"Come now, Adeline. I know better. You purr whenever my mouth touches you. Hell, even when you watch me eat, your gaze reveals that you are imagining all the wicked things I could do to you. Every inch of you." He was stalking her now, circling her as if this were a naughty game of blindman's bluff. "Surely in these fantasies, you are not fully clothed."

Her lips parted, not on a gasp but on a series of rapid breaths that caused her breasts to rise and fall beneath the ruffled layers of white silk. Pressing her lips together, she kept her gaze averted. "Nor am I fully undressed."

Damn! He nearly tripped. Her soft admission brought him to full, instant arousal. He expected her to *deny* dreaming of him, to taunt him in return. Now the hard length of him strained against the fall of his trousers.

Stepping behind her, he made the necessary adjustment. Thankfully, she did not follow his movement but remained still while he resumed his pacing.

Once he stopped in front of her, he held her gaze as he took the bundle of hair from her grasp and set it down on the foot of the bed. "Hmm... Then what are you wearing in these wicked thoughts of yours? A pair of stockings and your chemise?"

"Surely not." Adeline laughed softly.

The lush, decadent sound shuddered through him. He grinned, liking this game. Making another pass around her, closer, he trailed his fingers along her throat, around to the nape of her neck, taking pleasure in the quickening of her breath.

"Just stockings, then? With pink ribbons tied above your knees. My, my, Miss Pimm"—he stopped behind her and whispered into her ear—"naughty, indeed."

"Perhaps I am demurely covered from my neck to the floor in my nightdress."

Standing behind her, he gently grasped her chin, drawing her face to the side to press a kiss to her cheek. His fingertips trailed down her chin, to the hollow at the base of her throat, and paused at the ribbon that tied the collar of her nightdress closed. Then brushing small, nipping kisses along her jaw and down her neck, he tugged on the ribbon. "And does it slip off one shoulder…like this?"

She gasped, lips parting. "Perhaps."

He loved that she didn't shy away. Loved that she leaned back against him. Loved that her skin responded to his touch with an eruption of fine gooseflesh.

He tucked her hair behind her ear and kissed the corner of her mouth, her jaw, that sweet pear-scented place on her throat…"And in this fantasy, does my mouth press here? And here?"

Her answer was more moan than word, making his abdomen tighten. He drew closer. His hands roamed down to her hips. Threading her fingers over his, she followed his progress as he pulled the curve of her buttocks back against him.

Pleasure spiked through him and drugged him simultaneously. He felt dizzy with it. On a groan, his mouth descended to her shoulder, his gaze straying to the rounded flesh that hinted at the perfection of her breasts. How many nights had he recalled the delicious memory of her fluffing his pillow? Of that supple unrestrained weight?

Up until this point, his behavior had been practically chaste. He'd done nothing more than kiss her. Surely, he deserved a reward.

As if reading his desires, Adeline guided his hands upward over the valley of her abdomen. In the warm recess beneath her breasts, she hesitated. But the moment his mouth opened against her neck, she lay her head back on his shoulder and slid his hands over her supple flesh.

Instantly, her nipples pebbled against his palms. Arching her back, her taut buttocks nearly unmanned him with the glorious pressure of her untutored thrust. He groaned, loving her response.

Then with a single tug of her nightdress, he took her bare flesh in his hands.

Her skin was soft as petals, their pleasing weight warm, full, and yielding in his grasp. At their crests, a treasure awaited his attention. Those pink circles were so pale and perfect that they held a silvery sheen in the lamplight, like small coins from an undiscovered land.

"I've thought of this too," she admitted on a rasp as he grazed the ruched peaks. "I try not to, but the more I try, the more it happens. All day long. Each and every night…"

"Tell me no more," he pleaded, his erection threatening to rend the fabric of his trousers. His sac tightened, thoughts of seduction filling his head. He knew hundreds of ways to touch her, to coax her further, to encourage this event onward without a moment's hesitation. He could take her, fulfill this driving need... "We should not do this. There would be consequences, Adeline."

"I know you would not marry me," she said, turning her head to press her lips against his throat. "But since I am not marrying either, then I would not be ruined for my husband. So there is nothing to stop us."

It was the word *ruined* that finally jarred him enough to lift his mouth away from her skin. He lowered his hands from her breasts, then straightened. In that instant, his body revolted in a jerk, unwilling to leave her.

Forcing himself, he staggered back, his breath labored and burning through his lungs. Carefully, he lifted her nightdress in place, making sure to tie the ribbon at her throat before he moved to stand before her.

"You are two and twenty. So young. So passionate. Not jaded by the world. You will marry someday. I know it with a certainty that I cannot explain. And I..." Unable to help himself, he reached up and brushed the newly cropped tendrils away from her cheek. "I could not in good conscience repay the family who saved my life with your ruination."

She turned to press her lips to his palm. "No one but us would know."

"A statement which only proves your naivety." Her family was from the country, he reminded himself. They were good, kind people who had taken him in, sacrificing so much for a stranger. And this was how Liam would repay them?

No. He could not, or rather, *should* not. The fact that he could imagine himself taking Adeline—laying waste to that fragile barrier between them and making her irrevocably his—caused panic to rise up once more.

So, before she could tempt him further, he turned on his heel and left the room without another word.

CHAPTER FIFTEEN

In the morning, Mother decided they should take a drive in the park. It was the perfect day for it, with few carriages about at this early hour. Of course, Adeline would have rather walked, but felt that she'd put her mother through enough with the shock of her shorter hair.

The missing weight of her usual braid kept her reaching back to check on her chignon. That was when she remembered that Hester had been able to accomplish a new stylish twist on her crown. Adeline thought it made her look taller, older, and more refined. So then, why was she still so uncertain of herself inside?

Adeline wasn't sure, but she felt it had something to with Liam and how he'd left her last night. Especially when she'd given him every opportunity to stay.

She stared out the window, toward Rotten Row in the distance. "What was it like when you first met Father?"

"We've spoken of this before, Adeline. I'm sure you recall the story. Your father simply introduced himself and told me that I would be his wife. As you know, he was correct," Mother said with a laugh.

"And you knew without a doubt that he was to be your husband?"

"The truth is that I thought your father was an accomplished flirt."

"You weren't lightheaded or stricken with a terrible weight upon your breast? You didn't feel inexplicably tethered to him from the first moment?"

Mother shook her head. "Not at first. I fell in love with him straightaway. But I did not know that he was perfect for me until you were born." She looked out the window, her gaze far off. "During that time, I first felt the dizziness and that invisible chain you mentioned. Of course, your father had felt that way all along—that certainty is in your blood—and I'd felt foolish for not understanding the power of such a bond until we'd been married for nearly three years."

"Did you ever tell Father?"

Mother nodded. "Oh, he knew. While he was confident that I loved him, he was also rather smug in telling me that it wasn't as strong as the way he loved me. I thought he was just being romantic again."

All these years, Adeline had thought that the stories she'd heard about the Pimm family line falling deeply, inexplicably in love had always happened to *both* parties. Learning that they were—quite possibly—only quixotic stories left her feeling rather empty.

Her spirits plummeted. She told herself it was foolish to feel this way. "I'd always thought you both knew from the first moment."

"Are you worried that Wolford might not feel the same?" Mother's uncanny look of *knowing* lit her eyes.

"No, of course not." Adeline shook her head, adamant. "That would presume too much on both our parts. He does not want to marry and…neither do I."

She waited for her mother to look surprised, but she merely smiled instead and waited patiently, as if anticipating what her daughter would say next.

Adeline forged ahead. "You might have guessed that I did not come to London for the purpose of finding a husband. I came here to—"

"Prove to your father and I that you are a capable young woman. Yes, I have noticed things too," Mother said. "I've bitten my tongue to keep from asking if you were too warm or too cold. I've wanted to pack your things and hie you back to Boswickshire at least a hundred times. The other day, when Juliet and Ivy were here for tea, it took all of my willpower not to cover your ears so that you would not hear what the *ton* was saying. Not to mention the countless times when I've absently reached out to tuck a lock of hair behind your ear. And most of all, I've become all too aware of each passing year."

So Mother had taken her request to heart. She truly was trying not to coddle her any longer. And while Adeline appreciated the effort and love, those impulses Mother confessed to seemed as if she still thought of Adeline as a lame little girl. "You've never asked me to assist you with managing the servants or learning any of the duties expected of me. Most young women have that instruction from the time they are young."

"I suppose seeing you blossom into a woman has made me want to hold on all the more. I didn't want to offer instruction on how to run a household because I did not want to lose you to your own."

"Then it is not because of"—Adeline held her breath—"my leg or that you think me incapable?"

Mother's eyes watered. "Not at all. I'm sorry that you ever felt that way. That is my own failing. The burden of guilt over your leg dissipated long ago. You did that for me by being so brave all your life."

A choked sob escaped Adeline. This was the whole reason she'd wanted to come to London. If she had known...then she might never have left Boswickshire. Might never have met Liam. Might never have known what if felt like to feel utterly connected to another person. Then again, perhaps she would have been better off not knowing him. Especially considering that he might never feel the same about her.

Drying her eyes, a sense of certainty filled her. She would be better off returning home regardless. It was getting too difficult to think of her life without him, and therefore she needed to do just that. Live her life without him, before it was too late for her heart.

Standing in the study at Sudgrave Terrace, Liam heard the front door open. At first, he'd assumed it was one of the footmen from next door or even Boswick coming to look in on him. He did not expect to see his uncle stride through the open archway as if he owned the property. Although since Uncle Albert had been living abroad until recently, Liam chose to shrug it off as a difference between cultures. It might take some time for Albert to remember London ways.

Uncle Albert's walking stick rapped against the floor as he came to a sudden stop. Beneath a beaver hat, his yellowed and graying brows shot up. He stroked a hand over his trimmed though unfashionable beard and mustachio, before flashing a cigar-stained grin. "So this is where you've been hiding."

An odd greeting, but again, Liam was willing to make allowances. He set down the invoice that Rendell had left on the top of the crate and extended his hand. "Uncle Albert. I'm glad to see you. I trust both you and my fair cousin had a safe journey?"

"Couldn't have done it without Gemma. She speaks the native tongue wherever we travel. I daresay, even better than her poor sainted mother had." Albert removed his hat and grabbed his walking stick by the neck and—instead of shaking Liam's hand—began to stroll about the room, absently looking over the collection.

Liam lowered his hand and studied his uncle. "She was always a bright girl. I imagine she is eager to finish her studies."

Albert peered inside one of the crates. "She finished those ages ago. No. In fact, she expressed a desire to have a Season."

"Surely little Gemma is not old enough for a Season." His cousin had had a head full of bouncing black ringlets while scampering about in a pinafore the last time Liam had seen her.

"My thoughts mirror yours," Albert said convivially, while he continued his perusal around the room. "The truth is, she is one and twenty now."

Only a year younger than Adeline?

The thought gave him pause. Was it normal for him to compare every woman, even if only their ages, to Adeline?

Albert laughed. "It came as a surprise to me as well. It seemed as if one day she was a grinning girl, excited about riding to the dig site on the back of a camel, and then overnight she turned into a woman who thinks camels are smelly, disgusting creatures. Then again, she might be correct about that."

Liam chuckled. "So you intend to stay?"

"We have come home to roost, as it were."

Liam felt relieved. Not only for Gemma's sake but for Albert's as well. His uncle was far too naïve sometimes and prone to being deceived by unscrupulous men. Liam thought back to the day he'd made this discovery. It was only a year ago when Albert had returned to town for a few days. During the visit, he'd spotted one of Albert's new acquisitions—the head of Aphrodite.

Albert had boasted that it was one of the Elgin marbles that were thought to have been destroyed during their voyage to England years ago. Apparently, he'd paid a pretty penny to secure it for a colleague, who had backed out, leaving Albert without payment and in the weeds for his next excursion. Knowing that his uncle was too proud to admit that he was short on cash, Liam had offered to buy the head. At the time, he'd only thought of the amusement he'd have by examining it. Because no one had known that he already possessed the original. And now, only Vale and Adeline knew that he had both in his collection.

"But enough about me," Albert said. "Edith tells me that you intend to give a lecture at the Royal Society about forgery."

Liam concealed his confusion. Edith mentioned his lecture? But she had been the one most concerned about embarrassing Albert, should his purchase of the forgery be revealed. He was beginning to wonder if he truly knew any of his family.

Stranger still was the sudden change of topic, to be sure. And how odd that his uncle's thoughts had practically mirrored his own. Though perhaps, Liam reasoned, Albert had suspected the head of Aphrodite was a fake—but no. It didn't seem possible. His uncle had been too proud of the acquisition. At the time, he'd never given away an inkling of doubt.

Even so, Liam couldn't shake himself free of the notion that something seemed out of place in this visit.

"As a favor to Vale," he answered, choosing to believe that Aunt Edith had accidentally revealed his secret but without stating that Albert's Aphrodite would be the star of the exhibit. "As you might have heard, he is a new *fellow*."

"Hmm..." Albert smirked. "One would think Vale would present an invention of some sort instead. It sounds to me as if he thinks to do *you* a favor. After all, you are hardly the scholar that he is."

The statement had been made often enough over the years that Liam dismissed it with a mere shrug. His collection was seen as nothing more than a rich man's plaything. He rarely revealed his true passion to anyone.

Yet just now, Albert's laugh pinched at Liam's ego like a falcon perched on his shoulder, one that could not be dislodged with a mere shrug.

Feeling the tendons and sinew of his shoulders tighten, Liam adopted his characteristic persona, reverting to mockery, and self-mockery at that. "Vale has become sentimental since his marriage, so I do not doubt you are correct. Though

I would not dream of letting him down, even if only to give the *fellows* an hour of amusement at my expense."

Strangely, Albert frowned. His hand now clutched the head of his walking stick until his knuckles turned white. "Perhaps you should postpone it. After all, you were recently injured, and still hiding yourself away."

That was Albert's second mention of hiding. But Liam wasn't. In fact, he'd stayed here last night as if rooted to this place. Though perhaps it was not the property, but a certain young woman's hold over him.

Yet after last night, he knew he had to sever ties. He'd made the decision earlier this morning that it was time to return to his old life. It was safer there. He didn't need the cumbersome weight of his attraction to Adeline, nor his fondness for her parents, clinging to him. He wanted to shrug it off, go back to the way things had always been, and settle into a more comfortable skin. In fact, he'd already sent word to the infamous Lady Reynolds to expect him for dinner.

Thinking about the alternative—allowing Adeline to burrow beneath his skin, inside his heart—brought back a painful memory. He'd been foolish once, and the lesson had left a permanent scar on his jaded heart. He would rather remember Adeline as she was in his mind, instead of being proven wrong in the future, which seemed inevitable.

"I am well recovered, thanks to the kindness of my neighbors who took me in."

"Yes. Edith has told me all about Lord and Lady Boswick," he said absently. "Were you able to discover who attacked you?"

Liam shook his head. "I still cannot recall their faces. Likely one was a jealous husband. As for the other, I could not say."

"A jealous husband? Why would you assume that?"

Liam pressed a finger to his temple. "That night is still a bit foggy in here."

"Surely, you remember something. A voice? A face?"

Liam had been having dreams of that night, fragments of shadowed images and a voice asking strange questions. *Where is The…? If you let her go, we could end this.*

The instant he'd awoken, Liam repeated that first question, trying to hold on to the dreams. "Where is The—*what?*" Yet the words had been too garbled to comprehend. He was hoping for a name he recognized. Running through faces of the women he knew, he could recall none with a name that began with the sound of *The*. He knew a *Theodosia*, but she was Edith's aunt, and somehow he doubted those men were seeking an octogenarian with poor eyesight and at least forty cats.

The seemed important, his only link. Unfortunately, he could not wholly dismiss it as being dream fiction, nor could he add credence to it.

These thoughts caused his headache to return, like the ones that only Adeline had alleviated. Likely seeing her would make this one disappear as well, but it was best to withdraw from her for as long as possible. He didn't know how he would be able to see her at the ball Aunt Edith was hosting for Albert and Gemma at week's end.

Until that time, he needed to garner his strength by avoiding her. Even if it was only a wall that separated them now.

"Nothing, Uncle." Liam shrugged.

Albert's watchful gaze honed in on him for another moment before he drew in a breath and appeared more relaxed. Then he abruptly changed the subject. "Edith mentioned—*special guests*, I believe were her words—coming to the ball. She intimated that you hold a certain young woman in high esteem."

Now, Liam's attention fixed on his uncle, a sudden and keen sense of warning prickling over his skin, lifting every hair. It was one thing if Aunt Edith had slipped and mentioned his lecture on forgeries, but would she also start rumors that linked him to Adeline Pimm? No. Surely not.

After all, she'd been trying to ensure that an association with him had not sullied Adeline's reputation. She would not so casually propagate such a notion.

His uncle, on the other hand, had been away from town for too long and perhaps had read more into what might have been a passing mention. Therefore, to ensure that there was no misunderstanding, he laughed and shook his head. "There is no young woman I hold in high esteem. Perhaps my aunt merely wishes there were."

Albert flashed another stained grin and donned his hat with a jaunty pat against the top. "I must be off, Nephew. It is good to see that you are doing so well."

Then he rapped the head of his walking stick against the crate before taking his leave.

And when the door closed, Liam stared after the man who had seemed more of a stranger than kin. Though perhaps that was the effect brought by years of separation. Whatever it was, it left him unsettled.

CHAPTER SIXTEEN

The Season Standard—the Daily Chronicle of Consequence

Our Earl of W— has been seen a great deal around town. Conflicting reports, however, mark his attendance at various scandalous gatherings, as well as those far more respectable. While many still have great hopes for W—, one must wonder if our Original contender has been tamed at last, or has he returned to his wolfish ways?

As she read over the *Standard*, Adeline was not the least bit jealous. Whatever entertainments Liam sought were none of her concern. He'd made that clear enough in the past few days by his absence.

Not that it mattered. It wasn't as if he was hers…

She folded the page sharply and swatted the table with it as she stood. Was he afraid that she would begin fawning over him or clinging to his side? He probably assumed that her desire *not* to marry was nothing but pretense. Or worse, that after what happened the other night, she *expected* to marry him. The notion was nearly as infuriating as when they'd first met, and he'd thought she was plotting to trap him. *Of all the ridiculous...*

Adeline grew still.

While Liam hadn't confessed it to her, she'd guessed that such a circumstance had happened before. Perhaps even more than once. Surely, he was always on his guard against women seeking to marry a handsome gentleman with a fortune and title. And those weren't even his best qualities. He was brilliant and kind as well. Even his wickedness was appealing.

She could easily understand his desirability. After all, if she weren't so determined *not* to marry, even she would find herself wanting to marry him too, and to love him openly, unreservedly, instead of concealing her feelings as she had been since—

Adeline gasped for breath as the thoughts tumbled out of her before she even had the chance to think them through. *Love him?* Had she actually been foolish enough to fall in love with him? *True* love and not one born of a peculiar Pimm myth?

The walls of her heart squeezed sharply beneath her breast in answer. It had been doing this ever since they'd parted, as if throwing a tantrum. Stupid heart.

"There is no point in feeling this way," she told that petulant organ. She pressed a fist to her breast and glanced down at the paper that listed Liam's recent exploits. "He doesn't feel the same about you. So you're better off forgetting about him."

A fresh twinge twisted her heart, this one seemingly mournful. The pain of it traveled to the corners of her eyes where the sting of tears began. Liam did not—and would *never*—love her.

Hadn't he told her as much, countless times by revealing his ultimate goals? He was a hedonist, not a romantic. Even so, admitting it to herself felt like the death of a new unrealized dream and filled her with a fragile, futile yearning.

Adeline swallowed down her unspent tears and brushed the wetness from her lower lashes with an impatient swipe. It was good that she was going home so soon. By week's end, she would be on her way to Boswickshire. Perhaps with a greater distance between them, she would no longer feel this way.

Liam was restless. For days he'd done nothing more than live his life as he always had, filling it to the brim with revelry, lascivious parties, irresponsible gambling, and whatever else he damn well felt like doing.

In fact, last night he went to Lady Reynolds's dinner party, where an attractive young woman had lain in the center of the table. Her body had been nude, aside from vines winding up her lithe legs and arms and from the strategic placement of various fruits and delicacies. Amongst those, slices of grapes and strawberries covered her breasts. Dollops of cream and caviar adorned her abdomen. And for amusement's sake, slices of peaches formed a triangle over her mons.

This sensual cannibalism was a common occurrence at Lady Reynolds's. Usually, they made a game of it, clasping hands behind their backs and removing slices with their teeth. During these dinners, by the time their serving platter was bare, the orgy would have begun. They would have made a game of that too, using only their mouths. And Liam excelled in giving pleasure with his mouth, in addition to his hands, a well-placed thigh, and a usually generous appendage.

In these past few days, however, his appendage hadn't been displaying any sort of generosity. Behind the fall of his trousers, his flesh remained unmoved. Each time he'd made an attempt, his headache returned, splitting though his skull, turning his vision hazy, his mind dizzy, forcing him to abandon his entertainments for home.

The pain had become so terrible that he'd engaged his physician. After much prodding and poking, Fortier had prescribed a powder for his headaches. But even that did not work for long.

Liam was having trouble eating, concentrating on anything. He'd become a prisoner in his own bleeding skull, and it had all begun the moment he'd decided to avoid Sudgrave Terrace until the end of the Season, when the Pimms would be gone.

It was nothing more than a coincidence, he was sure. While his bruises had disappeared, obviously his brain had more healing to do. Though the thought had crossed his mind that it was his current location. That perhaps the servants were using a different liniment for the wood. Therefore, he moved from Wolford House to Brook Street, hoping to remove himself from the cause.

Unfortunately, that hadn't worked. His skull ached. And when his butler informed him that Thayne had arrived just now, Liam was tempted to send him away. Yet hoping a distraction could help, he allowed the intrusion.

A minute later, Thayne strode into the map room where Liam was studying the honey crock he intended to give Boswick as a parting gift.

"I had the devil of a time tracking you down. I don't even know if your servants know where you are staying."

"I must have forgotten to beg my housekeeper for permission to leave the house," Liam mocked, pinching the bridge of his nose as he took a moment to rest his eyes. Then, oddly enough, he caught a trace of familiar scent, and his headache dissipated somewhat. Curious, his eyes snapped open. "What do you have there?"

Thayne held a handkerchief, the corner displaying a W in green thread. "I went by Sudgrave Terrace to find you. Wound up running into Boswick instead. He welcomed me to breakfast, but when I explained I couldn't stay, he sent me on my way with one of his cook's muffins drizzled in Boswickshire honey. Then before I left, Miss Pimm obliged me to return this. Forgive me, it seems as though I've left a drop of honey behind."

Liam snatched the handkerchief out of Thayne's grasp. "You tasted the honey."

It was meant to be a question, but a sudden rise of anger made the words clipped. Harsh.

Thayne didn't seem to notice. "Everything Boswick claimed is true. I tell you it is the finest honey I have ever eaten. He offered to send me a jar when he returns, and I couldn't find a single reason to refuse him."

Liam could think of a reason. How about the fact that Thayne had no right to taste that honey! But that was absurd, the ranting of an insane man, a jealous man. And Liam had no reason to be jealous—or want to murder Thayne—over a taste of honey.

For that matter, Liam wasn't even sure this was his handkerchief, as his weren't monogrammed. But then he remembered that one morning and their race in the rain, and leaving one with Adeline.

She must have embroidered it. Brushing his thumb over the W, he imagined her carefully sewing each stitch, holding the linen in her soft hands...*plotting* for this very moment, *knowing* that Liam would be forced to think of her when he saw this handkerchief.

He curled his fingers around it, his hand forming a fist. Either he was going mad, or this was a ploy of hers, wanting him to think of her.

He was half tempted to ask Aunt Edith to remove her family's name from the guest list. Did it even matter that her family saved his life when he didn't even recognize himself any longer? When he felt as if he didn't belong in his own world, no longer enjoying his usual pursuits?

"Are you unwell, Wolford?" Thayne asked. "You seem...troubled."

"Bleeding headache," Liam snapped, then relaxed his glower. It wasn't Thayne's fault that he'd become a lunatic, after all.

"Then perhaps my news will aid in your recovery," Thayne continued. "All is not lost despite your recent...misdeeds. You are still a favorite. Your name tops the list of the column in the *Standard*, instead of buried like a whisper at the bottom. Once you make an appearance at your aunt's party, I may still win the wager."

Liam glared at his friend, incredulous. "Do you honestly believe I care about winning your wager or even who is named the *Original?*"

"No. I never once thought you cared. Do you think it has escaped my notice that you don't seem to care about anyone? Or even bothered to notice the hell I've been in these past months?" Thayne glared back, his jaw twitched as he gritted his teeth.

"Of course I noticed," Liam fired back. Then deciding that the root of all his madness might very well be Thayne's fault, he purposely goaded him into an argument. "Especially the way that Juliet has you so twisted inside out that you would turn your back on a friend, aiming to plot against him by naming him in a wager."

If it weren't for the damnable wager, then Thayne might never have pushed so hard to see Liam become respectable. Then the *ton* would never have considered him a candidate for the *Original.* And Liam would never have given a moment's thought to how his reputation might look to a certain debutante.

"Friend?" Thayne sneered. "All you care about is your collection. Tell me, *why* do you buy all of these artifacts?"

"Perhaps I simply abhor an empty house." Liam also used the collection to connect with his father's memory, but he'd be damned if he would share that personal detail with Thayne.

"And yet you keep purchasing more houses to fill." Thayne laughed but with more censure than amusement. "Have you ever thought, perhaps, that you might rather fill your houses with a family instead?"

Reflexively, Liam's fist tightened on the handkerchief. He looked down at it, a ready denial on his lips.

Then Thayne spoke again. "I already told you part of the reason why I named you for this wager. But the truth is, I only did it because I wanted you to show yourself. The real you that no one has seen for years."

Liam jerked up his chin. "What do you mean? This *is* who I am!"

"Not always." Thayne held his gaze. "Of course, you've always had a bit of the devil's mischief, but you were also noble and kind. And when you made a vow, you held fast to it. No matter what. That's what worries me—your vow not to marry until you are sixty. It isn't a favorable decision. You should think about your life and what you truly want."

Liam's back teeth locked. "I live exactly the way I choose."

"Behind a barrier that you've erected with your collection?" Thayne gestured to the pair of Oriental vases flanking the doorway.

Liam scoffed. While he may have been adding to his collection a great deal of late, that didn't mean he was building a *barrier*. Barriers were built by men who were afraid of being set upon or attacked.

"I was there when this obsession of yours began. Do you remember?" Thayne's dark brows rose. "We were seventeen and touring the Continent in order to put distance between you and that conniving debutante who'd tried to trap you into marriage."

Liam stared at Thayne, his memory flooding back to that trip and the Turkish dagger that he'd purchased. And up until recently, that dagger had hung in a glass case above his mantel.

"And you know something else? I think part of you wanted to marry her."

"No. You are quite mistaken," Liam said quickly. Perhaps there had been a time when the idea had appealed to him, but that ended when he discovered the truth. She had only pretended to be his friend, to like him, to love him. Her parents had done the same, often calling on him, bestowing pretty invitations to dinner, to the park, and even to stay with them during the holidays. At the time, Liam had been too naïve, too lonely, and too eager to be part of a family to know what their true designs were.

"Of course, I am," Thayne mocked. He walked toward the door, his own glower firmly in place. "Instead of a family, however, you started putting together a vast collection. Bravo! Now, you never need to get close to any new persons in your life—a young woman and her amiable parents come to mind—because you have all of this. Your *true* family. Hundreds, if not thousands of artifacts and statues…My, my, what a legacy you will leave."

Thayne knew nothing. The objects in this room weren't his family. If Liam wanted to have a real family then he would damn well have one, and no one would be able to stop him.

"You're absolutely wrong! Do you know that, Thayne?" Liam shouted as his friend exited the room.

Thayne had the audacity to laugh. "Then prove it!"

CHAPTER SEVENTEEN

It was the night of the Vale ball.

Standing in the receiving line, Adeline steeled herself for her first encounter with Liam in a week. So far, after greeting Ivy and Vale, she was doing admirably well. All she had to do was remember how to breathe.

While she stood in front of the dowager duchess, her parents were ahead of her, already exchanging a greeting with Liam and the guests of honor.

Adeline tried not to listen to Liam's voice or let her gaze stray even a single inch from her hostess's smiling face. Instead, she focused on her curtsy, keeping her corrective half boot flat on the marble floor.

"My dear Miss Pimm, you look positively radiant this evening in that pale coral gown. And your hair done up in a twist is quite flattering."

Adeline was just about to thank her when the dowager duchess tapped her nephew on the arm and asked, "Wouldn't you agree, Liam?"

But Adeline had come prepared for her encounter. She brought a fan of her own, and summarily dropped it on the marble floor. Then she *accidentally* kicked it, hard enough so that it slid between two potted topiaries behind him.

"Oh, do forgive me," she called out the moment Liam turned around to fetch it. Then she made direct eye contact with the next in line, assuming that Liam's uncle would introduce himself. Thankfully, she was right.

"I've heard a great deal about you, Miss Pimm, and the kindness you've shown my nephew," Albert Desmond said after their introduction.

"My parents and I believe we offered nothing more than anyone else would have done."

"Oh, how I wish that were true." His lips curled up at each end like his mustachio, but the smile did not reach his eyes. "It is a shame that my daughter was not well enough to attend the ball. I'm certain she would have enjoyed meeting you. Though perhaps some other time in the near future?"

"I'm afraid, sir, that we will be leaving London day after next." As she spoke, her gaze drifted to Liam.

Holding her fan and walking toward them, his steps suddenly halted and his brow furrowed, but he made no comment.

Adeline returned her attention to Mr. Desmond. "Please know that you and your daughter are more than welcome to our home in Boswickshire whenever your travels take you north of here."

And because the line of guests behind them were crowding closer, she did not wait for her fan. Instead, she took her father's arm and descended into the ballroom. This time, she did not take special care to ensure that her corrective half boot was concealed by the hem of her gown. By now, all of London—with the help of Miss Leeds and Miss Ashbury—knew about her limb. But Adeline walked with her head high and refused to let it bother her a moment longer.

This would be her last London adventure, and Adeline was determined to enjoy herself. So, as the evening progressed, she didn't look for Liam in the crowd at all. Well, hardly ever. Perhaps once—every five minutes or so, but no more than that.

Yet as she walked beside Mother after fetching a glass of punch, she saw Liam standing with her father near the open terrace doors. Trepidation slowed her steps.

It was almost time for the gong to ring for supper. Was Liam asking for permission to escort her to the dining room? She sincerely hoped not.

Her night was going along perfectly without him. Neither Miss Leeds nor Miss Ashbury had been invited. She'd already danced two country dances—one with Lord Ellery and one with her host, the Duke of Vale. And though she would never admit it, her foot was cramping. Which made it all the better that she'd taken Juliet's advice and filled her card for all the other dances.

When she finally reached the terrace doors, whatever conversation Liam had been having with Father abruptly stopped.

Liam greeted Mother and then bowed to Adeline, his hand extended. "Miss Pimm, would you do me the honor of this next dance?"

The musicians in the gallery above were already playing the first strains of the dinner waltz. Couples paired off on the ballroom floor, each of them twirling gracefully.

And Adeline went cold, feeling as if Liam were mocking her. He knew she did not know how. She'd confessed as much to him. "Thank you. No." Then she gave her father a pained look, feeling betrayed by him as well.

Turning away, she decided to adjourn to the retiring room. Liam stopped her, however, putting a hand beneath her elbow. She tried to shrug him off, but he was more insistent than she expected. Out of the corner of her eye, she saw her parents engaged in a quiet conversation, Mother frowning, Father shaking his head. Any moment now, all eyes would be upon their group. Therefore, to avoid a scene, she allowed Liam to escort her through the doors.

The air was brisk, and there were no stars or moon to guide them. The only light came from the ballroom, spilling over the wet terrace stones.

The instant he released his hold on her, she crossed her arms, warding off the chill she felt inside and out. "What could you possibly have to say to me that you could not have said at any time during this past week?"

"I did not ask you for a conversation. I asked you for a waltz," he said, his teeth clenched so hard that a muscle twitched over his lean jaw. He did not look pleased or even apologetic. Instead, those green eyes flashed in anger. "And the only reason I brought you out to the terrace is because I intend to hold you scandalously close, with your feet upon mine. Though with your parents nearby, your reputation is secure."

She refused to budge. "I decline your invitation."

He taunted her with a smirk and lowered his voice. "Come now, you know we've been this close before. Surely you haven't forgotten."

"Have *I* forgot—" Her hands curled in to fists and she untangled her arms, but only so that she could pummel him if the opportunity arose. "According to the *Standard*, it is you who has forgotten."

"There is no understanding between us, Adeline."

"Nor will there be in the foreseeable future. You are free to do whatever you choose."

"Correct. And this moment, I choose to waltz with you. Now cease this nonsense and step into my arms where you belong. For the dance," he amended with a glower.

Then he pulled her close beside him—hip to hip, leaving no space between them—without giving her the chance to refuse him again. Settling his hand against her back, he waited for her to do the same to him.

She did. But she hated that it felt so good to be in his arms, even now.

"We are both quite cross. I do not know why I am indulging you."

"Because you cannot refuse an adventure."

"True. That is all this is, after all," she said, embarrassed when her voice broke, and she felt a telltale stinging at the corners of her eyes. "Nothing more."

"Blink those tears away before you force me to kiss you," he commanded softly. His green gaze hard.

Knowing that she was only torturing herself, she blinked several times, just wanting to end this once and for all. Like the dancers inside, she lifted her arm, posing it with her hand extended in an arc above her head. Then he took that hand, and in that same moment, began their promenade.

Holding her gaze, he made a slow circle, each step making her aware of the warmth of his body and his hold on her. Once completed, he pulled her closer, shifting so they faced each other, stomach to stomach.

"Put your feet on mine," he ordered, his voice dropping. He settled both of his hands at the small of her back, making it impossible to resist. "And now fold your arms behind you."

The action caused her breasts to jut forward, pressing against his chest. "Are you certain this is—"

He didn't give her time to finish her question or even time to prepare herself for what came next. Instead, he swept her into a turn. One after another.

Adeline gasped, amazed that this was happening. She felt every bit of his strength, the thick muscles of his thighs, the shift of his abdomen, the security of his hands. He would not let her falter. She should have known better all along.

This was not a dance of humiliation or even of pity. He truly was giving her a last London adventure.

It was over all too soon. There was only time enough for a dozen turns, perhaps fewer. When the music ended, he set her on her feet and stepped apart from her. And she desperately wanted to do it all over again.

"I love you for the dance," she said on an exhale. She didn't know why she was breathing so heavily. After all, she hadn't done any of the work.

It took a moment before her own words filtered into her brain. But in that time she felt her lungs seize, her eyelids widen, and her mouth open.

And other than the rapid rise and fall of his chest, Liam went completely, utterly still.

"Oh! I meant to say 'thank you for the dance.' *Thank you*," she repeated stupidly. She wished he would say something to stop this torrent of embarrassment. "Because no one says 'I love you for the dance,' even if you're very fond of dancing. That doesn't even make sense. For if it did, then everyone would be—"

"Adeline, the dinner gong has rung," Mother called from the doors. Fortunately, she was standing far enough away that she couldn't have heard Adeline make a complete fool of herself.

With one last look at Liam, she whispered a final *thank you* and hurried off to join her parents, deciding to keep her mouth shut for the rest of the night.

Liam forced himself to remain still, rooting his feet firmly on the terrace stones. Yet every muscle in his body wanted to go after her. To haul her into his arms. To kiss her until there was only enough breath left in his body to tell her that he loved her for the dance too.

His head was spinning once more. This time it was not from a blow to the head but to the heart. How had he let this happen? How had he let her crawl under his skin and live in his veins? Hell, every breath he took was filled with her scent. Every sound filled with her wit. Every sight filled with her smile and her eyes. Especially when she looked at him as if he were put on this earth solely for her.

Thayne was wrong. He thought Liam erected a barrier to keep everyone at a distance. But if that were true, then his efforts had failed. Adeline Pimm had broken through.

She was not like any other debutante. Scheming and manipulation were foreign to her, not mother's milk. In fact, she was one of the few people he trusted. And when she said she loved him—even though she blundered it a bit—he believed her.

This was all new. He'd never felt this sort of certainty before, not even when he was seventeen. Back then his regard had been easily swayed. He'd been too eager for affection. Now he was different—reluctant and even jaded.

All the more reason for him to see where this would lead.

And if Adeline thought she was going to leave London day after next, she was sorely mistaken.

CHAPTER EIGHTEEN

Unfortunately, Adeline couldn't keep her mouth shut for the rest of the night.

She had, however, managed to survive the rest of Vale's ball without making an even bigger fool of herself. Yet by the time they returned to the townhouse, she hated herself for being a coward with Liam earlier.

Why hadn't she simply thanked him *and* told him that she loved him? She deserved to close the lid on London before she left it all behind. She did not need any open ends or regrets. Hadn't she faced all of her other fears?

So it was time to face this one. Sort of.

Instead of telling him, she decided to leave him a note. That way, she wouldn't have to look at his face and see that he—*she swallowed*—did not feel the same for her.

Having made up her mind, she went to the adjoining doors. Prepared to slip the note beneath them, she pulled on the painting. That was when she discovered something unexpected, something that piqued the interest of her adventure-seeking nature—the door on her side was unlocked.

Out of curiosity, she opened it and then pushed on the next door to see if it was unlocked as well. It was. Not only that, but she saw the flicker of light coming from down the hall.

Her heart raced at a fine clip beneath her breast. Was Liam here?

The parchment crinkled as she gripped the note in her hand. What if she did tell him face-to-face instead? While she knew the risk already, there could also be an advantage. She would never have to wonder about his response. Or spend years imagining—*wishing*—that he was thinking about her. Though, honestly, it was far more likely that he would completely forget about her existence.

"Happy thought, indeed," she murmured and quickly started to contemplate slipping her letter beneath his door instead. Or perhaps she'd drop it in the urn standing a foot away and leave the rest up to chance. Then again, servants might find it. And since this was a rather personal letter, she should just hand it to him and walk away. Or she could just leave it here on this demilune table. *Perfect.*

Without overthinking her decision—at least any more than she already had—she placed it on the table and turned back to the door.

"Adeline?" Liam's voice stopped her. "What are you doing here?"

She closed her eyes, feeling her heart thud with every one of his approaching footfalls as she faced him and offered a shrug. "I didn't want to leave without telling you good-bye."

It was a terrible excuse and made little sense.

Even with the lamplight behind him, she could see his smirk. "Are you leaving this very instant, instead of at daybreak the day after next, as you said earlier?"

She should simply hand him the note and walk away. But suddenly all of her bravery abandoned her. "I didn't think I would see you before then."

Dressed only in his shirtsleeves and his black trousers from the ball, he continued toward her with long, purposeful strides, avoiding the crates in the middle of the hallway. The closer he came, the more difficult it was to breathe. Her heart knew that this might be the last time she ever saw him, and now it was pounding so hard that it was surely deflating her lungs in the process. Her skin tingled too, aware of the diminishing space between them. And her eyes greedily swept over him.

He stopped directly in front of her, his dark, angular features more intense in the low light, his green gaze locked onto hers. "Adeline."

Just her name, nothing more, and it robbed her of her last breath. His chest expanded as if he was holding it captive. How dare he take her heart, her air, and leave her with nothing but this emptiness. She pressed a hand against her middle.

"How could you have known that I would be here?" he asked, his voice low as his gaze dipped to her mouth. In response, her lips pulsed, feeling warm and plump.

"I did not." She shifted on her feet and pointed her thumb back over her shoulder. "I merely noticed the door was open and the key"—as she spoke, he moved closer, forcing her to lift her face—"is missing."

And, without warning, he kissed her.

He hauled her to him, lifting her to her toes. His mouth slanted over hers, his hands delving through her hair, sending pins scattering. Sweet heaven, she was lost. Every excuse to leave disintegrated in the heat of this kiss.

She loved him—that was the only reason she was here. Not to say good-bye but to tell him properly, as she should have done before.

She said the words to him one thousand times in that instant, with every touch, every murmur of longing in her throat, every breath she took from him, and every breath she gave him back in return. She reveled in the taste of him, in the magic of his tongue gliding over hers. *Yes! I love you. I have always loved you. I will die loving you. And then I will love you for eternity…*

He growled, fierce and hungry as if he'd fed on those unspoken words and wanted more. She would give him more. And did as she wrapped her arms around his neck and pressed her body into his.

Taking her by the waist, he lifted her against him, never breaking their kiss. Not even as he strode back down the hall to the room with the glow of lamplight. He closed the door by pressing her against it, using his hips to anchor her. Instinctively, she tilted forward, rolling against him. With an urgency that matched hers, he devoured her mouth, her throat, her shoulders, tugging the satin sleeves down her arms. When he exposed the beribboned edge of her chemise, he paused and licked his lips as if she were a confection he was slowly unwrapping.

Catching her breath, Adeline looked down, seeing that the gauzy fabric merely acted as a veil over her breasts, leaving him an unhindered view of her pale nipples rising above her corset.

"Now is not the time to be bashful." Hot breath left his mouth, causing her flesh to tighten and ache.

"I'm not." She shook her head. "I want you to see me. And I want to see you."

He lowered her feet to the floor, his gaze a hot green elixir. She thought he might put a halt to everything they were doing. Instead, he stripped out of his shirtsleeves, giving her a display of his lean torso, matted with black hair over the sculpted lines of his chest and tapering down his stomach.

He was magnificent. Grinning, he took her hands and placed them on his bare chest. "Is this what you want?"

Her answer came out as an indecipherable mewl as she spread her hands over him, gliding up to his shoulders, marveling at how hard he was. Solid. Strong.

"And this is what I want." His mouth closed over her breast, chemise and all. She didn't even have time to gasp before she felt the swipe of his tongue, dampening the fabric, laving the taut peak. The heat of his mouth spread through her body, making her damp elsewhere.

She shifted, pressing her thighs together against the insistent pulse nestled in her sex. Instinctively, she wanted him there. Before she could tell him, he untied the ribbon of her chemise, tugged it down, and bared her flesh.

Cupping her breasts, he weighed them, kneaded them, increasing the ache. Then he clasped her wrists, lifted her arms, and pinned them against the door. He looked his fill. Dipping his head, he blew on her damp flesh, her nipples tightening even more, aching. Then, at last, he closed his mouth over her.

Oh...Her head fell back against the door as he suckled her, drawing her deeper. She thought she knew what it was like to be a morsel of food in his mouth before, but she was wrong. *This* is what it felt like. With the rasp of his tongue pleasuring her, grazing the crest in rhythm with the throb of her sex, she felt thoroughly devoured.

He elicited the same delicious torture from her other breast as well. Then her gown fell to her waist and with his help slithered down to the floor.

She was glad it was gone. It was far too hot in here. And she couldn't breathe either. But he remedied that soon enough by pulling her corset free. His hands splayed over her waist, thumbs toward her navel. Those sinful green eyes looked up at her as he sank to his knees, pressing kisses through the chemise over her stomach and down in a straight line.

She watched, fascinated by the way he closed his eyes with each kiss. The way he paused to inhale deeply. Her fingers brushed away the hair from his brow, wanting to see every expression. But when he gripped her hips as his mouth trailed lower still, to the hem of her chemise, she felt a rise of nerves. Leaning in, he nuzzled her there.

"Is now the time to be bashful?"

"Not yet. This is only the beginning. Just wait and I will tell you when." When he shook his head, his nose skimmed back and forth at the cradle of her thighs, burrowing closer with only the thinnest garment as barrier. "Mmm...Adeline, give me your hand."

When she did, he placed it against her sex, then settled his own hand over hers, cupping her. "What do you feel?"

Dampness met her fingers, completely saturating the thin chemise in between. Then she remembered their race on Rotten Row, and a flood of heat rushed to her cheeks. No wonder he had laughed so wickedly.

She realized she was holding her breath. It came out on a stilted exhale. "I am wet through."

"Very much, indeed," he growled with apparent approval. Then his kisses moved lower, his hands trailing down her legs. Past the ribbon ties of her stockings. Following the embroidered pink rosettes to the lump in her shin, that small protrusion of a broken bone fused without mending. He paid little heed to it and continued his course all the way to her half boots, untying and then removing one after the other.

She watched him with more caution now, not knowing what to expect or whether she needed to guard her heart. Standing before him, flatfooted and tiptoe, he pressed more kisses to her feet, her ankles, shins. When he reached the knee of her shortened limb, he slipped his hand in the sensitive hollow behind it. Then he lifted her leg and draped it over his shoulder. Those eyes met hers once more, a grin on those lips. "More?"

It was more command than question, but she nodded her head all the same. He pressed a kiss to the inside of her thigh. This conversation reminded her of their first, and by the gleam in his gaze, she believed he was thinking about that too.

"Again," she said, and he obliged, trailing kisses back up to the edge of her chemise.

This time when he took her hips in hand, he lifted the garment away, revealing a thatch of brown curls. The sound of an indrawn breath gave away her shyness.

"Not yet, darling." He nuzzled her again, murmuring something naughty about Boswickshire honey. Then he set his mouth over her sex.

She gasped again. But was it shock or pleasure? She had her answer soon enough when he began to lave her most sensitive flesh, suckling and flicking as he had done to her breasts.

She couldn't stop watching him. Indistinguishable sounds tore from her throat. The sheer bliss in his expression and in the guttural groans against her sex robbed her of words. But in her mind she was thinking, *Please. Yes. Again.*

Her senses overwhelmed her with pleasure, even as her leg trembled. Her hips rocked forward, but he held her still, devouring her. Then shifting, he draped her other leg over his shoulder too, his mouth pressing harder against her, filling her with urgency. Suddenly, an ache so sharp, so divine tore through her, and her entire body spasmed on a low, keening cry. It went on and on, shuddering through her and leaving her without any control, only a rush of pure euphoria.

She felt weightless, floating. In fact, she was only partially aware of Liam moving again and gathering her in his arms. But she knew the exact moment that he laid her down and lifted her chemise over her head. Her eyes drifted open to see a circular canopy above her, and beneath her a long chaise upholstered in blue silk. "This isn't your...bed, is it?"

He stood above her, his hungry gaze missing nothing of how she was lying nude, as if on a platter before him. "The mattress in the master chamber was too soft"—he stroked a hand down his side over the yellowish bruises—"so I've slept here instead."

She studied the lingering traces of the attack, grateful for the powerful build that protected him, kept him safe. Rising up, she touched him there, the tight flesh warm over his ribs. She wished she could heal him with a kiss. How strange it was to hate the men who did this to him and yet know that she would not have met him otherwise. How could she have lived without ever feeling this way? And her love was only growing stronger.

She wrapped her arms around Liam's waist, peppering kisses over his bruises. The hard length of him pressed against her breasts. Curious, she released him so that she could study the front of his trousers. Tracing the thick ridge with her fingers, she then imitated his action and set her mouth over him. This earned a choked sound from him.

"Not yet," she teased. Lifting her gaze, she pressed her tongue against the fine wool, feeling the heat and hardness of him through the fabric. She watched his eyes darken, shadowed beneath his heavy lashes.

He slipped his hands into her hair, framing her face, but shook his head. "Someday we will explore this more. But this time, I need to bury myself deep inside of you. Is that what you want, Adeline?"

Sweet heaven, how was she supposed to answer that when her mind just melted into jelly? A hot rush of liquid pooled low inside of her as if she could feel him there already. As if he were meant to be there. Now. "Yes."

She loved the way he looked at her, his gaze roving over her body. He unfastened his trousers, shucking them and covering her body with his so quickly that she barely had time to see that part of him. But the glimpse she caught of a column of flesh—darker than the rest of him—jutting upward caused a small surge of alarm. And feeling the hot length of it against her caused another. Though she did not have a moment to balk before his mouth was on hers once more.

And *oh* she missed him. How strange it felt to have been away from his kiss for a few moments and have this joy pour through her at his return. *I love you*, she thought again, wrapping her arms around him, pulling him closer.

Each time he moved over her, his springy chest hair brushed her flesh, teasing her nipples until they ached. Spirals of sensation burned through her body, making it so that her skin felt too hot where they touched. Yet she wanted more.

So, she told him against his lips, breathing into his mouth. "More."

He shifted, wedging one knee between hers and then the other, urging her legs wider. They trembled, and she couldn't seem to help it. She'd never done this, after all. And that thought struck her as so absurd that a giggle escaped.

Liam looked down at her in between nipping kisses over her lips and jaw. "Something amusing, darling?"

"I was just thinking about how I've never done this before," she admitted.

"I'd assumed as much." His grin altered, turning tender, but still somehow remaining wicked.

She blushed. "I know that I once implied that I was completely aware of what went on between a man and a woman, but I might have exaggerated…a little."

"Then perhaps a demonstration is in order." He lowered those sinful lips to hers. Slowly he eased them apart with his tongue, thrusting inside her mouth, shallow at first before retreating. He hovered over her, mouth open, eyes locked on hers, their breath intermingling, and then put his lips to hers again. Tongue easing her apart, thrusting inside, deeper this time and then retreating. Her lips trembled with want, eager for him to return. She arched her neck, urging him, inviting him. And he came back, thrusting, slow, deep, and then out again.

Now her entire body trembled but not with an ounce of fear. It was all desire. "Please. Again. More."

His eyes smiled at her, creasing at the corners. "Greedy."

Love and desire were wonderful elixirs, she decided. Clinging to him, she pressed every part of her body to his. That low throbbing pulse she'd felt before returned, insistent—and yes, *greedy*—making her arch her hips, seeking something to rub against. And he had the perfect something. So hot. So hard. She practically purred…until he moved, taking that part of him away. Before she could object, she felt the heat of him lower, nudging against that pulse, dipping lower still.

Liam's hand roamed over her hips, to her thigh, lifting her knee. She lifted the other, her thighs embracing his hips now. The movement seated him harder against her, where she was *wet through*. He groaned into her mouth, his thick flesh edging inside. Slowly he stretched her and then eased away, a lesson of thrust and retreat. Each time he pushed into her, the walls of her sex closed tightly around him, tugging on that pulse.

He broke apart from their kiss and reached for something above her head. She didn't want to stop, so she followed his hips with hers, rocking against him wantonly.

"Wait, darling," he rasped, his breath rushing against her lips. "You're very small and this will help."

He placed one of the cylindrical pillows at either end of the chaise beneath her hips and returned to their love play just in time. Her body was trembling again, her arms shaking as she held onto his shoulders. His flesh edged inside her, tugging on that pulse, starting slowly once more in shallow thrusts, until she was writhing beneath him.

There was no end in sight, and this ache was consuming her. She wanted to feel that euphoria wash over her again, but the need continued to build and build. Would she burst, or would she shatter first?

And the answer was *Yes. Oh, yes.* At last, she shattered, bursting out to the heavens on a cry and coming back again. A cool wash of starlight flashed behind her eyes. Every part of her tightened, contracting.

Liam groaned as she gasped his name, driving deep— deeper than before—and shocking her with a jolt of pain that interrupted the waves of her bliss. He filled her now, stretching her with each thrusting motion. Tearing away from the kiss, sweat glistened on his brow, his hips rocking, pumping faster, heated flesh and wetness urging her body to accept him.

Pain forgotten, she looked up at him in wonder at this beautiful frenzy they created. His gaze never left hers, his face tight with strain, his neck corded, his shoulders and chest solid, unyielding. And then she watched the moment when his eyes closed and a choked, guttural sound escaped him as he swiftly pulled out of her body, spending his hot seed against her inner thigh.

She never thought she could know such pleasure. But in the next moment, she realized she was wrong. When he pulled her to him, tucking her into his arms securely, contentedly, *that* was the greatest pleasure of all.

"What about now?" she asked on a sigh.

His fingertips skated over her brow, brushing her hair aside for a series of tender kisses that began at her forehead and ended at her lips. "*Do* you feel bashful?"

Fighting a yawn, she shook her head. Even when she'd been shocked by the wicked decadence of his mouth and tongue, she hadn't wanted to be anywhere else. She wanted to be right here, for as long as she dared.

CHAPTER NINETEEN

"*Where is the goddess? If you let her go, we could end this. Your choice, guvna.*"

Liam awoke with a start, lurching up in bed. Breathing hard and fast, it took him a moment to realize that the attack was merely a dream, a memory, and not happening again.

The next thing he realized was that Adeline was not next to him where she should have been, snuggling close while emitting heat like an ember.

The filmy light of dawn crept through his window, revealing a room that was too empty without her. He shivered, wishing to have awoken to the sounds of her sleep talking.

Yet even knowing that she'd slipped away in the middle of the night, he still found himself grinning and eager to start the day. Today he was a new man. Or perhaps he was the man whom Thayne had accused him of being all along. Either way, he felt good in this skin.

For the first time, he knew the certainty of love.

"*Love*, of all things," he said with a laugh. He never thought this would happen to him—that his jaded heart would suddenly abandon him, and in its place, he would find a pure, eager heart, ready to begin a new life. And Liam saw no reason to wait a moment longer.

Slipping into a pair of trousers, he wondered if this was how all would-be bridegrooms felt. If they did not, then they weren't as certain as he was. Of course, he would have to suppress his utter bliss while he spoke to Adeline's father. Even for a man as understanding and unconventional as Boswick, he still wouldn't like knowing what had taken place to cause the *necessity* of their nuptials. And Liam did not want to disappoint him.

Not to mention, there would be the matter of convincing Adeline. She was quite proud and stubborn when she wanted to be. He grinned, imagining all the ways he could explain his sudden transformation and realization.

These thoughts kept him company as he retrieved water from the kitchen below to wash and shave. A quarter hour later, Liam walked outside and made his way next door to request an interview with Boswick.

Finmore checked his pocket watch but announced Liam all the same.

"Well, good morning to you, Wolford. What a pleasant surprise." Boswick gestured with an open hand toward his study, and they both walked in together, taking chairs on either side of the desk. "I don't imagine you've had much more sleep than I. In fact, the only reason I am awake is because my eyes just pop open at the same time each morning, no matter how little sleep I've had."

"No, I haven't had much sleep either..." Liam scrubbed a hand over his face, suddenly feeling nervous. "I've had much on my mind."

"No doubt of it," Boswick agreed as he poured a cup of tea from the tray sitting on the corner of his desk. "With the burglary and the attack upon your person, I imagine it has been difficult to find much sleep at all. Though you must think of your health. We all worry about you. I'm certain that won't change once we return to Boswickshire."

Liam took the cup, murmuring his thanks. Absently, he took a sip while pondering his next words.

Guilt was getting the better of him. Boswick had been kind and generous to him. And how had Liam repaid his host? First, by taking his daughter's innocence and then by planning to take her away from the parents who loved and doted on her.

Setting the cup down, he stood. "Which brings me to the reason for my visit. You see, I was wondering if, perhaps, you might delay your return for a time. Not long"—he swallowed—"just until I marry your daughter."

There. He said it. At least, he thought he did. Yet when he looked at Boswick's bristly brows drawn together in puzzlement, Liam wasn't sure.

"Are you *asking* to marry Adeline?"

Liam went over the words he'd said and realized his mistake. "Yes. Forgive me. I'm a little out of sorts, it seems. I am, indeed, asking for your permission to marry Adeline." However, out of respect, he did not divulge that he would marry Adeline—permission or not.

Boswick's brow remained unchanged. "And have you explained your wishes to her? Because it was Adeline who requested that we end our time in London. She made no mention of this at all."

"We came to an understanding last night." Liam cleared his throat when Boswick's gaze sharpened. "Just after the waltz."

The baron's alteration came swiftly and with a hearty laugh. "Oh ho!" He stood as well and pointed a finger toward the ceiling. "That explains why Adeline was so quiet and withdrawn at the end of the night. *Out of sorts*. The pair of you certainly are, to be sure."

"So I have your permission?" Liam just wanted clarification.

"Have it? Why, you've had it from that very first moment we found you on our doorstep. One look at you with blood splattered all over your fine clothes, and Adeline knew."

Perhaps it was just a residual fogginess in his brain, but Liam found this confusing. "Knew what, precisely?"

"That you were the one for her, of course." Boswick clapped his hand on Liam's shoulder and smiled. "In that instant, I knew you would marry."

Something inside of Liam went cold. An old specter rose up to haunt him.

They'd known from the first moment? Impossible. No one could know by looking at a beaten and bloody man on the floor that he was going to marry their daughter. Then perhaps it was because of his *fine clothes*. Obviously, they'd taken him for a gentleman right away, and one with money to afford such finery.

Could it all have been a ruse? The kindness, the compassion, the desire to earn his trust? Liam didn't want to believe it. "You have no qualms over my reputation?"

Boswick gave him a pat. "That doesn't matter to us. We know the man you are."

And there it was. They couldn't have known the man he was when he'd been unconscious.

Now this fresh, new heart was learning a painful lesson—never trust.

The Pimms were the most cunning of all schemers. Liam had hardly suspected them. Imagine their satisfaction at having caught the eighth Earl of Wolford in their trap.

Liam had fallen for it. He'd convinced himself that Adeline loved him. That he'd been welcomed into the family…

"I should be going," he said, numbly making his way to the door.

"Stay, Wolford. Break your fast with us. I'm certain Adeline will be downstairs in a minute."

Liam offered a bland smile but waved him off. "Thank you. No. I have many matters to see to this morning." He would need to see his solicitor, Aunt Edith, and Vale. Not only that, but Uncle Albert had requested an early audience with him. He paused to draw a breath that burned in his lungs. "I will return this afternoon with the papers from my solicitor, and then we'll sign the appropriate contracts."

Waiting for the banns to be read, signing contracts, and negotiating dowries. Soon Adeline and he would marry in typical London fashion. It surprised him that only minutes ago, he'd been prepared to dash out the doors in search of a special license.

Adeline struggled to rouse from bed that morning. Her limbs were loose and languorous, but her breasts were tender. And when she shifted beneath the coverlet, she realized that other parts of her were tender as well, sore in an unfamiliar way. She blushed, thinking about the cause. Then she smiled, blissful, dreamy. And his name left her lips on a sigh.

As much as she would love to lie abed all morning, recounting every moment of last night, the sounds of servants in the hallway forced her to hurry.

Rising, she moved to the washstand and poured cool water into the basin. Using the flannel, she gently cleansed her sore flesh before drying off and slipping into a fresh chemise.

No sooner had she donned a green striped day dress than Mother rushed into her room and didn't stop—practically bowling her over—until she embraced Adeline.

"My dear, my dear! I am thrilled by the news!" Bunny Pimm was grinning like a madwoman, clapping, hugging Adeline tightly, and then gazing brightly, expectantly. "When you were so quiet last night, your father and I didn't know what to think. All we knew was that you would come to us in time. Ah, but Wolford has beaten you to it! Can you believe he was here at dawn?"

A fresh rush of heat flooded Adeline's cheeks. "Liam—Wolford was here?"

"And your father said his manner was perplexing at first but all became clear soon enough."

"Wolford spoke with Father?" Slowly, the warmth began to seep out of her as a sense of foreboding filled her. Liam had come here at dawn to speak with Father. Normally, this wouldn't have alerted her suspicions. After all, more than anyone else, Liam knew that Pimms were early risers and were not formal about calling hours. Yet after last night…

She shook her head. Surely, he wouldn't have suddenly been stricken with the need to propose. Liam wasn't the kind of man to change his mind about the life he wanted for himself. So then, was this alteration the result of his conscience getting the better of him? Was he worried about the stain upon his family name at the risk of an illegitimate birth? Yet she knew he'd taken special care against the possibility.

Besides, they'd been perfectly clear with each other. She was returning to Boswickshire tomorrow, and he would marry some young debutante in thirty years. Last night was simply a farewell.

There had to be another reason he'd come to see Father at dawn, and Mother was emitting so much joy that it hurt to look at her. At least, Adeline hoped there was another reason.

"Of course he did." Mother laughed and tucked a curl behind Adeline's ear. "No matter how capable and independent a young woman might be, it is only right to ask her father for permission to wed her."

Adeline swallowed, wondering if her complexion was turning as green as her dress. "Is Wolford still here?"

"Your father tried to keep him so that we may all sit in the breakfast room as a family, but Wolford mentioned a need to see his solicitor, arranging contracts and such. The banns will have to be read, of course."

"Oh," Adeline said on a breath. She remembered how he'd described London weddings with contracts and negotiations and how those were not the marriages of two souls bonded for all eternity. It was an agreement. Nothing more.

Obviously, he'd only decided to marry her because of what they'd done. He felt obligated. Yet he already knew she didn't want to be a burden. So then, what would make him think that she would be willing to be his obligation?

He'd never told her that he loved her. He'd made no promises. Nor had she expected them. She knew very well that he did not want to marry.

Surely, he didn't think her capable of trapping him? Adeline would never twist what they shared into a manipulation. But there was only one way to prove that to him—by leaving.

Mother opened the portmanteau on the floor. "I'll ask Hester to unpack your things, since we will be staying in London until the banns are read."

"We are still leaving on the morrow," Adeline said quickly. When her declaration received a startled and puzzled look, she offered an excuse. "Wolford knows that I would prefer to await our...nuptials in Boswickshire. I have grown tired of London."

Mother studied her carefully, then stepped closer to press her hand to Adeline's forehead. "Are you unwell, my dear? You look so pale all of the sudden."

Adeline needed to clear up this matter with Liam immediately before he did something he would regret. And Mother's concern was just the opportunity she needed. "Perhaps I need to lie down for a minute or two longer. Tell Father that I'll be down to the breakfast room in a few minutes."

The moment her mother left, guilt churned in Adeline's stomach. She didn't want to deceive her parents. They deserved more from her. But she didn't want to spend the rest of her life being her husband's biggest regret either.

Adeline went to the desk to draft a note to Liam. Abruptly, she recalled her previous note—the one that she'd left on the console in the hallway next door. Perhaps if she merely added a line or two to that, it would explain everything.

Especially why she was not going to marry him.

CHAPTER TWENTY

"Wolford, what brings you here this morning?" Vale asked after Liam cleared his throat from the study doorway. The duke was on his knees, tinkering with the gears and the pendulum. "Ivy was feeling a little peaked, and so I thought I could cheer her by finishing the automatic cradle."

"Uncle Albert asked me to meet him here this morning to look over his latest acquisitions, but according to your butler, he left a short while ago. So I thought I'd stop in here and tell you my news." Liam took a deep breath, ignoring the sting of betrayal he now felt. "Miss Pimm and I are to be wed."

Vale frowned and stood, dusting his hands together. "And yet this announcement comes from a rather severe-looking countenance. Shouldn't you be elated?"

An hour ago, perhaps. But he'd been proven a fool. "When you first knew you were marrying Ivy, I don't recall your being happy about it. In fact, you were downright terror-stricken."

"For good reason. My *Marriage Formula* was on the line, if you'll recall." Vale shrugged and laughed to himself, as if that were his favorite memory. "Everything I'd worked to achieve, all of my longstanding beliefs—they all meant nothing. Not if I couldn't have Ivy."

Liam wanted that luxury of having his longstanding beliefs—that no debutante was trustworthy—disproven in the face of an honest love. And for a brief time, he thought he'd had that, so he knew what he was missing.

For now, he'd rather not think about it. Distracting himself, he picked up a figurine on the desk. "What is this?"

"A gift from Albert for allowing him to stay while his own house is unavailable. Apparently, this was found in a tomb of the first pharaoh to build a great pyramid."

"Khufu's tomb?" Liam shook his head. Poor Albert. He'd been swindled again. "Did he say from whom he purchased this?"

Vale lifted his brows. "No. He said he unearthed this himself."

"That isn't possible," Liam said, walking over to Vale to show him the reasons. "This pottery is too new, likely forged within the past year. Here, you can see that the patina has been fabricated. And if you draw in the odor, there are remnants of a distinctive mossy creosote, likely used to make it appear ancient."

Vale took the figure in hand and scratched his thumbnail over the surface to confirm Liam's suspicions. "Such a pity. I'd actually held out some hope that it was genuine." He clucked his tongue. "Albert has been obsessed with artifacts for such a long time that one would expect him to know the difference."

"True," Liam agreed. "Though it surprised me to learn that he knows of the symposium I'm giving to the Royal Society. He said that Edith had mentioned it to him."

"That doesn't sound like Edith. After all, she was the one who asked us to conceal what we could about the bust to keep both Albert and Gemma from embarrassment."

"Those were my thoughts as well, nonetheless..." Liam shrugged.

"Come to think of it," Vale continued, "he recently asked me if I'd ever seen the head of Aphrodite in your collection. I evaded the question, mentioning something in regard to the head of one goddess being equal another."

Goddess... The mention abruptly brought back the memory of Liam's dream this morning. *Where is the goddess? If you let her go, we could end this.*

An inexplicable chill stole over him.

"When Albert visited me last week, he never once mentioned Aphrodite."

"I've often wondered if he ever suspected he was swindled. Perhaps that was the reason he asked about it."

"We should hope, for his sake. Yet if he suspected as much—especially considering the topic of my lecture—I doubt he would want to draw attention to it. Likely, he would speak to either of us directly, instead of all this skirting around."

"Not unless..." Vale scratched the patina from the figurine again. "Uncle Albert isn't as naïve as we'd thought."

They exchanged a look. Liam felt a peculiar tension spread through his shoulders. He didn't like where his thoughts were taking him.

"If that were true then he wouldn't have wanted me to lecture on the topic of forgery at the Society. He might have gone to great pains to ensure that I no longer possessed the marble he sold me." At the mention of pain, his memory took him to the night of his attack and then to the dream that woke him this very morning. What if those men truly were asking for the head of Aphrodite? What if this dream had been some amalgamation of the truth?

Vale began to move about the room, pacing, his brow furrowed. "Considering how odd Albert has been behaving as of late, and how we have witnessed his dishonesty, it is a fair assumption that he would not want his reputation sullied by the exposure. Just think of all the artifacts he has sold."

"That *is* how he earns his living," Liam added.

"To be certain, he would want to know where the goddess was. He might even search your houses."

"He's only visited one of which I'm aware. Of late, the only other uninvited guest has been a burglar." Liam blinked, eyes wide with sudden clarity.

"Normally, I would caution you against such a leap of imagination," Vale added in understanding. "However, I'm not entirely certain it is too far a leap."

It did not take long before the pieces began to fall in place.

"The burglaries. The Turkish dagger through the sketch of the Elgin marbles." Liam went still. "No wonder nothing of great value had ever been stolen. They were only searching for the goddess."

"He wasn't in town for those thefts, but it's possible that he hired some disreputable men to do the work. Others houses were ransacked as well, perhaps in order to keep you from figuring it out."

"Inspector Hollycott always thought the burglaries were linked to my attack."

Vale gritted his teeth. "And when those men grew tired of searching, they took a more direct approach."

"I am ashamed that I missed it all this time—" Liam broke off, remembering Albert reading over the invoice in his study. "Albert knows where the head is."

"The forgery is in a crate at the Royal Society already."

"No, the *real* Aphrodite. He likely thinks that is his copy. In fact, he might have sent his men to Sudgrave Terrace or even has gone there himself. After all, why would he ask me to pay a call—and then not bother to be here—unless he wanted to ensure he knew precisely where *I* was going to be?"

Liam started toward the door, Vale close behind.

Fortunately, Adeline discovered that the doors between their adjoining houses were still unlocked. Instead of darkness greeting her this morning, sunlight filtered in through the window at the end of the hallway. It made it much easier to locate the letter.

Picking it up, she held it to her bosom. She still felt every tender wish and promise she'd written, but those words were too revealing now. If Liam read this letter after what had transpired between them, then he might even think she was trying to manipulate him into marriage. She couldn't risk it. Speaking to him was the better option anyway. She needed him to understand that she wasn't trying to trap him, nor was she going to marry him.

Note in hand, she made her way to the room they'd shared last night, practicing how she would begin their conversation.

"After careful consideration..." No, no, that was far too dry and formal. He deserved more tenderness than that, and so did she, for that matter.

Then perhaps a simple, honest "I love you, but I won't marry you" would be better? She frowned, not liking that at all either. Telling someone you love him should never be followed by *but...*

She hesitated at the door, listening carefully. When she did not hear anything from within, she peered through the opening, but he wasn't there. She needed him to know that marriage had not been her goal last night. In fact, she hadn't even had an end in mind. When he'd kissed her, all her thoughts tumbled out of her head. Likely, she should have discussed it with him this morning *before* he sought out her father. Now everything was in a muddle.

A murmur of voices from below caught her attention. Thinking that he might be in his study with his solicitor— or worse, telling his family—Adeline quietly descended the stairs in search of him.

On the main floor, she heard a noise coming from the study and continued onward. Hesitating only long enough to draw in a fortifying breath, she rapped quietly on the door and nudged it open.

In the same moment, however, she discovered that it was not Liam in the study.

A strange, burly man in a bowler hat and brown coat stood near a crate. Because he held an iron lever bar, she assumed he was a footman sent to unpack Liam's things, and offered a polite smile. "Pardon me, but I was looking for Lord Wolford. Is he in, by any chance?"

Curious, she glanced down at the contents of the crate and saw the profile of a large, pale marble head.

"Nah," the man said, taking a step closer and effectively blocking her view. With a grin of his own, his gaze shifted from her to a point over her shoulder.

She looked back, surprised again, but this time to see Liam's uncle walking steadily toward her. "Oh! Mr. Desmond, how nice to see you again."

He touched the brim of his hat in greeting. "Miss Pimm, a pleasure indeed. But I'm afraid you've caught me at quite an inconvenient time," he said rather cryptically and offered a nod to the man behind her.

"I'm not certain what you mean, sir. I only came to see if I could find Wolford. Is he about?"

"He is not. In fact, no one was supposed to be here. Which is rather unfortunate for you, now that you've seen Aphrodite."

A terrible icy chill rushed down her limbs at the sight of his peculiar smile and the eerie brightness in his dark brown eyes. Then, without warning, a large hand clamped over her mouth and nose as an arm cinched around her waist, seizing her and trapping one of her arms by her side.

She screamed, panic and terror overtaking her.

What was happening?

She clawed at the hand, trying to pull it away, trying to catch her breath. Her lungs started to burn, her throat raw. She kicked. Punched. Scratched, but to no avail. None of her blows earned even a grunt of pain. Her limbs were starting to feel slow and weighted.

All of her struggling was only making her tired…so tired. And all the while, Mr. Desmond just stood and watched.

Her last thought before everything went black was sadness for Liam. He couldn't even trust his own uncle.

CHAPTER TWENTY-ONE

Liam spotted the missing crate the instant he strode into the study. Damn, he was too late to catch Albert in the act.

Vale followed him. "For a head of that size, they would have needed a dray and likely would have gone out the back."

They both turned to rush down the hall, toward the rear of the house. But then Liam caught sight of a note on the floor at his feet, his name written in a looped feminine scrawl. He paused to pick it up, knowing it hadn't been there before.

A sense of unease filled him and only grew as he read.

My dearest Liam,

After thirty years have come and gone, and you have at last met your young bride, please spare a thought for me—the one who loved you without expectation. For I will be thinking of you all the days of my life. And each night I will whisper your name in a prayer that you find more happiness than you ever have imagined.

All my love,

A

Liam's hand trembled, the words blurring on the page. Adeline was here. But when? Had she left the note early this morning, before the burglary? Clutching the note to his chest, he hoped that was the case.

It was only when he looked down at the straw strewn over the floor that he noticed the shoe. A green satin-covered half boot with a three-inch wedge of cork.

He went cold, shaking his head in fervent but necessary denial, even as he bent to pick up the boot. Perhaps she had meant to leave the note on his desk and—in her rush to run back home—it slipped out of her hand at the same time her boot fell off. Or she could have lost it simply fleeing to safety when she happened upon the intruders…

But he knew better. The men who attacked him, who beat him to near death, would not have let her escape.

"They have taken her." Terror like he'd never known before turned his body to ice but put fire in his veins too. He bolted out the door.

Without knocking, he rushed into Boswick's house and asked Finmore if he'd seen Adeline. Just then, Boswick himself appeared, descending the stairs.

"I just came from her room," Boswick said. "Bunny said she was ill. But when I went to check on her, she wasn't there."

Liam held up the note. "I believe she meant to leave me this in my study, but encountered"—his voice was shaking now, dread clawing at his throat—"burglars. I think they've taken her."

Dear Lord, he prayed that was all. If anything happened to her…he would murder every person responsible, family or not.

Boswick went white. "Finmore, send for Gladwin. We need the carriage."

Vale came running up behind him just then. "I spotted Albert hailing a hack around the corner. He was alone. We can't be too far behind. No more than a quarter hour."

A quarter hour. A lifetime. "Then we have to find the dray. They have taken Adeline," Liam said, desperate, fisting his hand in his hair. "I don't even know which direction to look."

If she encountered Albert and his henchman, then what could they want with her? Ransom? No. They wouldn't need ransom if they already had the head of Aphrodite.

"Albert would want to dispose of the evidence as soon as possible, believing there will be no other link to him and the forgery," Vale said, reading Liam's thoughts.

Albert might even want to *dispose of* anyone who'd caught him in the act.

"We are in Knightsbridge, so the closest and easiest way would be to"—a sudden wash of clarity and newfound terror hit Liam—"throw it into the Thames."

Briefly, Vale put his head in his hands as if he'd come to the same conclusion.

"There isn't time." Liam couldn't wait for Gladwin to bring the carriage around. "I'll move faster on horseback."

They both looked through the open door to find the streets filling with carriages and high-steppers.

With one purpose in mind, Liam ran straight out in the thick of it. "Ho, there! You! I need a horse."

"Is that Lord Wolford?" a woman in a feathered hat asked her companions from atop a phaeton. "What sort of scandalous deed is he up to now?"

Similar jeers followed, his past sins coming to haunt him at the worst possible moment. Didn't they know a desperate man when they saw one?

"You need a horse?" a man said from behind him.

Liam whirled around to see a somewhat familiar face beneath a gray John Bull. "I do. Please." He didn't even care that his voice broke.

The man—Viscount Ellery, if memory served—dismounted immediately. "Take care of her, Wolford."

"I will. Thank you." No doubt, Ellery was speaking of his mare, but Liam only had one thought. He had to find Adeline.

Wasting no time, he mounted the horse and headed toward the Thames.

Adeline awoke with a horrendous headache. She groaned. Her neck and body stiff, something hard digging into her back. And a wall pressed against her forehead. The air around her was dry and filled with debris, sticks poking her face, making her cough. She tried to lift her hands to brush it away from her mouth and nose, but her efforts were hindered by the confined space.

It took her a moment to realize that they weren't sticks, but piles of straw. And it wasn't a wall either. It was a box.

She was inside Aphrodite's crate.

The rocking motion beneath her forced the marble head to shift closer and made Adeline aware that she was moving, likely on the back of a cart.

Well, at least the men hadn't killed her.

She wondered where they were taking her. It was then that she noticed the sounds around her—traffic noises, horse hooves on stone, the jangle of carriage rigging, the echo of a bell near water.

Water.

"They didn't take care to make sure you were dead before, Adeline," she said, choking back tears, "because they are getting rid of the evidence…and you."

Even at this early hour, there were dozens of drays on the bridge, as well as men and women on foot and on horseback. Carts were everywhere, filled with wares to sell at market or stacked with the worldly possessions of those looking for a chance at a better life in London.

But there was only one dray driving out of town as if hell were on its heels. The crate had familiar markings too, but from this distance, Liam couldn't be certain. He had no fixed reason for following that cart in particular, just instinct.

"Do you see her?" Vale shouted. Having *borrowed* a two-horse carriage, he was close behind, sitting beneath the folding top over the driver's seat.

Liam didn't see her, but he knew she was there. Somehow he *knew* and prayed that he was right. "Up there. The fellow with the bowler hat heading south."

His voice must have carried, because the man turned sharply, looking over his shoulder at Liam. Abruptly, the memory of his attack returned. That was the man who'd beaten him. In fact, Liam likely would have died if not for the good crack he got at the thug's nose.

Then the man turned back to his horse, using a whip to spur it forward, faster.

The cart was close to the edge of the bridge where there was nothing but a small, upraised layer of brick to keep it from tipping over the side. Liam knew he had to hurry.

He didn't know this horse well enough to know if it was skittish, but so far she'd been steady under pressure. Weaving through the hoard, Liam kept his focus on the crate. It was jostling around far too much. One rough rut and it could bounce over the edge.

But as he watched, he saw something amazing. The corner of the lid began to lift, gradually at first, and then it shot upward all of the sudden. He caught a glimpse of a slender leg and a single green half boot as the lid tumbled over the side and down into the water below.

Relief and terror filled him simultaneously when he saw a bedraggled Adeline emerge from the straw. She was alive! But now the man driving the cart knew it too.

The henchman reached back for her with one hand, grabbing at whatever he could, taking hold of her hair. Adeline's head snapped back, and she cried out.

Twisting, she managed to free herself, but only just. She was still trapped on the back of that cart with nowhere to go.

Liam rode faster, Adeline nearly within his reach.

There was one good thing about being underestimated, Adeline thought. Her attacker had not thought to bind her arms or legs. Nor had he taken the time to secure the crate properly. There were gaps above her that let in plenty of light, enough to see how the lid shifted up and down on the nails with every bump they hit. She'd simply needed to give it a swift kick.

And once she was free, she took a moment to feel pleased by her accomplishment. Unfortunately, she'd celebrated too soon, and found herself within her captor's reach.

She wrenched her hair free, the shortened locks slipping through his fingers. Then, scrambling up on her knees, she made it to the opposite end of the crate where the marble head stared at her with blandly interested eyes, as if waiting to see what would happen next.

Adeline contemplated jumping, but then she saw where they were. The cart was on the very edge of the bridge. One slip of the wheel and she would go down a very long distance to the water.

"Adeline!"

Liam! Her heart leapt when she looked up and saw him riding pell-mell. He found her! "Be careful!" she shouted, hating how close the horse was to the edge.

He seemed to take care, because he came around to the other side, wedging between the cart and the crowd of people lining the bridge. It was so strange to see that no one paid much attention to them or even moved out of the way. They were so determined to get into the city that they likely wouldn't care if the dray went over the side.

Her captor seemed to think the same thing and veered the cart closer to the edge. At the same time, he reached for something beside him, but whatever it was fell to the floor. So he used the coachman's whip in his hand instead.

Turning, with only one hand on the reins, he lashed back at Liam. The crack split the air around them. Liam's horse threw her head back, careening to the side. The whip flicked again, but with less force because he had his wrist locked. Liam gained control of the horse and rode back up to them.

On a curse, the man dropped the whip onto the bed of the cart and turned, hunting beneath his seat once more. This time, he came up with a gun.

Pointing it at Liam, he cocked the arm with his thumb.

"No!" Adeline reacted on instinct. Reaching over the edge of the crate, she grabbed the abandoned whip. Years of practice told her that this man had underestimated her for the last time.

With a single strike, she lashed the henchman's fingers. He screamed, dropping the gun, a stub of crimson flesh where his finger had been.

Adeline was stunned for an instant, staring in horror as the man released the reins to clutch his wounded hand. The horse and cart careened toward the edge.

Numbly, she turned her head to Liam, whose face went stark white. Reaching out, he called out her name, but she couldn't hear him. All she heard was the sound of blood rushing in her ears. Not knowing how she managed, she stood up on the moving cart, one foot in the straw and the other on Aphrodite.

Then, without hesitation, she'd leapt off the side and into Liam's arms.

By the time Vale had caught up to them, Uncle Albert's henchman was at the bottom of the Thames. Along with

Aphrodite's head. But the most important part was that Adeline was safe.

Now, they'd crossed the bridge, Vale beside them. Liam was still traumatized and shaking from the events of the morning. He held Adeline in his arms, unable to think about how close he'd come to losing her.

When it started to rain, he tucked her safely into the carriage and spoke with his cousin. After a negotiation, he traded Vale's borrowed carriage for Ellery's horse and asked his cousin to settle up with the owners of both.

"I'm heading to Arborcrest," Liam said, looking forward to returning home at last. For him, London had lost its luster. All he wanted was a simple life that was pure and honest. "Please inform Boswick of his daughter's safety and whereabouts. I imagine they'll follow shortly thereafter."

Of course, it would be a wet ride, with the driver's seat exposed to the rain.

Vale clutched Liam's shoulder in something of an embrace. "You will need a special license, I imagine. I can help with that."

With a glance toward the carriage, Liam nodded. Waiting for the banns to be read was not an option any longer. He planned to abscond with a debutante, and nothing but a hasty marriage would save both of their reputations.

Chapter Twenty-Two

"Are you not happy with your first sight of Arborcrest, Miss Pimm?" Liam asked with a peculiar smile as he rubbed a flannel over his damp hair.

No. Adeline was furious.

For more than three hours, she'd been sequestered inside the carriage, and now he expected her to be glad?

Besides, she barely had a glimpse of the estate with the way that she'd been covered with a greatcoat, rushed inside and up the stairs. She'd caught a blur of pale stone and a wide oaken door and then dozens of faces, all eagerly saying, "Welcome home, my lord. Welcome to Arborcrest, my lady."

Now, she was standing in a vast, *and yes, elegant and splendid*, rose-colored bedchamber. Beyond the window lay an expansive grove of white-blossomed pear trees, all lined up in rows, extending to the rolling hills that crested the horizon. But the fact that she liked what she had seen of Arborcrest so far did not matter in the least.

She set her hands on her hips and glared at Liam. "How dare you tell your man at the door that I am your countess!

You never even asked me to marry you. Regardless, I absolutely *will not*."

Liam tossed the cloth to the upholstered bench at the foot of a large bed with four ornately carved posts. He seemed unaffected by her outburst and began stripping out of his wet clothes. "You will marry me. By now most of London will know that we left town without a chaperone."

"I don't care about that," she said, trying not to watch him tug his wet cravat free, revealing his corded throat. Next, he shrugged out of his waistcoat, offering a view of black hair and the firm muscles of his chest and shoulders beneath the transparent linen of his shirt sleeves. She tried not to remember how it felt to have her hands on him or to feel him pressed against her. She swallowed. "You tucked me away in the carriage. Then you carried me inside, not even allowing me to walk on my own."

He pulled his shirtsleeves over his head and padded to her, wearing only his trousers. His hands skimmed over her arms, pulling her closer, inch by inch. "I put you in the carriage because you were shaking and it was beginning to rain. And I carried you into the house, not because I thought you incapable of doing so, but because I needed you in my arms."

Oh. Her breath came out all at once, gooseflesh and tingles dancing over her skin. She felt herself softening a bit until…

"I needed to know you were safe," he said, his statement sounding far too much like something her parents would have said.

She shrugged away from him, only to have him follow.

"How could I not be safe after having been imprisoned in a carriage the whole journey?" she asked, ignoring the quick tug of her heart. "I will not be coddled."

"Very well. Next time we drive in the rain, I will put you in the seat beside me so that we are both"—he flashed her a wicked grin—"wet through."

How dare he make her blush at a time like this! Not only that, but did he have to touch her this way, brushing his fingers up and down her arms, eliciting sensations that made her want to step into his embrace?

Against her will, her resolve began to weaken. She lifted a hand to his forehead, his skin smooth and emitting a pleasant, temperate warmth. "You were the one foolish enough to ride the entire journey in the rain. It is dangerous to put your health at risk."

She almost lost him once today, and she didn't want to think about him falling ill too. It was taking all the strength she had not to fall apart.

"Do you think I require bed rest?" Even though he teased, his expression was both heated and tender. He took her hands and settled them against his chest, over his heart.

She nearly gave in, ready to offer him whatever he wanted and gladly. But when he started to undress her, she stepped back. Or tried to. He didn't let her go too far.

"I can undress myself," she assured him. Since she did not have a change of clothes, however, she saw little reason to remove her dress. Although, this one was covered with bits of straw and quite dusty. It also reminded her of the horror of being trapped in the crate, of watching as Liam was almost shot, and then seeing the cart drive over the edge of the bridge...

She shivered.

"I have no doubt of it. However, your hands are trembling." He pressed a warm kiss to each of her fingertips as if to prove his point. "And you need the warmth of a bath. There is a large copper tub waiting in the dressing room that joins the master suites. I believe the servants have finished filling it."

Suddenly, a bath sounded like the perfect idea. She nodded, allowing him to help her with the tiny fastenings of the bib front dress, knowing her hands were shaking too much to do it herself.

"Good." He stepped closer, his fingers deftly working the enclosure. Heat emanated from his body, warming her. He leaned in to whisper, causing those tingles to return. "Besides, as you might have guessed, this is what husbands enjoy doing the most, and wives, I imagine. They undress each other."

"Likely they do," she agreed, her heart squeezing with regret. "But I am not going to be your wife."

He kissed her throat, nipping down to her collarbone as he slid her dress from her shoulders, then freeing her from her corset. "It is too late for that."

"Are you forgetting that you don't want to marry me either? Or how you believe I had a grand scheme all along to trap you?"

He lifted his head. "How could you know that?"

She fought the tears that stung her eyes. "The instant Mother told me that you left to see your solicitor, I knew. I remember what you said about London weddings—contracts, dowries, and waiting for the banns to be read."

His clover-green gaze pinned her. "Your father told me that you knew from the first moment that we would marry. Do you deny it?"

She shook her head. "No. You see, my family believes in love at first sight. According to the stories, my ancestors have claimed to have known the moment they'd met their future spouse. I come from a long line of romantics who married for love. It is nothing more than that—no scheming involved."

"And it happened to you." He held her gaze, and he never stepped away from her.

Again, Adeline shook her head. "I did not fall in love with you at first sight. That took time." She decided not to tell him about the strong reaction or how she felt tethered to him instantly. It would only cause problems when she refused to marry him.

"But you do love me." He grinned and waggled his eyebrows.

"Yes. I love you," she began. "But you know my reasons for not wanting to marry. I will not be a burden to anyone or a source of pity."

He grasped her shoulders. "Have I ever once made you feel pitied, incapable?"

When she opened her mouth to reply instantly, he silenced her with a finger against her lips.

"I will answer that for you," he said. "From the beginning, I have thought you everything that is brave, capable, and perfect."

She remembered back to the night she'd cut her hair and how she thought she'd heard him say something similar, but at the time it was too easy to convince herself that it was merely hopeful yearning. Knowing that he felt this way filled her with wonder and complete elation.

But still, it was difficult to obliterate all of her doubts. After all, he had never professed any deeper feelings for her. Could they build a life on admiration?

Likely not. "But who is to say that would not change?"

"And this is why you are willing to let me live for the next thirty years before I found a young bride, hmm?" His jaw clenched, his gaze hard, but his hands were tender upon her flesh, drawing her into his embrace. "Oh, yes, I read your letter. Perhaps you are right, after all. I might fare better with a bride who is more determined than with one who will let her fear be the barrier between us."

"You have no idea how much that letter cost me." Her hands settled over his chest once more to push him away. Yet the rhythm of his heart began thrumming through her own body. She closed her eyes against the power he held over her, against wanting to wrap her arms around him and hold on to him forever. Then she met his gaze. "I was the brave one, willing to let you have your dream, even knowing that you were mine."

"Then make me yours, darling." A flame ignited in his eyes at her bold declaration. He pulled her to him, lifting her as he made his way toward the bed. "If you like, you can display your capabilities by being the one on top."

They fell together through the bed curtains, tumbling onto a satin coverlet. He turned her so that she was straddling him, her chemise rising up, the hard evidence of his arousal between them.

She was out of breath once more and staring down at his sinful smirk. "This is not a jest, Liam. My heart is trembling, and I don't know if it's out of fear or longing. All I know is that I want it to stop."

"It won't stop." He took her hands and threaded them with his. "Perhaps it is a mixture of fear *and* longing. This feeling is inside of me too. It is far worse when we are apart.

Every single moment I've spent away from you has been pure torture. My only reprieve from agony is when you are near. Then my head clears, my heart beats strong in my chest, and I am suddenly filled with certainty."

Did that mean he felt their connection too? Just as strongly as she?

The answer was there in the happiness that flooded her, pure and magnificent.

"Adeline, you cannot make me wait thirty years."

Make him *wait?* "If you'll recall, the thirty years was always your—"

He stopped her by pulling her down for a kiss. "I'll have to keep you here for all that time. I refuse to live without you for even a single day. I love you far too much."

She grinned against his lips, letting his words fill her. "Unmarried for thirty years… What will our children think?"

He turned, shifting so that she was beneath him now. "Then it is fortunate that Vale will be here tomorrow with a special license for us."

No banns, no contracts, no negotiations… "No London wedding?"

"I've long held the belief that marriage is *a union between two souls who will be united forever*," he said, quoting her own speech to him.

She laughed softly, adoringly. "Oh, you have, have you?"

"Always. Since the moment we met." As he brushed the hair from her face, there was no humor or wickedness in his gaze, just complete sincerity. "So when are you going to say *yes*?"

"As soon as you kiss me."

And so he kissed her.

EPILOGUE

The Season Standard—the Daily Chronicle of Consequence

Rumors abound, dear readers, over the fate of our Original who has yet to be named!

The committee surely has candidates aplenty. Though we must wonder if all of our favorites have not suddenly married, making them ineligible. A curious thought, is it not?

Which brings our attention to the esteemed Earl of W— and his recent symposium at the Royal Society. This astounding transformation has us all atwitter and looking to his fair bride.

In the style of the lovely Countess of W—, we have seen a rise in debutantes flaunting silk-covered half boots from their phaeton perches. Even our goddess, Lady G—, was spotted in the park, wearing a bold pair in turquoise blue. Sources state that they certainly earned the Marquess of Th—'s admiration.

Every sighting brings a new report, whetting our collective appetites over these rivals. Yet, until the Original is named, we shall have to wait…

"Do you think Thayne is terribly upset that you weren't named?" Adeline asked from across the coverlet, her legs folded beneath her and her hair mussed from a rather thorough morning.

Liam grinned, licking a drop of honey off the pad of his thumb and watching his bride's eyes follow, her cheeks flushing with color. Likely, she would never see honey without blushing again—he'd made sure of it. "Not at all. In fact, he lives for the challenge of it, not the result. I'm certain he will figure out how to tempt Juliet into a new wager. One that she won't be able to resist."

"Hmm…likely so." Adeline slathered another piece of dark, grainy bread with soft cheese—a main staple of their frequent coverlet picnics.

They'd been married a week now. The ever-competent Mr. Ipley had seen to all the arrangements in a mere day—a wedding in the chapel, filled with friends and family fresh from London. It almost seemed too convenient to Liam that such a feat were possible. But then Ipley confessed to having received a letter from Aunt Edith weeks ago.

Apparently, she had known from the beginning that Liam and Adeline would marry in short order. He still wondered what gave him away. Nevertheless, their wedding party, complete with houseguests, lasted until Liam and Adeline returned to London for his lecture.

Now they were back at Arborcrest again. The Pimms were staying in the east wing for a time, Serge taking great pains to set up a bee colony to *marry* Boswickshire honey with Arborcrest's pear orchard. And Liam was more content than he could imagine.

"It was kind of the *Standard*'s editor not to mention any part of your uncle's scandal," Adeline said, coming closer to lay her head on his shoulder.

He tucked her beside him as they shared bites of bread. "I believe they are in shock—as we all are—even more so now that he has fled the country."

"Poor Gemma—abandoned by her unscrupulous father and then left to endure the scandal."

He kissed her head, loving her pure heart. "Aunt Edith says she's up to the task of separating the *ton*'s opinion of Albert from Gemma. But I do not envy my cousin at all. She will be forced to endure the *dullest* affairs of the entire Season."

"Then perhaps we should return, to help her have a London adventure."

Liam stiffened, pulling Adeline closer. "Do you want to return to London?"

Finishing the last bite of bread, she tapped her fingertip against her lip as if in contemplation. Then, tilting her head, she pressed a kiss over his heart. "I think I would prefer...an Arborcrest adventure." She kissed him again, higher this time. "A waltz in the orchard." Another kiss. "A race in your carriage toward that copse of trees at the bottom of the hill...The one you showed me the other day, where the grass is lush and soft beneath us..."

By the time her kisses reached his mouth, she was straddling him. And Liam completely agreed that an Arborcrest adventure was exactly what he needed too, for the next thirty years, and more.

The scene at Hanover Square was a complete disaster. Traffic converged into one colossal mash-up of closed carriages, open barouches, horse carts, and every type of conveyance one could image.

And here they sat. Red-faced coachmen were shouting, horses whinnying, the cart owners cursing, and all of their wrath seemed to be aimed at one young gentleman in a single-horse gig. The man at the center of it all appeared dumbstruck, his gaze fixed toward the corner townhouse.

From atop his horse, Max followed the young man's gaze and was suddenly no longer surprised. For standing on the pavement was none other than Juliet.

The woman frequently left wreckage in her wake.

After steering clear of it, he dismounted and tied off his horse on a post before walking in her direction. "My, my, Lady Granworth, you do cause quite the spectacle."

Her gold-trimmed hat tilted upward as she coolly watched his approach. "Do not think to blame me. All I did was direct Mr. Wick to the portmanteau beneath the driver's perch and then this…" She tsked and gestured with a wave, raising a lace-gloved hand up from where it rested elegantly on the tip of her closed parasol.

Max paid no heed to the maelstrom on the street. Instead, he focused on the true culprit, his gaze skimming over her and down the length of her fitted blue walking costume. He could hardly blame the lad in the gig. She was a veritable siren. At one time, even Max had lost his bearings over her.

But that was years ago. He was a different man now.

With a shake of his head, he glanced toward the small set of stairs leading to the townhouse as Mr. Wick, portmanteau in hand, disappeared through the door.

Max frowned. "Shouldn't you be directing your carriage to be filled with luggage instead emptied of it?"

"For what reason?" Her pale golden brows arched, all innocence. Yet the glint of contention in those vivid blue eyes told him that she knew exactly why.

"To return to your home in Bath, of course. After all, you did not win our wager."

"Nor did I lose. Until there is a formal announcement in the *Standard*, I may still reclaim my home." Lifting her closed parasol, she rested it against her shoulder as if it were a musket and then turned toward the townhouse.

He glared at her retreating figure, his back teeth grinding together. "You have no hope of winning."

"Dear Max"—she glanced over her shoulder, a small smile curving her lips—"our true battle has only begun, and I am not about to surrender."

Not quite *The End*.

Max and Juliet are next!
The Season's Original series continues with

When a Marquess Loves a Woman

Coming October 2016 from Avon Impulse!

ACKNOWLEDGMENTS

This book wouldn't have been possible without the great team of people at Avon/HarperCollins. Many thanks to my new editor, Nicole Fischer, for your special flair and for your patience and kindness throughout the process. Thanks to Angela Craft and Libby Collins for all the behind-the-scenes work of marketing and publicity. And thanks to Gail Dubov for this stunning cover.

Thanks to Stefanie Lieberman for the brainstorming session that birthed this awesome title (and potential earworm).

Thanks to Lisa Filipe for your completely amazing Tasty Book Tours and the special banners you make.

And thank you to the fans who make my job even more of a dream come true. Seeing your "likes" and reading your comments and e-mails fill me with such gratitude that I feel blessed every day.

Wishing you all the best and more...

ABOUT THE AUTHOR

USA Today best-selling author **VIVIENNE LORRET** loves romance novels, her pink laptop, her husband, and her two sons (not necessarily in that order...but there are days). Transforming copious amounts of tea into words, she is an Avon Impulse author of works including *Tempting Mr. Weatherstone*, The Wallflower Wedding series, The Rakes of Fallow Hall series, "The Duke's Christmas Wish," and the Season's Original series.

Discover great authors, exclusive offers, and more at hc.com.

Give in to your Impulses . . .
Continue reading for excerpts from
our newest Avon Impulse books.
Available now wherever ebooks are sold.

THE VIRGIN AND THE VISCOUNT
A BACHELOR LORDS OF LONDON NOVEL
by Charis Michaels

LOVE ON MY MIND
by Tracey Livesay

HERE AND NOW
AN AMERICAN VALOR NOVEL
by Cheryl Etchison

An Excerpt from

THE VIRGIN AND
THE VISCOUNT
A Bachelor Lords of London Novel
By Charis Michaels

Lady Elisabeth Hamilton-Baythes has a
painful secret. At fifteen, she was abducted by
highwaymen and sold to a brothel. But two days
later, she was rescued by a young lord, a man
she's never forgotten. Now, she's devoted herself
to save other innocents from a similar fate.

Bryson Courtland, Viscount Rainsleigh, never
breaks the rules. Well, once, but that was a
long time ago. He's finally escaped his unhappy
past to become one of the wealthiest noblemen
in Britain. The last thing he needs to complete
his ideal life? A perfectly proper wife.

Bryse.

He had introduced himself as Bryson that night, so long ago, and despite her residual horror, she had clung to the sweet intimacy of that introduction. She'd devoted years of foolish fantasies to guessing whether those close to him referred to him as Bryson or Bryse or perhaps Court . . .

She looked up at him. *Bryse.* And now she knew. Now she was being invited to become one of those people close to him.

Cowardice compelled her to back away and retake her seat. "Forgive me, my lord." She spoke to her knees. "I don't know what to say, and that is a rare circumstance, indeed."

"I would also speak to your aunt," he assured her. "It felt appropriate to suggest the idea of a courtship to you first."

She laughed, in spite of herself. "I'd say so. Unless you wish to court my aunt."

"I wish for you," he said abruptly, and Elisabeth's head shot up. It was almost as if he knew she needed to hear it again, and again, and again.

I wish for you.

He crouched before her chair, spreading his arms, putting

one hand on either side of her chair, caging her in. "How old are you, Elisabeth?" he asked.

"How old do you think I am?" A whisper.

"Twenty-six?" he guessed.

She shook her head. "No. I am the ripe old age of thirty. Far too old to be called upon by a bachelor viscount, rolling in money."

"Or"—he arched an eyebrow—"exactly the right age."

She laughed and finally looked away. And she thought he'd been handsome at nineteen. Her stomach dropped into a dip. She reminded herself to breathe.

"Why me?" she asked, looking out the window. "Why pay attention to *me*?"

His voice was so low she could barely discern the words. "Because I think you'd make an ideal viscountess."

An ideal what? Hope became a living, pulsing thing in her chest. It became her very heart. She fell back in her seat and closed her eyes, but the room still swam before her.

He went on, "You are mature, and intelligent, and poised. And devoted to your charity, whatever it is."

A thread of the old conversation. She sat up, determined to seize it before he could say another thing. "I've just told you what the charity is."

"You spoke in vague generalities that could mean a great many things. I let it go because I hope for more opportunities to learn."

Elisabeth breathed in and out, in and out. She bit her bottom lip again. She watched his gaze hone in on her mouth.

She closed her eyes. "My lord." She took a deep breath.

"Rainsleigh . . . Bryson." She opened her eyes. "If your far-reaching goal is to earn an esteemed spot in London society, you're going about it entirely the wrong way. My charity is . . . unpopular, and no one has ever asked to court me before. It's really not done."

"Why is that?"

Because I have been waiting for you.

The thought floated, fully formed, in her brain, and she had to work to keep her hands from her cheeks, to keep from closing her eyes again, from squinting them shut against his beautiful face, just inches from her own, his low voice, his boldness.

"I'm very busy," she said instead.

"Then I will make haste."

"Is this because of last night? When I . . . challenged your dreadful neighbor?"

The corner of his mouth hitched up. "It did not hurt."

"It's very difficult for me to stand idly by when I hear a person misrepresented."

"And to think I was under the impression that you could barely abide my company. Your defense came as a great surprise."

"Oh . . . I am full of surprises."

"Is that so?" His words were a whisper. He leaned in.

She had the fleeting thought: *Dear God. He's going to kiss me . . .*

An Excerpt from

LOVE ON MY MIND

By Tracey Livesay

Tracey Livesay makes her Avon Impulse
debut with a sparkling and sexy novel about
a woman who will do anything to fulfill her
dreams . . . but discovers that even the best
laid plans can fail when love gets in the way.

Chelsea Grant couldn't tear her gaze away from the train wreck on the screen.

She followed press conferences like most Americans followed sports. The spectacle thrilled her, watching speakers deftly deflect questions, state narrow political positions, or, in rare instances, exhibit honest emotions. The message might be scripted but the reactions were pure reality. If executed well, a press conference could be as engaging and dynamic as any athletic game.

But watching this one was akin to lions in the amphitheater, not tight ends on the football field. Her throat ached, impacting her ability to swallow. She squinted, hoping the action would lessen her visual absorption of the man's public relations disaster.

He'd folded his arms across his chest, the gesture causing the gray cardigan he wore to pull across his broad shoulders. The collar of the black-and-blue plaid shirt he wore beneath it brushed the underside of his stubbled jaw.

When he'd first stepped onto the platform, she'd thought he was going for "geek chic." All he'd lacked were black square frames and a leather cross-body satchel. Now she understood he wasn't playing dress-up. These were his everyday clothes, and as such, they were inappropriate for a press conference, unless he was a lumberjack who'd just won the lottery.

Had someone advised him on how to handle a press conference? No, she didn't think so. *Any* coaching would have helped with his demeanor. The man stared straight ahead. He didn't look at the reporters seated before him. He didn't look into the lenses. He appeared to look over the cameras, like there was someplace else he'd rather be. His discomfort crossed the media plane, and her fingers twitched where they rested next to her iPad on the acrylic conference table.

A female reporter from an entertainment news cable channel raised her hand. "Mr. Bennett?"

The man turned his head, and his gaze zeroed in on the reporter and narrowed into a glare. Chelsea inhaled audibly and leaned forward in her chair. His eyes were thickly lashed and dark, although she couldn't determine their exact color. Brown? Black? He dropped his arms, and his long, slender fingers gripped the podium tightly. The bank of microphones jiggled and a loud piercing sound ripped through the air. He winced.

"How does it feel to be handed the title by David James?" the reporter asked, her voice louder as it came on the tail end of the noise feedback.

The camera zoomed in and caught his pinched expression. "Right now, I feel annoyed," he responded sharply.

"Annoyed? Aren't you honored?"

"Why should I be honored?"

"Because *People Magazine* has never named a non-actor as their sexiest man alive."

"An award based on facial characteristics is not an honor. Especially since I have no control over the symmetry of my features. The National Medal of Technology. The Faraday Medal. The granting of those awards would be a true honor."

The camera zoomed out, and hands holding phones with a smaller version of the man's frustrated image filled the screen. Flashes flickered on the periphery, and he rubbed his brow, like Aladdin begging the genie for the power to disappear.

"How does one celebrate being deemed the most desirable man on the planet?" another reporter asked.

"One doesn't." His lips tightened into a white slash on his face.

"Is there a secret scientific formula for dating Victoria's Secret models? Didn't you used to be engaged to one?" A male reporter exchanged knowing looks with the colleagues around him. A smattering of chuckles followed his question.

"Didn't she leave you for another model six weeks before the wedding?"

"So you're single? Who's your type?"

"What's your perfect first date?"

"Can you create a sexbot?"

Questions pelted the poor man. The reporters had found his weakness: his inability or unwillingness to play the game. Now they would try to get a sound bite for their story teaser or a quote to increase their site's click-through rate. The man drove his fingers through his black hair, a move so quick and natural she knew it was a gesture he repeated often. That, and not hair putty, probably explained the spikiness of the dark strands that were longer on the top, shorter on the sides.

"This has nothing to do with my project," he snapped, then scowled at someone off-camera.

Chelsea glanced heavenward, grateful she wasn't the recipient of that withering look.

An Excerpt from

HERE AND NOW
An American Valor Novel

By Cheryl Etchison

Former Ranger Medic Lucky James feels right
at home working long night shifts in the ER, but
less so during the day, when his college classes are
filled with flirtatious co-eds. When his 19-year-
old chem lab partner shows up at his work with
dinner for "her Lucky," he quickly enlists the
help of Rachel Dellinger, a nurse and fellow third
shift "vampire." From there a friendship is born
between two people just trying to make it through
the night. Neither are living in the past or planning
for the future—until one day changes everything.

When the phone kept ringing non-stop and the desk clerk asked her to take a set of scrubs to exam room seven, Rachel didn't think much of it. It was, after all, an ER and she assumed they were for a patient whose clothes were ruined and was in need of something to wear home. She gave a light tap to the exam room door and pushed it opened further, expecting to find someone at least sitting on the exam table and requiring assistance. What she did not expect was to see a fine physical specimen, upright and most certainly able-bodied, whipping his shirt off over his head in one swift, fluid motion. Nor did she expect to be greeted by strong shoulders, a broad muscular back, and narrowed hips.

Holy moly.

This guy was by far the best looking man she'd seen in the flesh in a very long time. Maybe ever. And she hadn't even seen his face.

She clutched the scrubs to her chest and stood silent and tongue-tied, watching, appreciating, as the muscles in his back and arms flexed and strained as he unfastened the leather belt around his waist and released the button. All those finely sculpted muscles worked in unison to create a stunning physical display of power and strength as he shoved his pants to the floor.

Wearing only white crew socks and gray boxer briefs, he turned to face her and she nearly forgot how to breathe. She thought the back was nice? The chest. The abs. The dark trail of hair that began just below his navel and disappeared beneath the waistband of his briefs.

"You could've dropped them on the table and left instead of just standing there."

Her gaze shot upward to see one corner of his mouth lifted in a half smile and as dark brown eyes stared back at her she was immediately struck by the feeling she knew this guy. There was something so familiar about him, but she couldn't quite put her finger on it.

She swallowed hard in an effort to unstick her tongue from the roof of her mouth. "You knew I was standing here?"

Instead of answering, he simply held out his hand, his eyes flicking to the scrubs she held in a stranglehold against her chest before lifting to meet hers once again.

"How?" She relaxed her grip, felt the blood rush back to her fingertips as she placed the scrubs in his hand. "How did you know?"

"Spatial awareness," he said taking the clothes from her and immediately tossing the shirt onto the gurney. "That and you knocked on the door before you came in." He flashed that half smile again before stepping into the pants and tying the drawstring. "Thanks for the clothes, Rachel. I can handle it from here."

Immediately she looked down to see if he'd read the name from her badge, only to realize her crossed arms were covering her ID. Clearly, he knew her. So she looked harder this time, doing her best to ignore the chest—and abs and arms—and focus on his face. As she mentally stripped away the disheveled hair, the heavy scruff covering his face, the laugh lines around his eyes, the earlier feelings of lust were replaced by a sinking feeling in the pit of her stomach.

There was little doubt the man standing in front of her was the one and only Lucky James.